ONE LOST SOUL

HIDDEN NORFOLK - BOOK 1

J M DALGLIESH

First published by Hamilton Press in 2019

Copyright © J M Dalgliesh, 2019

ISBN (Hardback) 978-1-80080-775-4
ISBN (Trade Paperback) 978-1-80080-354-1

EXCLUSIVE OFFER

ONE LOST SOUL

PROLOGUE

HOLLY WAS grateful for the shelter of the dunes. The wind had a habit of rattling along the coastline, sweeping across the flatlands and cutting through even the hardiest of winter clothing. Where they were sitting, beyond the thick pine forests of the Holkham estate, there was shelter of sorts. She watched the others building a fire on the beach below, gathering driftwood and any fallen branches scavenged from the nearby woods. In the summertime, the estate routinely sent groundskeepers out to ensure open fires were not set but not at this time of year. Early spring could be lovely on the Norfolk coast, bright sunshine, warming on the skin. As long as the prevailing wind wasn't whipping in off the North Sea, at least. The sun had long since set and the chill of the evening was beginning to bite.

In a month or so, the tourist season would begin. All the local businesses running skeleton opening hours over the winter would be up and running once more. The seasonal workers would soon return, maybe. There was a lot of talk amongst the locals that this year would be different. Applications for job vacancies were down on last year and her father commented that even agencies were struggling to fulfil the roles.

It must be amazing to be one of those people with the freedom to

2 J M DALGLIESH

travel beyond the confines of where they grew up, able to go to another country and experience different lifestyles and culture. The prospect of learning a new language, trying strange food or simply watching the sun set over an alien landscape was exciting, exotic. One day that would be her. Not that she could tell anyone, nor would she when the time came. She would vanish on the breeze, carried away by an unstoppable force. Maddie came to mind, watching her as she danced with her friends a short distance away. What will become of her when I leave? That last thought dampened her enthusiasm, tempering the future vision.

The fire was lit now. They were singing, the others. It wasn't a song she cared for, not one she even knew the words to but it was popular. Their shadows danced on the sand around the fire as they moved, linking arms and singing louder as more voices joined in the chorus. Holly felt a hand on her shoulder. The touch was gentle. She didn't look round. Mark slipped his arm across her shoulder, coming to sit alongside her on the blanket he'd laid out for them. Part of her wanted him to suggest they move closer to the flames. He didn't and she knew why. He would no doubt try to slip his tongue into her mouth soon. To be fair, it was to be expected. The location, the fire, and their being alone, away from the others and sitting in the darkness made for quite a romantic setting. She would probably oblige.

Mark was a nice guy. Most of their year group steered clear of him but that was less to do with his outbursts and more to do with the family reputation. If she knew of anyone less deserving of such scorn, then it would be news to her. Releasing his grip on her shoulder, Mark retrieved a bottle from a plastic bag at his side and unscrewed the cap. He offered it to her first. She could smell the alcohol and it made her stomach churn. The waves of nausea were getting more frequent but she kept quiet. The last thing she needed was another lecture on visiting the doctor. How could she? The thought of drinking made her feel worse and she declined the offer. He said nothing, sipping from the bottle and pulling an odd face as the liquid burned his mouth. That was the issue with Mark. Immature.

The bonfire was well underway. The colours, the crackling of the wood and the spiralling wisps of smoke and flame dancing into the night sky with the waves crashing on the beach was somewhat hypnotic. Holly imagined her fears being consumed by the heat, with the glow at its heart a depiction of her dreams and fantasies. One day soon she would leave this place and everyone in it behind, travel somewhere where no one knew her and become an artist, make things… jewellery perhaps. All of this would be but a memory.

She felt Mark's hand stroke the small of her back. Looking to him, he smiled. She said nothing, returning her gaze towards the bonfire and spying the whites of the breakers beyond as they approached the shoreline. Mark was a nice guy. Even so, he still couldn't come with her. There was no place for him. There was no place for any of them.

CHAPTER ONE

THE FROSTY CHILL of the dawn was now rapidly becoming a warm Saturday morning and Tom Janssen sat on the bonnet of his car, sipping his takeaway coffee and watching Saffy in the nearby play area. Only a couple of short months ago, she would have insisted he accompanied her to every piece of apparatus whether he could fit in, under, or on top of it. Not so now. She was a precocious seven-year-old, confident and enthusiastic for any new experience and she would seek out a challenge at any opportunity. That wasn't to say she took everything in her stride. As he observed her interactions with the other children, none of whom she was familiar with as far as he knew, he felt a swell of pride within, which felt odd. Occasionally, her little head would pop up, similar in style to that of a meercat, and he would see her blonde curls framing her rounded face and piercing blue eyes just checking on his presence. Sometimes, if he wasn't observant enough, there would be a call to ensure he was still paying attention.

He waved with his free hand, offering a broad smile to go with it. Saffy set off across the rope bridge in pursuit of another little girl, whose mother looked on nervously from the side lines. He could understand, more or less. He wondered at what point a parent would cease worrying about how their children might damage themselves. It seemed to him that from a very early age, they were practically indestructible. That was his experience where Saffy was concerned. Once, she had bounced from a sofa, pitching forward in an unplanned somersault and landed head first in a heap on a hardwood floor. There were a lot of tears and blood-curdling shrieking but once the initial shock subsided, no harm was done and she was off in search of more stimulation.

Perhaps there was no set timescale. The fears only shifted along with the perspective as the child grew up. Today's playground would become tomorrow's gymnastics and then, soon enough, her first driving lessons.

Sipping more coffee, he shielded his eyes from the glare of the sun. It was still sitting low in the sky and he regretted not bringing his sunglasses. His head felt foggy and a mild headache gnawed at him. On another day, he could be cursing the bottle of wine drunk the night before but he hadn't had a drink in months. Thinking about it, it could be much longer. He couldn't remember. Not that it mattered. It wasn't a choice to stop drinking, merely something he fell into by accident. Either way, his lips were dry and his tongue felt like sandpaper. *A hangover but without the fun of the night before.* Maybe he should be drinking after all if this was what abstinence felt like.

"Penny for them." He looked to his left as Alice approached. He hadn't heard her. She clutched a jute bag containing whatever it was she was picking up this morning. She must have said but he was preoccupied and hadn't really been listening.

"What's that?"

"You were miles away."

Tom smiled. He was lost in thought but with nothing in particular. That wouldn't be an acceptable answer, so he chose to say nothing. Alice was much like her daughter, very inquisitive. Others would call her nosey but not him, he wouldn't dare.

"Did you get me coffee?" She looked around expectantly, frowning at the absence of an extra cup.

"Sorry, I didn't know how long you would be."

"No problem. Did you manage to keep a hold of my daughter, at least?" She was only semi-serious, her tone mocking as always. Even when they were children, Alice used to take the position of the authoritarian despite being several years younger than Tom. He pointed towards the play area and as if on cue, her head popped up again. Catching sight of her mother, the suddenly animated girl jumped up and down letting out a whoop of delight. Alice waved. "Seems to be enjoying herself."

"Saffy always does."

"I wish you wouldn't call her that." Alice was curt. He knew the shortening of her name irritated her.

"Well, what did you think it was going to be shortened to?" Now it was his turn to stir things.

"We didn't really think about it."

"So, what do you call her?" he asked, wracking his memory for an occasion when she'd used a nickname but couldn't recall one.

"Sapphire." Alice was matter of fact. "It is her name after all."

He frowned, then flicked his eyebrows to indicate his understanding. At that moment, the girl in question appeared and hurled herself into her mother's arms, momentarily throwing her off balance.

"Hey, Saffy." He cast a sideways glance at Alice just as Sapphire extracted herself from her mother's hug and launched herself into him. "Was that fun?" She nodded affirmatively. "Where should we go now?"

"The beach!" He laughed and Alice shook her head. The little girl always wanted to go to the beach, it was the destination of choice if ever given the option.

"We're not going to the beach this morning, young lady." Alice was firm. The way she managed her daughter's expectations was commendable. One day, he would be a parent himself and he might adopt a similar approach. Although, in reality, he knew he was more likely to be a pushover or delegate all responsibility regarding tough decision making to his partner.

His attention was drawn to raised voices. The type of altercation you hear when a couple are having a very public argument, unable to hold themselves back until behind closed doors but, at the same time, attempting to continue their heated discussion without anyone else overhearing. *An impossible task.* Fortunately for the man and woman in question, the car park was pretty quiet at this time on a Saturday morning. Those in the play area were preoccupied with their children and only the three of them were there to witness the display.

The woman caught his eye appearing to notice the attention, not that he was particularly interested, and she dropped whatever she was saying mid-sentence. She was in her forties, dressed in riding trousers and boots, the stereotypical garb of someone getting into a nearly new Range Rover on the weekend in affluent rural Norfolk. She was either on her way to tend to her horses or had already done so. Her make-up was immaculately presented, fastidiously applied but still looked understated which was quite an achievement in his book. Her partner, on the other hand, was a little older, perhaps pushing fifty. A tall man, heavy set with a portly belly and once black hair, now shot through with grey, swept back in a quiff that stood to attention. He wore mustard coloured corduroy trousers and a thick green khaki jumper. His cheeks were flushed, whether as a result of their heated discussion or he was a naturally red-faced individual, Tom couldn't be sure.

Both doors to the Range Rover slammed shut and the debate restarted. *Today was going to be a long one for some people.*

"Well, I hope that's sorted by Monday morning, whatever it's about." Alice sounded concerned. Tom looked to her and realised she too had been watching the exchange. Saffy was oblivious, already onto an exploration of a patch of daffodils and a number of ducks who were approaching her in the belief she might feed them.

"You know them?"

"Yes. Don't you?" Alice sounded surprised. He shrugged. The engine fired up and reversed out of its space at a more measured pace than he'd anticipated. Alice noticed his watchful gaze whereas she had already averted her eyes, focussing on her daughter. "That's Colin and Marie."

"From the surgery?" Tom spoke, watching the vehicle approach the main road, indicate and pull out, accelerating away. Alice nodded. "Do you think they saw you?"

"Yes. Certain of it."

"That'll be awkward when you're making tea."

Now it was Alice who shrugged. "I expect they'll pretend it never happened."

"They often like that?" He wasn't really into gossip but the atmosphere where you worked could really affect your mood. He should know, after all.

"I don't really see much of them." She sounded disinterested. "Once I'm onto my patient list and they are seeing theirs, you don't really come up for air until the end of the day." He admired how much energy Alice put into her job. As far back as he could remember, she wanted to help people. Her graduation from Nursing College, and subsequent move to Norwich, coincided with his acceptance into the job and he relocated at a similar time. It seemed like their childhood friendship would remain exactly that, something in their past. Now though, somewhat happily of sorts, they both found themselves back home, each with their own story to tell – and equally reticent to share it.

"Maybe it was a cross word that quickly passed."

She looked down the road, the car having long since disappeared from view. "More likely they saw me and took an educated guess at who you were."

Tom found his curiosity piqued, intercepting her gaze with a half-smile. "So, you talk about me, then? At work, I mean." She flushed, much as she used to years ago when embarrassed but didn't reply. "What do you tell them?"

"To make sure their cars are taxed." The jibe was cutting. Alice was back on form and it made him laugh. Sapphire reappeared, begging for something to feed the ducks with, swearing blind that crisps would do. *Everybody likes crisps.* "Now, can you unlock the car, please? This bag is getting heavy."

JANSSEN PICKED his way along the access road running up to Holkham Beach, aware of the number of children charging about excited at the prospect of the day ahead. The road was dead straight, lined on both sides by pine trees, with parking allocated to both left and right.

Despite early spring returning to a cold snap, today promised to be glorious and the spaces were filling up with families keen to exploit the four mile stretch of golden sands along with the nearby nature reserve. It was still early for most and therefore they managed to park close to the barriers, cutting off the road from the reserve, the last point where members of the public could drive to.

Sapphire trilled away cheerily in the back seat and Janssen exchanged a knowing smile with Alice. The little girl had been looking forward to this day all week. Leaving Alice to get their coats out of the boot, the wind may have dropped but the temperature was still only a touch above freezing point, and he walked the short distance to buy a parking ticket. Baulking at the price, he only just managed to gather together enough coins to pay for half of the day. It would be enough. Saffy would get bored. By the time they'd eaten the picnic they brought with them, she would be ready for something else.

Retrieving the ticket from the slot, he returned to the car. Saffy and her mother were standing alongside the car, playing patty cake as he approached. Both offered him broad smiles as he came past, reaching in through the open passenger door and sticking the ticket to the windscreen.

"How long did you get?" Alice asked casually.

"We'll be okay until lunchtime." Stooping, he picked up the bags containing their food and another with assorted spades and sand castle buckets, along with a frisbee. "Let's go!" If the truth were known, he was as excited as Saffy at the prospect of a morning on the beach. Some of his favourite memories were of days spent with his parents and friends hanging out on the sands. Not necessarily here, but Norfolk was blessed with a magnificent coastline. Some days they would be out in the depths of November engineering architecturally unsafe castles and their associated fortifications. If they were solid enough to stay up until the tide came in, there was an equal chance that the children would gang together and destroy them themselves at the end of the visit, just for the fun of it.

Within two steps of leaving the car, his mobile rang. Reaching into his pocket, he took out his phone. It was Eric Collet. He was manning

CID today. There was no way he would bother him unless it was important. Waving the others on, he held back to take the call.

"I'm sorry to trouble you on the weekend." His tone was genuinely apologetic. He could hear the squawking of gulls along with the sound of waves crashing in the background. Eric wasn't in the station.

"That's okay. What's up?" Janssen looked towards the beach. Alice was slowing as they walked up the incline not wishing to get too far ahead despite Saffy pulling on her outstretched hand, begging her to get a move on. Alice smiled in his direction and he returned it. His was forced. The sixth sense of his police intuition, along with years of past experience, told him their plans were about to be interrupted.

"We've found a body. A young girl, out on the path running along the cliffs through Holkham reserve. You're going to want to take a look." Eric sounded nervous. He understood. Recently transferring into CID from uniform, Eric was still to find his feet, although he had everyone's confidence but his own. "I'm down at Holkham beach myself, not far away. Send someone to pick me up from the main gate, would you?"

Taking a deep breath, Tom forced another smile as he tried to draw Alice's attention. She appeared to recognise the significance of the call because her own faded as he put his mobile away, trotting over to join them.

"I'm sorry. Something's come up and I'm going to have to work today, after all."

"That's okay." Alice was despondent. A touch of guilt tugged at him but it was a suspicious death and he couldn't ignore it.

"We can do this another time." Saffy realised what they were talking about and threw him a dark look. The feeling of guilt grew. Dropping to his haunches, he addressed the girl. "I promise, I'll come back with you another day."

"I'm not talking to you!" Saffy crossed her arms and turned her back to him. Stamping one foot on the ground as she spoke for dramatic effect. He looked to Alice, who smiled. Clearly, that wasn't the first time she'd witnessed such a reaction.

"We'll be fine, Tom." Alice reassured him, reaching over and relieving him of the two bags. "Honestly, it's okay. Go and do what you have to. Just be sure and call me later."

He was relieved, feeling his sense of guilt dissipate. Passing her his car keys, he leaned in and gave her a kiss on the cheek. She smiled warmly. "They're sending someone to pick me up, so you can take my car. I'll pick it up later." Saffy flatly refused to acknowledge the fact he was leaving or even to look at him, so he leant down and kissed her on the top of her head, ruffling her curls. She responded with a deep *harrumph*.

Waving them off as they headed for the beach, he turned and set off for the gate a little over three hundred metres away. "Tom!" He looked over his shoulder to see Saffy, standing on the wooden boardwalk leading to the beach, jumping up and down and waving at him with both arms fully extended, flapping in an arc motion. He returned the wave with a broad grin. Then she turned away and ran ahead of her mother along the path, cutting through the pine forest in the most direct route to the beach.

CHAPTER TWO

THE ROUTE to the crime scene was barely a five-minute drive away. Eric was waiting for him at the edge of the police cordon, a thin blue and white barrier taping off the access to the path through the nature reserve. Despite his assurances, Janssen had the impression the detective constable was still on edge about calling his senior officer on his day off.

"I'm sorry to call you out." Eric repeated his apology but Janssen waved it away with a dismissive flick of his hand.

Slipping beneath the tape, Eric led them along the path, apparently keen to demonstrate what he'd already achieved prior to his arrival. He spoke at a rate of knots and Janssen struggled to keep up, having to ask him to slow down and start again.

"The call came in from the paramedics shortly after half-past eight. They pronounced her dead at the scene and immediately suspected foul play." Eric looked at him with a serious expression, conveying the gravity of the scene.

"And who called the ambulance?"

Eric consulted his notebook. "A local lady, out for her morning walk. She came across her on the path."

They rounded a bend and the path descended, lined on both sides by banks with assorted brush and wild grass growing to knee height. They were in a natural hollow where the path ran close to the cliff edge. The sound of the waves thundering against the rocks below carried on the breeze making them feel much closer. At high tide, the sound would be greater still as the low-lying land making up the Holkham basin would fill.

From here, the legs of a woman were clearly visible protruding onto the path. Her waist and upper body were lying on the shallow incline of the bank behind her. Coming closer, he wondered whether a woman was an apt description. She looked far younger. Maybe in her late teens. It was hard to tell. Her make-up was neatly applied, understated. Bright red lipstick and dark eye-liner accentuated her cheekbones and angular jaw. If it weren't for the pale grey skin, one could be forgiven for thinking she was asleep, so peaceful was her expression. A sheen of frost covered her from head to toe. She had been out here much of the night.

"It's the bruising around the neck," Eric said, as if his boss may have missed it. He hadn't.

Careful not to get too close to the body, he shifted his position in order to get a better look. Eric was right. He had seen enough strangulations before to know that this girl had been throttled. The bruising followed the lines of two grown hands closing around the girl's throat. He assessed her. She couldn't be much more than five-foot-three, petite. Her weight was hard to judge but she was slight. It wouldn't take a lot for someone to overpower her, he was sure about that. *What a tragic waste of a young life.* Oddly, she wore no shoes. Inspecting the soles of her feet, they were dirty but not blackened, suggestive of her having walked a short distance barefoot recently, if not actually to this place.

"Any idea who she is?" he asked, looking to Eric.

"Yes. She's the Bettany girl."

"Colin and Marie's daughter?"

"That's right. You know them?" Eric asked, sounding surprised. He always did when outsiders knew the locals. Those without form at least. Not that Tom Janssen was a true outsider. He grew up in Sheringham, along the coast from the more famous seaside town of

Cromer. However, when you moved away only to later return there was still the scepticism regarding how *truly Norfolk* you really were.

Janssen shook his head. "No, just by name. I didn't know they had children. I saw her parents this morning by pure coincidence."

"They have two, although the other one's name, I can't recall. I'll check." Eric confirmed his superior knowledge of the local community. "They have the GP practice just outside Burnham Overy. They'll be devastated. I called in forensics as well as the coroner. They'll be on their way."

"Good. What do you make of them, Colin and Marie?"

Eric took a moment, his expression a contorted mixture of sincere thought and concentration. "Professional. Well respected and hard working. Posh."

"*Posh?*"

"Well, you know… wealthy, moving in the right social circles and stuff like that."

Janssen wondered whether there was an edge to Eric's tone. He was a lovely young man, dedicated, but every now and again a little chip would appear on his shoulder, often without notice and at the strangest of times.

"Right. What about the witness, the lady who found her, where is she?"

"I took her details and sent her home. I said we'll call round later and take her statement. Is that okay?"

Janssen nodded his approval, focussing on the deceased. "What did you say her name is?"

"Holly. Holly Bettany," Eric confirmed.

"How old was she, do you know?"

"Sixteen or seventeen, I think. I know she was studying at the local sixth form."

Janssen blew out his cheeks, massaging his temple with the fingers of his left hand. *Too young to go out like this.* "We'll need to go and speak to the parents. Word gets around and I don't want them hearing about it from anyone but us."

THE VILLAGE of Burnham Market was a hive of activity. The warm sunshine had brought people out to visit the independent shops, galleries and artisanal establishments the area was known for. At the centre of a conservation area, it was the quintessential chocolate box representation of a rural Georgian market village. Eric turned off the high street and picked his way down the narrow side street, negotiating the parked vehicles of early season tourists and residents alike.

Brancaster House was easily identifiable by the large plaque mounted to the side of the entrance, fixed to the huge perimeter wall. The tyres of the car crunched on the gravel lining the driveway as they pulled up before the front door.

Janssen rang the doorbell, hearing it chime within. Moments later, a figure appeared on the other side. It was Marie Bettany, Janssen recognising her from earlier in the day. She had changed out of her earlier clothes. Now she was wearing a long summer dress, predominantly blue with a floral print. Her hair, worn up that morning, now hung to her shoulders and she sported a pearl necklace. There was a flicker of recognition when Janssen revealed his warrant card but she pretended to acknowledge him only for the first time there and then. He introduced Eric behind him, also brandishing his identification. To Janssen it came across in a stylistic way reminiscent of a television crime programme. The young man really hadn't settled into his new role yet.

She welcomed them into the house but it struck him as a begrudging gesture which he found odd.

"Could your husband join us as well?" Janssen asked, looking around the entrance hall. It was suitably grand, far larger than the biggest room in Janssen's own home, with hardwood panelling lining the walls and continuing on up the ornately carved staircase to the first floor.

"I'm sure, yes. Please, do come through."

She led them along the hall towards the rear of the house. The ticking of a grandmother clock echoed off the walls and the polished parquet floor. Janssen noted Eric's discomfort, resolving to enquire about his strange behaviour later on. The kitchen was huge, a real farmhouse affair. Obviously, a modern installation and yet with a traditional inspiration. Marie Bettany stepped across to the threshold of the French doors and called out into the garden before returning to them. She met Janssen's eye and he thought he saw a glimmer of embarrassment. He was surprised she wasn't pushing to know why they were there.

Colin Bettany arrived shortly after, appearing at the entrance from the garden, beads of sweat on his forehead and looking decidedly unhappy at the interruption.

"For Pete's sake, Marie, what is it?" He pulled up when he caught sight of the detectives. His facial expression changed in an instant along with his tone, adopting a far more gracious manner. "I'm terribly sorry. I didn't realise we had visitors. It's just that we have guests arriving this afternoon for drinks before we head out for a meal and I have so much to organise."

Janssen spied the dining table in the adjoining room. It was laden with plates of food, all neatly laid out and wrapped in cling film. By the look of it, they were expecting a fair number of people.

"No need to apologise, Mr Bettany." Janssen smiled warmly as he spoke.

"Dr Bettany," he replied coolly. Janssen was taken aback but then again, some people could be spiky when it came to their titles. In contrast, Marie didn't seem to be particular about hers though.

"My apologies. Perhaps we could sit down." His tone was serious, conveying the gravity of the reason for their visit.

"What is it?" Marie asked, in a worried tone.

"I'm afraid we have some distressing news for you. We found the body of a young woman this morning in the Holkham nature reserve. I'm sorry to have to tell you but we believe it to be your daughter, Holly."

"Impossible!" Marie stated emphatically. "Holly travelled to Norwich yesterday evening for a recital. They are practising today before this evening's performance." She was unequivocal. Janssen glanced at Eric but he remained firm, confirming his own certainty with an almost imperceptible nod.

"We strongly believe it is her. Obviously, we need to carry out a formal identification but that will have to wait."

"Wait?" Colin Bettany cut in, flabbergasted. "Wait for what exactly?" His tone returned to hostile as he continued on. "You only ever wait if you are treating it as a crime scene. Is that the case?"

Marie gasped, throwing one hand across her mouth and bracing against the worktop alongside her with the other. Eric appeared ready to leap over and catch her if she fell but she steadied herself seconds later.

"We are investigating the circumstances surrounding her death, Dr Bettany. I'm sorry but it does appear your daughter was the victim of an attack and therefore, potentially a murder." Janssen watched as the detail sank in. It was too early for him to know the cause of death, albeit the evidence was suggestive but not as yet conclusive.

Colin Bettany pulled out a chair from the nearby breakfasting table and sank into it, a look of bewilderment crossing his face.

"Marie is right. Holly was supposed to be in Norwich last night." He spoke softly, with no sign of the previous aggression and hostility.

"When was the last time you saw her?" Janssen asked, taking out a notebook.

"Yesterday afternoon," Marie replied. "I dropped her at the bus stop. I offered to take her all the way into Norwich but she said she would rather make her own way and besides, Colin and I both had plans and I needed to get ready."

"Plans?"

"Yes, that's right," Colin cut in. "Nothing exciting. A meeting of the rotary club to discuss fundraisers, that type of thing and then I had work to attend to."

"When was Holly due to come back?"

"Later tonight. I don't know when exactly," Colin replied. He appeared to Janssen to be lost but there was more than that. Clearly overwhelmed, he was also agitated and unfocussed. Unsurprising, bearing in mind the news he'd just received but clearly the reality of the situation was yet to really hit home. Colin looked to his wife. "I guess we should phone round everyone and cancel today." Janssen was surprised at the cool, almost offhand nature of the comment but he said nothing.

"For heaven's sake, Colin!" Marie muttered, tears welling in her eyes. Janssen agreed with the sentiment. "I... I should make you gentlemen some tea..." She began to hunt around the kitchen, almost as if it was the first time she had been in there, seemingly unable to locate anything she would need to enable the process.

"That's okay, Mrs Bettany. There's no need." He tried to put her at ease but the offer of the tea was merely a distraction for her, an opportunity to focus on something monotonous and thereby remove her from reality if only for a few minutes. "Tell me, if the concert recital was this evening... why was she due to travel yesterday?"

"We pay for private tuition," Marie explained, glancing at her husband. He looked to the floor, sitting forward and resting his elbows on his knees and dropping his head into his hands. "Holly's grades have slipped and she wanted to make it to medical school... without the extra support, she was never going to make it."

"We'll need to check up on whether she made the appointment. Can you think of anywhere she might go if she decided to ditch it or the recital? Did she have any close friends or a boyfriend perhaps?"

Colin Bettany sat upright, a flash of irritation momentarily crossing his face. "No! She didn't have time for boyfriends or any of that nonsense."

"You're sure?" Janssen knew that often the parents were the last to know what their teenage daughters were up to. He could still remember dating them when he was a similar age, although the clarity of those memories was fading. "What about friends?"

"If she did, I'm sure we would know. Am I right, Marie?" His wife nodded, retrieving a tissue from a box alongside a set of cookbooks, stacked on a low shelf. "As for friends... she didn't have many. Amelia was probably her closest."

"Amelia?" Eric double checked, making a note.

"Yes. Amelia Harding," Marie confirmed.

"Fraser and Angela's daughter?" Eric asked. Janssen was once again blown away by his detective constable's connections. *Did he know everybody in this part of Norfolk?* Marie confirmed it and Eric scribbled away in his notebook. Janssen put his away.

"Is there any reason you can think of that might explain why she stayed here last night, anywhere she may have planned to go?"

Both parents shook their heads. Marie spoke. "She had her overnight case along with a change of clothes for today. Not forgetting her uniform for tonight's performance. I guess, she could have been planning to stay with a friend. I can check in her room and see what she took?"

Marie moved towards the inner door, presumably to head upstairs but Janssen stopped her. "It might be best if you let DC Collet take a look first? With your permission, it will be important for us to go through her things. Doing so may shed some light on her motivations." Marie nodded but her husband bristled.

"Is that really necessary? I mean, we're just talking about some clothes."

Janssen ignored his protests, indicating for Eric to take a look.

"Perhaps you could show DC Collet the way, Mrs Bettany."

"You should be out finding whoever did this to my daughter!" Colin Bettany snapped at no one in particular, dropping his head and burying his face in his hands. Janssen thought he was crying. There were some days when he hated his job.

CHAPTER THREE

Eric let Marie guide him through the house. The first floor was as grand as he imagined it would be. The landing was so wide in places that it could accommodate various pieces of furniture. Each appeared well worn and could have been expensive antiques or picked up in a local charity shop. He didn't know about such things. He was out of his depth in the company of these types of people.

Eric was a Norfolk boy, born and raised. He had never seen the appeal of the bright lights of the capital or any other city for that matter. He joined the police straight out of school, working hard and wanted to build a career here, among the people and places he knew and loved. Not that it had been easy on him. His father passed away shortly before he left high school, leaving his mother to raise both Eric and his two younger sisters.

His mother had been diagnosed with cancer the following year and it was Eric who stepped in, providing for the family. His sisters eventually made it through school and college. One, Elizabeth, set off for university while the other, Angela, now lived in the north. He didn't begrudge them their choices. He didn't have the same freedom as they'd enjoyed but that was okay. He wouldn't have played it differently even if he had. His mother once worked for people *like the*

Bettanys. Cooking or housekeeping. Taking care of all the tasks they couldn't be bothered with or considered beneath them. Working her fingers to the bone and barely being noticed except for the days when she wasn't at work or required payment. When she fell ill, her employment was terminated. She could no longer keep up with the pace of the job. Even when in remission, the most she could manage was a part-time position at the local co-op. She loved it, mind you. There was a far lower expectation on her to assume responsibility and that was a welcome change.

They approached a door. It was ajar and Eric could see pink wallpaper and a poster stuck to the wall above the bed. Marie noticed his hesitation as she continued on. "That's Madeleine's room." As soon as she said her name, he recalled her. Madeleine was several years younger than Holly.

"Where's Madeleine today?"

"She was due to sleep over at a friend's house last night. Colin was working late and my choral practice was rescheduled from earlier in the week." Marie took on a faraway look, pained. "Probably for the best she isn't here at the moment, I suppose."

Eric bobbed his head, saying nothing. He was glad to not be witnessing the child's reaction to the news. That made him feel selfish and he focussed on the task in hand. At the other end of the house, Marie came to a closed door, indicating it was Holly's. She went to open it but Eric stopped her with a gentle touch to her forearm.

"Probably best to leave it to me, if you don't mind? I'm sure you've seen these types of things before on the telly."

"Yes, of course." She seemed flustered. Understandable under the circumstances. "I'll leave you to it, then." Marie stepped back, anxiously fiddling with hands. She didn't seem comfortable meeting Eric's eye and he waited quietly for her to take the hint and actually *leave* him to it. Seconds later, she did exactly that. Nodding nervously, she set off to return downstairs, pausing briefly on the landing and watching as Eric donned a pair of latex gloves he pulled from his pocket. A full forensic search of the room could be done later, if the cause of death turned out as expected. In the meantime, all he was looking for was an indication of whether Holly intended to skip her recital or not. He slipped into the bedroom, gently closing the door behind him.

The room was tidier than he expected a teenage girl's room to be. Not that he had ever set foot in one before, apart from the one shared by his sisters obviously, but that didn't count. There were no posters of popstars lining the walls nor any celebrity magazines casually left on the floor. All her clothing was either in the laundry basket or put away because nothing was left on show. There was a dressing table on the far side of the room, inset into the alcove alongside the chimney breast, but even this had very little in the way of what he expected to see. A hairbrush and straightening tongs lay in front of the vanity mirror, the latter still plugged into the socket on the wall. He eased the drawers open, examining the contents. It felt odd going through her underwear and he flushed, feeling the heat on his cheeks and at the base of his neck, imagining the reddening of his skin. Passing over it quickly, seeing nothing of note, he found no further make-up or cosmetics. *Presumably, she took them with her to make herself up.*

Thinking back, he couldn't remember any bags being found near the body, suitable as either a travel bag or for toiletries. Maybe the search team would locate them in due course. Moving to the wardrobe, he opened the doors wide. There were two lines of clothes hanging from the rail with jumpers, trousers, and what appeared to be skirts, either rolled up or folded neatly on the shelf above. He saw nothing suggestive to indicate where Holly may or may not have planned to go.

Crossing the room, he addressed the bedside table. A digital clock radio was present, pointing towards the bed, the numbers blinking red. Perhaps there had been a power cut overnight. Opening the single drawer to the unit, he found what looked like a diary and again, feeling strange about doing so, he flicked through the pages. Most of them were blank and those that weren't were filled with inane drivel that he quickly grew bored of reading. Replacing it in the drawer, he pushed it closed, sitting down on the bed and looking around. The mattress was soft and springy, he sank into it. The thought occurred that it must be dreadful to sleep on. He much preferred a stiff mattress himself.

As an afterthought, he slid off the bed and dropped to his knees. Bending over, he peered under the bed. It was a divan but with no pull-out drawers, leaving a narrow gap between the base and the carpet beneath. Using the torch on his mobile phone, he lit up the area, excited at possibly finding something presumably stashed out of sight. It would have been easier to retrieve with the slender fingers of a petite teenager, he was sure, but eventually, Eric managed to tease the laptop out from its hiding place. It was incredibly slim and lightweight, crafted from one sheet of pressed aluminium he figured. Eric knew his hardware and this cost a small fortune. This was an expensive piece of kit for a teenager, even for people as wealthy as the Bettanys.

With one last glance around, he retreated from the room, closing the door behind him. Setting off downstairs, he found Janssen still in the kitchen holding a discussion with the parents. Conversation ceased as he entered with all eyes turning to face him.

"Anything?" Janssen asked expectantly.

"No uniform, no," he replied, noting the look of consternation on the faces of the parents. "But I did find this, though." He held up the laptop triumphantly.

"That's not Holly's," Colin Bettany said flatly before looking at Marie. "It's not, is it?" Suddenly, he didn't sound so sure. Marie shook her head.

"We'll have to take it back to the station with us," Eric said, apologetically.

"And it might be best if the two of you stayed out of Holly's room for the time being," Janssen added. "I know it might be tempting to be close to her possessions and thereby to your daughter, at this time, but please, we may need to carry out a more detailed search and if you were to touch anything or remove—"

"For goodness' sake, man! Why would we want to move anything?" Colin said, the hostility returning. Janssen appeared irritated with him. Eric could tell. He was a relaxed boss, although that was probably the wrong choice of word, *calm* would arguably be more suitable, but when his back was put up, he could be a nightmare to be around. One of those times was in danger of manifesting now. He also found himself making an early assumption that Colin Bettany was used to getting his own way and not one keen to relinquish authority.

Janssen explained how they would assign a family liaison officer to them who would keep them abreast of the investigation but, for the moment, they were to bear with them. Once Holly was able to be seen, they would be offered the chance to sit with her along with carrying out the formalities of the identification. He gave them his contact card and Eric fell into step as they saw themselves out.

Closing the door behind them, Eric blew out his cheeks. He was grateful to be outside. Janssen appeared to notice his reaction and Eric quickly unlocked the car, scurrying round to the driver's side and getting in, wishing for the moment to pass. His discomfort was not only a result of delivering this type of news and witnessing the ensuing grief; that alone was a terrible experience, but also, he wasn't comfortable around people of this class. He found their social status intimidating, reminding him of his roots. He felt somehow inferior to them, unworthy of sharing space as their equals and that annoyed him.

CHAPTER FOUR

THE CHILDREN WERE SQUABBLING over what to watch on the television when Jane returned. A flash of annoyance passed through her mind at the pettiness of the debate. William's insistence on his choice of a superhero cartoon series he'd become obsessed with recently, seven series' worth of episodes and every one virtually identical to the last. Rosie, on the other hand, wanted a cartoon featuring children in the form of a variety of animals, attending craft classes managed by an affable canine. The latter was the most preferable but instead of getting involved, she tuned the disruption out.

A pile of fresh mail sat on the worktop, next to the kettle. Her thoughts passed to her husband. *At least you managed to walk to the gate and retrieve that.* The coffee machine was on, the filter head still set in place and somehow, she doubted he had left it ready for her. Not wanting to bother with the hassle, she flicked on the kettle. Sifting through the post, the first three she picked up were flyers or generic advertising mail shots and she set them aside for the recycling bin with barely a glance. The next was a utility bill and she tore it open, removing it from the envelope and scanning the total sum, nothing more.

The water reached temperature and the kettle switched off.

Reaching into a high cupboard, she took down a mug, putting in a heaped teaspoon of instant coffee granules and two sugars. She would need to reduce her sugar intake at some point soon. The process wouldn't be pleasant, it never was. She'd put on weight since the move despite walking the surrounding landscape on a daily basis with Archie. Her eyes were drawn to the next letter. The envelope was handwritten, addressed to Ken and came without a stamp. Scooping it up and glancing over her shoulder towards the children, she saw their heated debate was over. The animals were planting vegetable seeds by all accounts. Rosie was happy. William lay in the crook of the corner sofa, his head buried in his tablet with a flash of green reflecting from the screen onto his face.

Scrunching the envelope up, she stuffed it into her pocket with one hand, pouring water into the mug with the other as the back door opened and her husband entered. "Would you like tea, love?" She reached for another mug before he could reply. Ken wouldn't drink instant coffee, so there was no point in asking but she wasn't going through the palaver of making a fresh coffee for him if she couldn't be bothered to do so for herself.

"Yes, please."

He walked past her and into the living room, casting an eye over the children. Even though he was facing away from her, she knew he would be frowning. *You hate the television.* He disliked streaming services even more but it kept the children quiet, up to a point. Something he never managed to do. He turned back and she looked away, hoping he wouldn't read her thoughts by way of her expression.

"Did you get a paper?" Ken asked, looking around.

"Oh… no, sorry." *What am I supposed to say?* Suddenly, she was lost for words. It wasn't as if she hadn't spent the entire walk home playing out different scenarios in her head, how to frame the news, what she should be thinking… or feeling. "Something came up."

"What was that then?"

He sounded disappointed, annoyed even. *Sorry you didn't get your blasted paper. Go to the shop yourself if it means that much to you.* "I… I'll tell you in a minute. Can you finish making the tea?" She left the kitchen, retreating into the cloakroom. Putting the lid to the seat down, she slid the lock across the door and took the envelope out of her pocket. Sitting down, she fought for calm. The cloakroom smelt funny. That mixture of fresh paint tinged with a touch of damp. Ken insisted it would dry out once the summer kicked in but usually she chose to go upstairs such was the strength of the odour, particularly on rainy days. This morning was different.

The glue on the seal hadn't taken firmly and the flap came apart from the sleeve with ease. The envelope itself appeared old and battered. Perhaps the glue had dried out. Carefully removing the letter from inside, not wishing to make a sound despite there being practically zero chance of anyone hearing her beyond the door, she unfurled the crumpled paper. The handwriting was poor, barely legible and with several crossings out at various points. The letter was short, the message clear. Reading to the end, her eyes flicked heavenward and it took a few seconds before she realised her hands were involuntarily shaking.

Taking a deep breath, she closed her eyes and sought to calm herself once more. The sound of a car pulling up in the yard outside carried to her. Standing up, she could make out a dark shape through the frosted glass of the cloakroom window. Silently cursing, she folded the letter flat several times and secreted it in her back pocket, along with the envelope. Lastly, she depressed the flush and unlocked the door, hurrying back towards the kitchen.

By the time she reached the kitchen, Ken had already ushered the men inside. The kids were both leaning over the back of the sofa eagerly inspecting the new arrivals. She recognised the young detective constable although his name escaped her. He must have told her earlier but, what with everything else, she hadn't taken it in. He was nice enough, a bit drippy for her tastes. The other wasn't present when she left, of that she was certain. She would have remembered. He was tall, athletic, with a shock of floppy fair hair but, unusually, with a Mediterranean complexion. His expression was serious, his features chiselled and angular and yet offered a promise of kindness.

The younger officer deferred to the taller and Jane deduced he must therefore be senior. He eyed her approach, smiling and offering her his identification. She gave it a cursory nod before chancing a glance into his dark eyes, yet another contradiction when considering his hair colour. She was sure the latter was natural.

"You found a *body*?" Ken was overly dramatic as he was often prone to be. Accusatory. The children were wide-eyed with excitement, the response that only those without the ability to process the enormity of the events could generate. "Why didn't you say?"

"Because you disappeared into your studio." *As you always do on the weekend in spite of promising you would spend more time with the kids.* She chose not to voice the thought, bearing in mind the company they had. "I was about to just now." Whether the explanation was satisfactory or not, he didn't comment further.

"I was just making tea, if you would care for some?" Ken suggested, looking between the two officers. His tone was light, upbeat. He had slipped into the mode of a welcoming host, much as he used to before when they lived back in Fulham. Ken could be a charming man when he turned it on. "Look at the time, it's nearly lunch. We could put some food out seeing as you are here. It will only be bread and cheese, perhaps some fruit."

The young detective looked eager. His eyes lighting up as the presence of his appetite made itself known. The other appeared ready to decline but Jane stepped in, asserting control like she usually did.

"I'm sorry, I didn't catch your name," she asked, approaching and extending her hand with an accompanying broad smile.

"Detective Inspector Janssen, Tom Janssen." He took her offered hand. The grip was firm, his hand was large and yet gentle, feeling soft to the touch. *He must use moisturiser. Takes care of himself.* As he returned her smile, she took the initiative. "Ken is right. You *must* have something to eat with us. Who knows when you'll next get the chance?" He looked about to object but relented against the tide of her persistence, instead accepting graciously.

Jane set about preparing lunch, busily pulling everything together. The kids would have their usual weekend lunchtime offering, a pizza with some carrot sticks, sliced avocado and a few fresh tomatoes, if she was lucky. They could eat in front of the television today, leaving the adults free to talk. For them, she found three quarters of a loaf of olive bread that was still fresh enough to serve if she were to sprinkle it with water and heat it through in the oven. Retrieving the cheese box from the fridge, she placed it on the kitchen table while Ken busied himself setting out plates and gathering cutlery. He hadn't been this productive domestically in months. There was also a carton of fresh soup, still within date, at the back of the fridge and without asking, she emptied the contents into a pan and set a heat beneath it.

Occasionally, she glanced at the policemen out of the corner of her eye. The drippy one appeared awkward, apparently unsure of how he was expected to behave whereas the other, Inspector Janssen, appeared impassive on the surface, quietly observing the goings on around him. She had the distinct impression very little passed by him unnoticed. She would need to tread carefully around him. Very carefully indeed.

CHAPTER FIVE

JANSSEN OBSERVED the couple beavering away at preparing lunch. The prospect of taking a statement whilst breaking bread seemed odd. They would need to make casual conversation while they ate, possibly touching on the discovery of Holly's body, which in itself would also feel odd, and he resolved to take the formal statement afterwards. The husband's ease with which he openly questioned his wife's experience seemed strange bearing in mind the presence of the children, too young to hear the details in his opinion. Maybe when he was a parent, he might feel differently but somehow he doubted it.

The man, Ken Francis, was busy making himself useful, keen to offer himself up as the competent, domestic contributor. The modern-day husband and father but it didn't take a career as a detective to figure out he was playing the role. Quite badly as it happened. The man frequently paused, looking around with an expression of bewilderment as he sought to locate items for the table. Whether it was the correct cutlery, soup spoons specifically, or napkins, he kept having to refer back to his wife for directions on where he could find them.

For her part, she hid her exasperation at his increasingly feeble attempts at assistance relatively well. Janssen interpreted her occasional frown or eye-roll as a judgement on her husband's ability, no doubt much preferring him to leave her to get on with it in the belief food would be delivered much sooner. The children received their food first. The pizza was cut into manageable slices and arranged alongside their vegetables. Both protested at the volume of the latter and demanded more of the former but to no avail. Distracted by the television and the food, they hunkered down on the sofa and Jane returned to the table as the three men took their seats.

Ken set about slicing the warm bread, although, hacking at it was probably more accurate. Janssen caught Eric looking in his direction. The constable knew the approach with the knife would irritate him. Aware of his almost obsessive desire for neat lines and presentation, there was a good reason as to why he was well-suited to this profession. Attention to detail, organisation, a methodical approach were all key attributes to his success.

At the invitation of his hosts, he reached over and helped himself to some bread, burying his frustration at the uneven cut. Gratefully accepting the butter, he caught Jane's eye. First checking the children were not listening, they weren't, the volume on the television was up further; no doubt a desire to filter out the adult voices for the novelty factor had already lost its appeal.

"Tell me how you came to be out at the reserve when you were?"

She glanced at her husband but he was intent on loading his plate and didn't notice.

"I was on my way to the shop for a morning paper," Jane replied.

"Bloody forgot it though, didn't you?" Ken replied, blowing on a spoonful of soup before taking a mouthful. "Understandable, I guess." Janssen ignored the comment, encouraging Jane with his eyes.

"The path isn't the route I took, mind you."

"I thought that," Janssen agreed, letting her know he had already mapped out the probable route in his head. It was a deliberate admission.

"But I saw something... someone." She appeared edgy. Nervous about something but whether it was the shock of finding a dead body, Janssen couldn't be sure. "That strange lad from up the way. Oh... what's the family? The ones you always complain about." She glanced at Ken, this time he noticed. Janssen gauged his reaction. His eyes narrowed while he thought.

"You mean the McCalls?" She nodded. Ken returned to his lunch, tearing a slice of bread in half and dipping it in the soup.

"You mean Mark?" Eric chipped in, chewing a mouthful of tomato and frowning as he queried the comment. Jane nodded. Janssen didn't add anything, preferring to let her continue. He found it was easier to remain silent on occasion. Most people sought to fill any gap in conversation with more words which was useful when investigating a case. The McCalls were well known in the area, by the police as much as by the locals. There wasn't an officer stationed in the parish who hadn't needed to speak with one of the family in relation to their inquiries at least once.

"Yes, he was there, looking at the body when I saw him." Jane directed her answer towards Janssen, even though it was Eric who asked her the question. If the constable minded, he didn't show it, merely setting about his food once more. Janssen picked at his own. There was nothing wrong with it. The soup was okay. Shop bought. He could do better himself but it was flavoursome enough. Similarly, the bread was good. The oven revived it. Almost any bread product could be salvaged by a splash of water and a blast in the oven. "He ran off as soon as he caught sight of me, though."

"Why would he do that, do you think?" Janssen was intrigued. Ken looked over at him.

"Funny in the head, that boy." He tapped at his forehead with two fingers, emphasising his point. The words were more of a statement as if that put the question to bed.

"Mrs Francis?" Janssen encouraged her.

"Jane, please," she replied with a smile. "I don't know really. He was standing there. I was a little way away but he had this strange look on his face, almost mesmerised by it, I would say. As soon as he saw me watching him, he was off."

"And then?"

"I went over to see what was going on." She cast her eyes downward, staring into her bowl and absently stirring the soup with her spoon. "Then... I... saw her. To be honest, I didn't know what he was doing there until I found her."

"What do you think he was doing there?" Janssen asked, noticing Eric's attentive attitude towards his question. His tone certainly changed. He was curious about her veiled intimation. She backtracked almost immediately.

"I've no idea... not really..." She stammered, appearing to register Janssen's interest and judging it negative. "I mean... he was there. I'm not saying he did anything."

"Of course." Janssen found her response interesting. Quite possibly, a narrative of events was already starting to take shape and he wanted facts, not opinion, to guide the case. "Did you see him touch the body?" She shook her head. "Did you?"

"I did, yes. I touched her leg. She was cold. I've never seen a... anyway, she was gone. It was obvious. I called an ambulance anyway."

"Did you know her, Holly?" This was a small community. Everyone knew everyone else as well as their business. It was that type of place. Even newcomers found out pretty quickly their privacy was seldom their own even if they sought to maintain it. He found his eyes drift to Ken. He was approaching his food with less enthusiasm than before, toying with the food on his plate and paying less attention to the story. Janssen found Jane looking directly at him as he studied her husband. Her expression was impassive, hard to read.

"We knew her a little, yes. She's been here before."

Janssen failed to mask his surprise. He hadn't been expecting that. "Here, at your house?" Jane nodded.

"That's not unusual. Many people in the community have been here. Ken is quite the celebrity. His artworks, both paintings and sculptures, are quite sought after. We sell them abroad, run exhibitions at galleries and the like. We're hoping to convert the old byre into something of a gallery of our own, one day. A second phase of the renovations. Isn't that right Ken?"

Her husband was lost in thought, almost failing to register she was talking to him. He looked up, seeing all eyes on him. Raising his eyebrows, his mouth dropped open and he glanced between them.

"The gallery, Ken." Jane was stern, inclining her head slightly to one side.

"Yes, absolutely." He finally responded, momentarily flustered before resuming the more familiar role of consummate professional. The performance part he'd adopted since their arrival. "Hopefully, later in the summer. It would be nice to encourage visitors early next year, perhaps in the spring. Catch a share of the tourism pound that drives the local economy, you know?"

Janssen nodded. There was something in the exchange between the two of them. Something unspoken, not comprehensible unless you were in on the information that only a husband and wife shared with each other. The nuances of their relationship were tough to decipher. He chose to let it go for now.

"What happened then, after you checked whether she was alive?"

Jane shrugged, picking up a glass of water. "Like I said. I called the ambulance. I knew it was too late for poor Holly but... I didn't really know what else I should do."

Eric piped up from the other end of the table. "You didn't mention to me that you knew her." To Janssen, Jane seemed startled by that question, slightly taken aback.

"Did I not? I don't remember. It was a bit of a shock. I wasn't really thinking." She took a mouthful of water, replacing the glass gently on the table and reaching for the jug. It was closer to him and Janssen picked it up first, refilling her glass. She thanked him but didn't meet his eye.

"Well, I think that will do for now," he said, smiling at their hosts in turn. Eric here, can take your official statement later on, if that's okay but I wanted to hear your story first hand. Thank you for lunch. It's very kind of you to accommodate us."

"Not at all, Inspector. Call round anytime." Jane smiled at him warmly. There was something behind the smile, held back. No matter how hard she tried to disguise her reticence there was more to be said but perhaps not right now.

"Agreed. You're more than welcome." Ken's voice boomed. Their imminent departure took his enthusiasm up a notch, almost as if he was maximising to fill the space.

Janssen stood, Eric following suit, cramming in another mouthful of bread as he did so. Janssen wondered if the young man had skipped breakfast. He would have said goodbye to the children but any interest in the visitors had long since dissipated. Jane escorted them to the door and they stepped out into the early afternoon sunshine. The day was warming as expected. In Janssen's mind at least, so was the investigation.

CHAPTER SIX

GETTING into the car neither of them spoke but Eric was itching for Jane Francis to go. As soon as she disappeared back inside, closing the door, he looked across. "She definitely gave me no indication she knew Holly." He felt it necessary to explain himself, almost to plead his case. He was relieved when his boss waved away the statement.

"There's more going on in there than either of them is letting on. You can drop me back at the station. They'll want to bring in an SIO for this one, so I'll make the call."

Eric nodded but wondered what their next step should be. A senior investigating officer would have to travel up from Norwich. They would need to progress the investigation in the meantime. Starting the engine, he looked over his shoulder to determine the best method to navigate their way out of the courtyard. The turning circle was tight, the exit gate narrow, and the residents' vehicles were awkwardly parked. For what had once been a working farm, space was limited.

Janssen ignored his obvious anxiety at the manoeuvre, setting out their next steps. "Then, I want you to go and have a word with this friend that the Bettanys directed us to. You're closer to their age group than me, so she might open up to you more if I'm not there."

"Really?" Eric was uncertain and he heard it reflected in the tone of his voice. "Teenage girls don't really talk to me. At least, they never did."

"Teenage girls confide in their friends. If anyone knows what was going on in Holly's world, then it will be her."

ERIC WAITED PATIENTLY in the sitting room of the Harding's home. Amelia's parents had been shocked to learn of Holly's death, offering any support they could to the investigation. Eric met Fraser Harding for the first time three years previously. Their home was burgled while they were attending a harvest supper at the village hall, barely two hundred yards away. Theirs was one of a spate of burglaries that took place over the course of a few weeks; seven in total on that very night. Eric had been one of the uniformed officers on duty, attending to the calls that flooded in once the residents returned home to find their belongings and in many cases, their lives, turned upside down.

Oddly, he didn't feel the same sense of anxiety around being in the company of the Hardings as he did at the Bettany residence. He should. They were of equal standing, if not superior to the latter. Fraser Harding was a senior executive with one of the global oil companies, or had been but the last he heard, Fraser was looking into taking early retirement following a health scare. He couldn't remember which company he worked for. Perhaps it was the fact he came across as a self-made man, speaking much like everyone else and did not carry any of the associated mannerisms that niggled Eric, such as the ones exhibited by Dr Colin Bettany.

Angela Harding appeared bearing a tray of cups and a teapot. She smiled broadly at Eric as he stood out of politeness. That was what you did when a lady entered the room. His mother taught him his manners. *You'll always go far if you remember your manners.* Those words stuck with him although they often felt like they might belong in a bygone age. Some people held preconceived ideas about those at the lower end of the economic scale, imagining their existence being rough, somewhat unclean and relatively squalid in comparison. His experience was the total opposite. It was the kids on the estate like him whose parents always insisted they wore clean clothes, nagged at them to brush their hair and mind their manners every time they left the house. Fewer people seemed to act that way these days. Or maybe he was struggling to see things as he once did. Angela Harding set about pouring them a cup of tea and Eric spied the plate of assorted biscuits. The lunch provided to them was nice and everything but soup, bread and a bit of cheese didn't quite fill the gap, so to speak. She noticed, encouraging him to help himself. He selected an oat biscuit, topped with milk chocolate.

The mouthful he took was ill-advised as he was still chewing when Fraser entered the room, a nervous looking Amelia half a step behind. It was obvious to him she had been crying. He stood up, taking the offered hand of her father, biscuit crumbs visible down the front of his shirt and lap. Everyone was far too polite to comment. He swallowed as fast as he could. He introduced himself to Amelia who perched herself on the edge of one of the two sofas in the room. Eric sat opposite her. Fraser Harding stood to his right, folded arms across his chest.

Eric glanced at Angela and then shot a fleeting look to her husband. Nobody spoke. "Perhaps, it might be best if you left us to have a word in private." The silent bridge between words lasted barely a few seconds but felt like minutes. "Amelia's not in any trouble. I just need to speak to her about Holly." Her father appeared unconvinced, immoveable. "This isn't a formal interview situation." Eric explained, appealing to Angela with a hopeful smile.

"Come on, Fraser. Let's leave the kids to have a chat." Angela got up and practically hauled her husband from the room. He didn't offer much by way of resistance but it was clear he would prefer to remain. As the sound of the latch clicking into place could be heard, he breathed a sigh of relief.

"Does it bother you, my mum referring to the two of us as *the kids*?"

The reference passed by him unnoticed and therefore he shook his head, suddenly self-conscious as the dark eyed teenager focussed on him. "I need to ask you about Holly. Her parents thought she was attending a tutorial in Norwich and then heading to a recital tonight." Amelia scoffed. A derisive gesture. Eric figured he would return to that. "Did you see her last night?" Her reaction was cagey. "It's important, Amelia." Eric laid on his most serious tone. He had practised it once he knew he was moving to CID.

"Yes. I was with her for a bit." She lowered her voice in case one or both of her parents were eavesdropping at the door. "Not that I talked to her much."

Eric lowered his voice too. "Where were you? What were you up to?" For a moment, he worried he'd overcooked it and pushed too hard. He sensed she might clam up. "You'll not be in trouble, I promise." Flicking his eyes towards the door, acknowledging that he recognised her concerns, he sat back in an attempt to appear casual. It worked.

"We had a party at the beach. It wasn't planned but we all came together. Nothing heavy. A few drinks and a bonfire, you know?"

"Right." Eric was happy. They were making progress. "Your parents don't know?" She shook her head. He tapped the side of his nose with the end of his pen. She laughed, leaving him with the impression it wasn't necessarily him she found amusing. "Who was there?"

"Friends from the sixth form mostly. Some of the older guys came along later."

"And Holly?"

"She was around but like I said, I didn't speak with her very much."

"Who did?" Eric was keen. Perhaps too keen. Amelia hesitated. "You may as well tell me. I'm going to find out eventually. It's my job."

She shrugged, dropping the pretence of a code of silence. "She was hanging out with Mark a lot." Eric raised his eyebrows, encouraging her to continue as he made notes. "Mark McCall. She was with him when I saw her. It was weird, though."

"How so?"

"She sat with him away from the rest of us. Away from the fire. It wasn't warm last night but she sat apart. I'll bet he was loving it." She glanced out of the nearest window, mulling something over. "I don't know what she saw in him. I mean, he's nice enough and that but he's a bit of a weirdo."

"You think so?" Eric didn't look up from his pad.

"Yeah. Doesn't everyone?" It was more of a statement and she seemed offended at the possibility of him not agreeing with her. "Anyway, I saw them together, then they weren't there."

"What time did they leave?" She shook her head to indicate she didn't know. "Mark McCall. How long have they been seeing each other?"

Amelia shook her head. "I'm not even sure they were an item. She never confirmed it to me but he seemed to think so. Like I said, he was a strange choice." Eric was very interested to hear she was last seen with Mark McCall bearing in mind Jane had placed him alongside the body that very morning. "She knew how to make life hard for herself, that's for sure." Eric met her eye with an unspoken request for her to continue. He'd watched Janssen operate enough times to know when to keep quiet. "Well, her parents would have a fit if they knew she was knocking about with the likes of Mark, and I don't think his dad cared for their relationship too much either, whatever it was they were to each other."

"Why do you say that?"

"I know Holly took issue with Mark's dad, that's all. I saw them going at it in town the other week. Old man McCall grabbed a hold of her and Holly went mental." She sank back into the sofa. He gazed at her, poised to continue writing but she shook her head, accompanied by a brief shrug. It was an act of childish petulance and he figured he had got as much from her as he was likely to. "I've no idea what it was all about. Holly never said. You'll have to ask him about it."

CHAPTER SEVEN

THE SUNLIGHT STREAMED in through the window. Not for the first time, Tamara Greave bemoaned the lack of a curtain to pull across to shield her. The driver's voice came over the intercom once again, announcing as soon as the signal change took place they would pull up to the platform at Downham Market. She checked her watch. They had been waiting there for almost fifteen minutes already. Peering up the track, she could see the platform and could easily have walked it three times over in the time they'd been waiting.

On another day she would have swapped seats but for some reason, the train was almost at capacity. Being a Sunday service, there were only two carriages laid on and this had been the only available ticket unless she was willing to travel in the afternoon. That wouldn't do. The call came through the previous evening. DCI Marcus Galbraith had fallen ill and they needed an SIO up on the coast, so the request fell to her. Richard, her fiancé, wasn't happy about it. The family gathering in Peterborough, arranged six months prior, was scheduled as a weekend affair and an early departure was negatively received, by him at least. *Aunt Christine's tales would have to wait until Easter or, with a bit of luck, perhaps the Christmas holidays.*

Not that she owed her departure to him in that way. The reality was she wanted her promotion to be confirmed. Having worked damn hard to make DCI before turning thirty-five, she wouldn't jeopardise it now by appearing inflexible. Besides, Richard fell for the woman who would up sticks on a whim and take off somewhere new at the drop of a hat. That was her thing. A hangover from an upbringing at the hands of arty types in *bohemian Bristol*.

Oh, how she loathed those large family occasions. Not only with Richard's family but hers equally so, but arguably for altogether different reasons. Richard's family were so staid, civilised and quite dull. Hers, on the other hand, were radically opposed to almost everything that passed as state apparatus, the police included. *The police in particular*. That's one reason why she was happy to leave the west country when Richard proposed and move to the other side of England. The excuse of work requirements as well as the distance of travel were beneficial when invitations arrived in the post.

The carriage jolted and for a second she wondered if the engine had detached leaving them to fend for themselves but then she felt movement as the train lurched and juddered forward. Internally she let out a silent whoop of joy. The journey, short as it was, was proving arduous. Richard insisted on keeping the car and Sunday trains were far from frequent, particularly in the direction of the East Anglian coast. Maintenance works had led to further cancellations. This was as close to her final destination as she could get. Which was to say, not very close at all.

Standing, she navigated her way past the other passengers assembling their coats and bags, bracing herself on the headrests of the seats as she angled in the direction of the luggage racks. The train screeched to a halt alongside the platform and she joined the queue of people waiting for the automated doors to unlock. The light blinked from red to green and a young man, wearing a multi-coloured beanie hat and low-slung trousers she was just itching to pull up, tapped the button. The doors hissed and whooshed as they parted. Everyone shuffled forwards, stepping down onto the platform.

People hurried off in the direction of the exit and Tamara looked around, blinking to minimise the glare of the sun sitting low in the sky. She'd never been here before. Extending the handle of her case, she followed the herd. Finding herself at the back of the group, the station emptied quickly and soon she stood alone as family and friends picked up the new arrivals and those travelling on to other stations boarded the bus set aside as a replacement for the cancelled train. Thankfully, she would be spared this particular torture. Scanning the car park, her eyes fell on a tall man standing in the sunshine and leaning against a dark blue Volvo, seemingly preoccupied with his mobile phone. He didn't appear to be meeting anybody and in the absence of anyone else fitting the bill, she approached him. He glanced up, eyeing her arrival. He was fair-haired but carried a natural tan and dark eyes in stark contrast. His appearance was slightly scruffier than she might expect. She found herself wondering if this is the standard that passed for the senior officers on a rural beat.

"DCI Greave?" he asked, greeting her with a smile, revealing white teeth. She approved of good personal hygiene.

"Inspector Janssen?" she replied, offering him her hand. He took it. "You seem surprised."

"I didn't know who to expect."

He sounded sheepish and then it clicked. All he had was a name. He must have been expecting someone else, perhaps another man. *Back in the provinces*, she thought, mocking, *but he doesn't speak with a broad Norfolk accent*. Then again, she shed her own west country twang years ago. Whether that was a conscious choice or a result of the social circles her family moved in she was unsure but most people found it hard to place her accent.

"Is this us?" she asked, indicating the car he was leaning against when she arrived. He nodded, releasing the boot with a touch of a button. The lid elevated and he reached for her case. Normally, she would object, always one to manage herself but on this occasion, she let it slide.

"I've got you booked into a B&B. It is more of a hotel and you can eat there in the evening but I figured this way you could make your own choices. I'll take you there first, so you can freshen up. Then—"

"No!" Her tone was harsh, not intended as such but she was inclined to get up to speed as soon as possible. "I'd rather take a look at where you found the body, if you don't mind?"

"No, not at all." Janssen didn't seem perturbed by her desire to crack on. That was a positive for she wasn't one to let the grass grow under her feet. "I've brought a summary of the case notes compiled thus far. You can familiarise yourself with them on the way. It'll be a good three quarters of an hour drive from here."

She climbed into the passenger seat, noting the child seat in the rear. There was no wedding ring on his left hand, though. Not that it bothered her. Not everyone was as uptight or as traditionally focussed as Richard and his family. The differences between a strong family culture, based broadly along Christian values, versus her own humanist background made for interesting conversations at shared mealtimes. Interesting in her mind at least. She spared a thought for her long-suffering other half. He didn't share his parents' beliefs, but he toed the line for a quiet life. Arguably, he was marrying the wrong woman if he thought she would do the same.

Janssen got into the other side, reaching into the rear and producing a folder that he passed to her. Starting the car, he reversed out of the space. The car park was deserted save for one vehicle in the far corner. It looked like it may have been left there for the weekend. She had no idea of her bearings being so unfamiliar with where she was. Reading the sign indicating a distance to King's Lynn, she thought of yet another place she'd never set foot in. Janssen didn't appear to have much to say. He seemed to be a man of few words. Either that or she was intimidating him. Flicking through the case file, she wondered whether they could pass by a drive-through and pick up a coffee. The after effects of the night before were still present and she needed to sharpen her mind.

They passed over a large roundabout where multiple routes appeared to intersect with each other before they set off in a direct route towards the coast. The road was elevated above the surrounding farmland and she realised how flat the region was. A modern housing development nestled below them off to one side and she considered how realistic the likelihood of them flooding must be.

Reading through the file, she asked the occasional question seeking clarification or elaboration. Janssen seemed on top of his information, being able to answer most of her queries. If he didn't know, he would say so. That was refreshing. In Norwich, she was forever surrounded by those who felt it a weakness to admit they were unsure of something, let alone confessing to their ignorance of a subject.

They took a turning to the right at a small roundabout signposted towards Fakenham. He was talking now, filling her in on the background of the victim. She was the eldest daughter of a well-connected family with a long history in the medical profession. Apparently, the parents hoped she would follow in their footsteps and go on to medical school. She wondered if the girl felt the pressure. Thinking back to her own childhood she could see similarities of sorts. Tamara's own parents were both academically gifted and they were strong influences on her life, so her education was better than many of those who went through the state system. They also went to great lengths to instil a strong ethical foundation in her.

Despite their overall parenting style aiming to bring up confident, socially responsible children, there was always the undercurrent for them to aspire to ecologically responsible careers. Tamara's brothers were currently senior partners in overseas NGOs and her younger sister was a Green Party candidate at the last general election, so they had succeeded in their mission. Tamara, on the other hand, was considered something of a misfit. Although, judging from some of the kids she'd come across in her work, many parents would love to have a daughter as driven as she was but her decision to enter the police force was met with disappointment at best and on other occasions, disdain.

Listening to Janssen talk about the case, the involvement of the boyfriend piqued her curiosity. He was seemingly cut from very different cloth to the victim. The artist's wife also required some looking into. Janssen appeared to have a nose for when something was off but as he rightly pointed out, at this point it was purely instinct. This case appeared to be revolving around internal family dynamics and how they might reach out and draw others in from the periphery. In Holly, Tamara saw a young girl not too far removed from her own experience, keeping secrets, mixing with those her parents would disapprove of and her true personality may prove to be far from the one she presented to the world.

CHAPTER EIGHT

TOM JANSSEN HELD BACK, watching Tamara Greave assess the place where they'd discovered Holly Bettany's body. She had been removed the previous afternoon, transferred into the care of the pathologist to determine the cause and method of her death. The path through the nature reserve remained closed off to the public with a uniformed presence required at both ends of the cordon. A fingertip forensic search took place on the Saturday afternoon but there were no signs of her shoes, bag or any other items that may have belonged to the teenager. They were maintaining the integrity of the scene until the pathologist delivered his results.

He was impressed with the DCI so far. She had a no-nonsense approach, eager to get involved but, at the same time, seemed happy enough to listen. At first, the prospect of a newly promoted SIO, even if only in an acting capacity, taking charge of the investigation concerned him. Not because he had any preconceived ideas surrounding how things should be run but it was more the rapport that they may or may not have. Usually, it was Marcus Galbraith who would travel across the county in this scenario. They got on well, knew each other's strengths and weaknesses. The two of them complemented one another and he enjoyed working alongside him. He was perhaps a little bit old-school but you knew where you stood. Greave on the other hand, was an entirely new proposition. New to him, as well as new to Norfolk.

She knelt alongside where Holly was found, staring at the bank. What she was looking at, or for, he had no idea. Rising, she turned and looked up and down the coast. The coastal fog that rolled in overnight was rapidly burnt off by the rising sun and once again, they were now blessed with a beautiful day. "Stunning here, isn't it?" she said to him and he nodded in agreement. "Any thoughts on how she came to be out here?"

Janssen glanced out to sea. A cargo ship was making its way north hugging the coastline having circumvented the huge offshore wind farm to the south. "She was out with her boyfriend and her peers earlier in the evening. We're working on the theory of her either coming here with her boyfriend or alone with the intention of meeting someone else. I didn't see any signs of defensive wounds on her body but we will have to wait for confirmation of that."

He watched as Tamara looked back to where Holly had lain, possibly recreating the scene in her mind from the pictures taken and supplied in the case file. "When can we expect the report?"

"Monday." Which was tomorrow but somehow it didn't feel like the weekend anymore and Janssen was losing track.

"Where do you think her shoes went?" He got the impression she was genuinely puzzled by the missing shoes and not that she expected him to know the answer.

"Her feet were dirty but that doesn't mean she didn't have shoes, only that she wasn't wearing them all the time."

"Uncomfortable?"

"Possibly. These paths aren't the best. If you're in trainers or walking boots it's not a problem but if not, you could be tempted to remove them."

"Bit cold." Tamara flicked her eyebrows as she voiced the thought. He couldn't disagree. It didn't make a lot of sense. "Have we spoken to the boyfriend yet?"

Janssen shook his head. He had been about to do so first thing but he'd got the call to divert and pick her up so had put it off figuring the

SIO would most likely want to attend. They set off back to the car. The McCalls lived further inland on an old strip of common land that had been the subject of many disputes among local landowners over the years. No one ever successfully laid claim to it with competing titles repeatedly overturning each other in the courts. The upshot of which meant the McCalls managed to stay there with no one ever securing their eviction. On one occasion, a local petitioned the council to have them removed but they were in such a remote location, away from anyone else, that it wasn't deemed worthy of the expenditure from the public purse.

The address was difficult to find. The McCalls lived at the end of an unmade track, churned up by both farm machinery and livestock being driven between grazing land. The car bobbled around as Janssen picked his way along it, doing his level best to avoid the peaks and troughs. The winter may have been mild with little rain but in the flatlands of Norfolk, the ground remained boggy. Tamara held onto the door handle, sometimes glancing in his direction with the odd disapproving look. He was tempted to offer her the chance to drive them back but thought better of it.

Reaching the end of the track, tucked away alongside a small copse of Silver Birch trees was the McCall house. It wasn't really a house. By the look of it, it was an old railway carriage the likes of which hadn't been seen on the network for decades. The exterior to the frontage was lined with windows. They were ingrained with dirt and it was impossible to imagine you could see through them with any clarity. The remains of the carriage were no longer on wheels and as they got out of the car, Janssen figured they'd actually stripped the panels and reused them to fashion a makeshift dwelling with other structures precariously attached in something of an ad hoc fashion.

The roof was made up of an odd assortment of corrugated metal sheets, similar plastic ones and a hodgepodge of felt linings, the likes of which would be commonly used on domestic sheds and garden out-buildings. Janssen noted a cable running up the exterior side of the ramshackle accommodation before angling off and disappearing into the trees. *I wonder where the power is drawn from?* There was no possibility the property was connected to mains water and he assumed they must have access to a natural spring or something nearby. The family were about as close to living off grid as one could get without a lot of green technology and a significant budget.

They approached but didn't get far before the door creaked open and a man stepped out and headed them off. He was short for a man, probably around five-foot-six in height but stocky. He wore grubby jeans and a white vest, now greying with age. He sported several day's worth of stubble growth and his hair was unkempt. Callum McCall scratched at his crown eyeing them warily. "I've nae seen him and I don't ken where he is. Not that I'd tell you if I did!"

Tamara looked to him and Janssen inclined his head. "Good morning, Mr McCall. How do you know we're looking for Mark?"

"Well, aren't you?"

"We are, Mr McCall," Tamara said, displaying her warrant card. "DCI Tamara Greave and this is Detective Inspector Janssen." She indicated in his direction and Janssen nodded a greeting towards him. Callum disregarded her and addressed Janssen.

"Janssen? That's not a Norfolk name." He seemed quite serious, his expression was fixed, disdainful. "You don't look local either. That name sounds more Scandinavian to me. Is that where you're from?"

"When did you last see Mark?" he asked, ignoring the question. "Are you expecting him back soon?"

"No idea." Callum didn't appear to be in the cooperative mood.

"It's very important we speak with him, Mr McCall." Greave asserted herself, coming over to stand slightly in front of Janssen. She clearly wanted to display her authority to Callum. That was fine with him, if she felt the need. "I'm sure you're well aware of how these things go."

"Well aware, aye." Callum fixed her with a stare. "Don't worry about finding the real perpetrator when a McCall will do just as well."

"Seeing as your son isn't here," Tamara said, glancing around the surrounding area, "perhaps you would like to tell us about your relationship with Holly. You did have one, didn't you?" The last was framed as a question but she sought to make it a statement of fact, forcing an admission or a flat-out denial. She was canny, Janssen had to give it to her. Callum thought about it, probably conceiving the question in the same way.

"Yeah. I knew her. She was Mark's girl. Of course, I did." He sniffed loudly, wiping his nose with the back of his hand.

"And the altercation you had with her in town a while back. What was that about?" Tamara wasn't messing about, going straight in on him.

Janssen judged Callum was going to offer a considered response, choosing his words carefully. He didn't want them coming back to bite him. "That was in the coffee shop in town. She pushed in front of me in the queue. Trying to wind me up, that's all. I told her what's what. Nothing more."

"Anyone around to corroborate that?" Janssen asked.

Callum glared at him and nodded. "Loads, yeah."

Tamara exchanged glances with him, turning to go back to the car. "Tell Mark to get in touch, would you?" she said over her shoulder. Janssen took out one of his contact cards and passed it to Callum who accepted grudgingly. He glanced at the card.

"*DI Tom Janssen,*" he said slowly, rolling his tongue across the inside of his lower lip. "*Tom,* eh? Trying to make yourself sound English doesn't count, you know? You'll always be an outsider with a name like that." He fixed Janssen with an impassioned stare.

"Right back at you, *Mr McCall,*" he replied, with a flick of the eyebrows. Callum smiled, apparently enjoying the confrontational exchange. Janssen took a couple of steps backwards before turning and opening the car door. He climbed in alongside Tamara who had already fastened her seatbelt. Starting the engine, he pulled the car forward, coming alongside Callum and lowering his window. "Have Mark call me, for his own sake." He then depressed the accelerator and moved off gently.

Callum watched them go. Tamara adjusted the rear-view mirror without asking, enabling her to observe the man as they drove away. He remained fixed in place, watching the car leave with an expressionless face. She kept her eye on him until they cleared the copse and he disappeared from view. She angled the mirror back to roughly where she imagined she found it. She was way off but Janssen didn't comment, merely setting it back as he desired.

"Pleasant man." Her sarcasm was barely masked.

"He has form for all manner of things. Came out after a short stretch for assault just last summer. I'm surprised he was as helpful as he was."

"Is it true, what he said?" Tamara asked him. He glanced across at her with a questioning look. "I know there isn't necessarily much in a name these days but are you Scandinavian? I see it with the hair and possibly your build but not your complexion or eyes."

He was momentarily thrown. Then he laughed. Tamara echoed it with one of her own.

"Not far off. My grandfather was Dutch, from Friesland, north-east of Amsterdam up on the coast. He was part of the free Dutch army stationed in North Africa when the country was occupied during the war." She nodded along as he continued the story once they'd passed back along the track and re-joined the highway. "He met my grandmother while he was over here, prior to the build-up of the D-Day landings."

"So, he stayed on after the war?" Tamara asked, appearing genuinely interested. He shook his head, smiling.

"Not quite. After the war, he returned to The Netherlands to help rebuild the country but… he missed her, I think." Glancing across, he assessed her interest. She was listening intently. "They were always a bit sketchy on the details. I imagine there were some complications they never wanted to share with the rest of the family, but he came back for her a couple of years later. They never left."

Tamara looked away, staring off into the countryside. He didn't feel the urge to elaborate further, worried perhaps he'd misread her level of interest. A couple of minutes later, he caught her looking over at him.

"That's a beautiful story." She spoke softly before turning her gaze back towards the passing landscape.

CHAPTER NINE

HE'LL HAVE CALMED *down by now. It will be safe.* The thought was more hopeful than assured. Of all the times to have triggered an angry response from his father, this came as the least expected. *He can't blame me, I didn't do it.* Putting his foot through a stick lying on the ground, it launched sideways into the brush. Sheep muttered to one another in the field alongside the path. It was lambing season.

Mark's stomach groaned. He was hungry. Unsurprising when he thought about it. He couldn't eat yesterday. The shock of coming across Holly... like that... the thought of it made him feel physically sick. Seeing her, so pale, so peaceful. She could have been asleep, if it weren't for her eyes staring to the heavens, cold and lifeless. *Then there was the mad woman.* The one Holly always referred to as the neurotic, psychopathic witch, standing over him, watching. He had run as far and as fast he could until his legs gave out beneath him and he'd fallen to the ground gasping for air. The fright was something else, a new experience, and he thought he knew everything there was to know about fear. He was wrong.

There was his stomach again. A sense of betrayal coursed through him. Admitting to and feeding such a base level need felt somehow deceitful, guilty. It was strange. Holly was gone and he couldn't understand it. Eventually returning home the day before in the early afternoon, he found his father up and about. Gingerly wandering about nursing his sore head… his ever-present sore head, he had told him about Holly, immediately feeling the need to protest his innocence. After all, his father always told him to be careful where he went and who he confided in. *The rest of the world aren't like you son. You can't trust them. You can only trust us.* He meant the family, himself and the other children, his siblings but not his mother. Definitely not his mother. She had proven the point by vanishing one night, years ago, when Mark was barely into double figures. Disappearing as they slept, without a word, and leaving them all to get by without her.

Thinking back on his father's reaction, it had surprised him. First, he stared at him, straight-faced and silent. At school, his English teacher once quoted Shakespeare as saying *the eyes are the windows to your soul.* That was a wonderful expression. If so, his father's soul was a terrifying place. Having gazed on him, Mark remembered the feeling of nervousness under the scrutiny, he had sniffed loudly, a habit he had when he was under stress and then dismissed it. *Dismissed Holly's death like it meant nothing!* Anger flared within him then. Just as it did on occasions when people came too close. *Penetrated his personal space*, his support worker once said.

The night had been cold, unforgiving, but it wasn't the first he'd spent outdoors and undoubtedly, it wouldn't be the last. The words exchanged the previous day were harsh, bitter. He thought on it. Things would be calm now. Both of them would be calm.

Approaching the rear of the house, voices carried on the gentle breeze. His father was talking to someone. He was irritated. It was evident in his tone although he wasn't letting on. If you knew him as well as any son knows their father you would easily recognise the tension. The other man was addressing him politely but, in a stern, authoritative way, just as the teachers did at school before he'd moved up to the sixth form. Now they were kinder, speaking with him and the others more like they were grown-ups. Holly flashed into his mind, still and lifeless. Dead. She would never get to grow up.

Hanging back, he dropped into the nearby tree line and crouched low, skirting around his home and taking up a position behind the brush to enable him to observe the exchange. There was a woman there as well, serious looking and attractive, but she didn't speak. He watched as she got into the car. His father exchanged another word with the man. He was taller, blond and didn't seem to take to whatever was said to him. Mark couldn't hear his response, try as he might, but his father didn't like it. He tensed. Mark knew that look well. He half expected him to land a punch on the tall stranger but instead the man backed away and got into the car. They were police. There had been enough of them calling by over the years for him to recognise them as such.

A feeling of dread manifested in the pit of his stomach. His hunger all but forgotten. *They were here for me.* The car disappeared from view but he remained where he was. Shifting his weight saw him snap a small branch at his feet. His father looked around staring directly at the place he was hiding but still he didn't move. He was rooted to the spot.

"Get out here boy!" his father called to him. "I think you and me need to have wee chat."

CHAPTER TEN

JANE FRANCIS STOOD in the garden to the front of their house, turning her face to the sun. Cupping the mug of tea with both hands, she warmed her fingers. The temperature outside was climbing but there was another mild frost overnight thanks to the clear skies and lack of wind. Soon, the onset of spring would march forward unabated and the freezing, mist-shrouded days would be quickly forgotten. Thankfully, the children were no longer badgering her for details about the macabre scene they envisioned their mother stumbling across the day before. William in particular was decidedly put out about the apparent lack of blood at the scene. Not that she would have said if there were. His persistence was eventually rewarded with the briefest of descriptions. She was careful to say just enough to satisfy his curiosity but offered nowhere near enough detail to feed his enthusiasm.

I'm sure it's those damn computer games, she thought, remembering the gleam in his eyes as he asked her to recount what she'd seen. Ken didn't see an issue, putting it down to the naivety of youth and a lack of understanding between action and consequence. *Like he could lecture anyone on that subject.* She found herself picturing Holly as she had seen her on the path, a far stretch away from the arrogant child with the haughty expression. She was a girl playing at being a woman. Still with so much to learn but already acting like the master. *She was better off dead.* Catching the thought as soon as it popped into her head, she immediately felt guilty. That wasn't fair. The girl was misguided, intentionally so in her opinion, but she hadn't deserved to die.

It's still okay not to like her.

Stepping back into the house, the children were nowhere to be seen. The sound of thundering feet on the wooden floorboards above carried to her and she realised they were upstairs. Ken was sitting at the table in the kitchen, sketching something on his notepad with a pencil while he drank his coffee. She had slept in this morning. Ken, on the other hand, was up remarkably early for him. She pretended to be asleep not wanting to engage in conversation, but she knew he had been awake for some time before he got up and went downstairs having spent half an hour pacing around the bedroom.

Her husband appeared drawn and haggard. A far cry from the man she married years ago. He was older than her by nearly a decade at that time. Now, the distance between them was greater still, more so than just years. Everyone changed, grew older and less attractive. She knew she had peaked. The kids helped to drive that point home but she felt good, still looked great and attracted attention. Just not from Ken. Their marriage had become a trade-off. *Had it always been so?*

"Do you want more coffee?" She adopted a lighter tone than she normally offered, seeking to draw him out of his trance-like contemplation. Perhaps she was interested in what he might have to say after all. He had certainly gone quiet once the police left yesterday.

"No, thanks. I'm off to the studio."

She watched as he finished his coffee, standing and placing the cup alongside the dishwasher but not in it. He sat down in order to put on his shoes. He hadn't showered this morning or shaved. He was scruffy but didn't manage to carry it off anywhere near as well as that fair-haired detective who visited the day before.

"You haven't said anything about her." Ken paused. He was bent over, tying up his shoe lace but he didn't look up. Seconds later, he continued on with it.

"What's there to say?"

Well, you could say how much you're going to miss her. You could bemoan you won't be having sex with her anymore because you were, weren't you? But you won't ever admit it, will you? These were all valid questions that came to mind but she voiced none of them. He stood up, avoiding her eye and walked to the rear door. He stopped at the threshold to the kitchen, placing a hand on the doorframe, turning to look at her over his shoulder. He seemed about to speak but his eyes were drawn to William coming down the stairs on the far side of the room and instead, he shook his head.

"I will miss her," he said, almost in a whisper.

I bet you will. Then you'll have to replace her, like you did with the last one... and the one before that.

As William clattered into the kitchen in search of food, Ken slipped out. Jane watched him through the open window, crossing the yard right up until he disappeared into his studio.

"Mum, I'm hungry." William whined. The words didn't register. "Mum, I'm hungry. I *really need* something to eat."

"What was that?" she asked, turning to him. He was about to repeat his statement for the third time when they heard a shout. It was one born of desperation and anguish rather than anger.

"Is that Daddy?" William asked with a nervous frown.

"Wait here," she told him, putting her mug down on the work surface and heading outside. She scampered across the yard, careful not to slip on the uneven cobbles, still damp from the melting frost. They'd dry out once the sun breached the ridgeline of the house.

Converted from one of the old barns, the studio was twelve metres long, six wide and open to the roof trusses above. Ken utilised one end for his ceramic works, sculptures and standalone pieces with the other set aside for his canvas works. She gasped. These were strewn around the studio. Some were destroyed, the canvas torn and, in some cases, practically shredded. Ruined beyond repair. Other works, whether sketch outlines in charcoal or pencil or part-painted pieces were daubed in various colours or a whole tin of paint had been thrown over them. The space was in utter disarray.

Jane glanced to the far end and she could see debris everywhere. The sculptures were lying on the floor, some smashed beyond recognition whereas others lay on the floor chipped or missing sections.

"Oh, Ken... what's happened?" she spoke softly, the damage was devastating in its level of destruction. Her husband was facing away from her. He didn't utter a single word in reply. His shoulders began to vibrate and his head tilted forward. She realised he was crying. The sound grew and he sank to his knees, his breathing turned into loud gasps for air as the tears became sobs.

"What's wrong with Daddy?" a quiet voice came from behind. She turned to see the children standing at the entrance. William's mouth was open and his eyes narrowed as he looked upon them both. Rosie stood slightly behind him, to his left, peering around her brother at the interior of the studio, frightened. She shooed them back towards the main house with the promise of chocolate biscuits and fizzy drinks. Rosie came willingly but William was reticent, clearly worried about his father. Begrudgingly, at her insistence he followed on.

Once they were settled, instructing them to stay in the house, she ran back to the studio. Ken was sitting now, with his back to the wall. His composure had returned but it was still evident he'd been crying. His face was tear lined with streaks down both cheeks as he scanned the destruction. His eyes flicked to her as she entered. She stopped for a brief moment before coming to him and kneeling alongside. Reaching out, she placed a comforting hand on his shoulder. It was the first physical contact they'd shared, at least that she'd initiated, in months. Without a word, he leaned in to her and she nestled down alongside him allowing his head to fall against her chest.

They remained there in silence. Jane looked around. The double bed that Ken used both as a set for his models to pose on and as an occasional sleep pad for himself, had several different colours of paint thrown over it. The white duvet and bedlinen were now highlighted with yellow and purple. The walls, too, were not spared. *Scum* was legible in one place, *nonce* in another. Alongside the bed a pair of red high-heeled shoes lay haphazardly near one another.

She looked down at the broken, shell of the man she fell in love with, now cradling his head. Running her free hand through his hair a phrase came to mind. *For better or for worse.* Turning her thoughts to the note she found in the post the previous morning, she remembered it was still in the pocket of the jeans she was wearing yesterday. They were now in the dirty linen basket. Fortunately, Ken would never bother to attempt the laundry but she made a mental note to retrieve it later. *Things were starting to get out of hand.*

CHAPTER ELEVEN

THE STATION WAS QUIET. It always was on a Sunday. Eric was alone in the ops room. Pushing aside the folder on the desk in front of him, he made room for his lunch. Initially he objected but bearing in mind the limited options available, in the end, he relented and allowed his mum to make him lunch to take with him. She had a point. There was no time limit on his working day, not in a case such as this. Secretly, Eric was concerned that was one of the driving factors for why his transfer to CID was rubber stamped. The way working contracts were set up these days uniform officers could claim overtime or rest days in lieu if they were kept beyond their allocated shift. CID officers had no such recourse. If you caught a major case, then you were expected to run with it. It was no wonder CID were struggling to recruit and retain officers.

That was where he fitted in. He didn't have a family. Well, he did but his mother didn't really count. Without children, he considered himself far too young for all of that, or even a girlfriend to speak of there was no danger of his caseload getting in the way of his personal life. Not that the cases crossing his desk up until now were particularly beguiling. DI Janssen was keeping things from him of that he was certain but what he didn't know was *why*? The confident side of his nature advised it was to allow him to bed in, find his feet before the pressure would ramp up. Then there was the nagging little voice, the one that told him why he couldn't attract a girlfriend. This voice implied that Tom Janssen didn't rate him, nor want him on his team and therefore couldn't trust him. Time would tell.

Unwrapping the cling film from his sandwich, he took a bite. Home-made Coronation Chicken filling with a fresh salad to accompany it and a piece of cake. *This is why I would be mad to find a place of my own,* he thought, regardless of what his friends said. Voices in the corridor announced the imminent arrival of his boss. Sitting up in his chair, he chewed furiously and tried to swallow the mouthful before they entered; but failed.

Tom Janssen walked in, glancing at him. The woman alongside him was a new face and he looked past her, seeking DCI Galbraith but it was quickly apparent the two were alone. Janssen must have read the look of confusion on his face.

"Eric Collet. Meet DCI Tamara Greave. She will be the SIO on the Bettany case."

Realising she was the new boss, he practically leapt out of his chair, keen to make a good impression. The chair slid backwards on its wheels, striking his desk. The impact rocked his open bottle of coke and it toppled, spreading fizzy pop across his paperwork. He swore, righting the bottle and frantically rescuing as much of the paperwork as he could while the liquid fizzed and spread everywhere, running to the edge of the desk and falling to the floor below. He swore again, flushing red with embarrassment.

Greave noticed a box of tissues on an adjacent desk, passing it across. Eric thanked her and began the clean up operation. Inwardly cursing his clumsiness, he knew they were off to a poor start. Glancing in their direction, Janssen looked on with an expression depicting a mixture of pity and mild amusement. As for the DCI, she merely frowned. He wished the ground would open up and swallow him whole.

"You went back over to the Bettanys' house yesterday, right?" Janssen asked him as he finished the mopping up. He nodded. "What did you pull out of Holly's room besides the laptop?"

Eric felt much more comfortable. He had something constructive to share. Producing a large evidence envelope, he took it over to another desk, one without fizzy cola residue. Removing the contents, a clutch of sheets of plain paper, he lay them out alongside each other. The two senior officers came to stand behind him, looking over his shoulder.

"I found these in a folder stashed at the back of her wardrobe."

"Stashed?" Tamara asked.

"Yes. They were underneath a pile of clothing towards the rear. But I don't think they are old works and forgotten about. Look," he pointed to them, "the paper is not faded and the edges aren't tatty or creased. She took care of them and I think they're recent works."

"So, she was a budding artist?" Janssen said, admiring one of the drawings. Eric noted his interest in that particular sketch. It was black and white, sketched with charcoal by the look of it. It was also a stunningly accurate representation of Holly.

"I don't think she did that, though," he said. Both senior officers looked to him. Feeling suddenly self-conscious he continued. "Look at this." He reached past them and scooped up another piece. This one was of a male face only this time it was drawn in pencil and the lines were of a far lesser quality. "Either she was excellent one day, in self-portraits, and forgot how to draw the next or…?"

"She was responsible for some but not all," Tamara finished, nodding her approval of his conclusion.

"That's right. I reckon someone else was sketching her and either she took it or it was a gift."

"Is it signed?" Janssen said, leaning in for a closer look. It wasn't, not even initialled. Eric reached for another work, passing it over to Janssen but Tamara misread the intent and took it from him instead. The image was of another male, only this time there was more definition to the figure. He appeared to be drawn bearded, an attempt at designer stubble possibly.

"A different person to before," Tamara said. "Perhaps she was part of a true-life artist's class? Do you have anything like that around here?"

Eric didn't know of anything like that but both of them appeared to be looking to him. He knew Janssen was impressed by his local knowledge of people but arty hobbies weren't his interest. He shook his head. "I'll ask around." If anyone was disappointed with the contribution, they didn't show it.

"We could always ask Ken Francis. He would probably know," Janssen suggested. Eric was annoyed he hadn't thought of that. It was fairly obvious. "Did you ask the parents, Colin or Marie, about these drawings?" They looked to him once again. He hadn't. Shaking his head, he felt that was another mark against him today. He was playing a blinder. "Any joy with Holly's laptop?"

"No. It's password protected and the encryption on this brand is pretty decent. We will have to get the tech guys in Norwich to have a look at it." Janssen appeared deflated. With Holly's diary recording next to nothing aside from a few choice references regarding her mother's insistence she continued her musical endeavours, they knew very little about what made Holly tick. There was always the hope she was more open in the digital world than the written.

"What about her digital footprint, aside from the computer? Does she have a mobile phone?" Tamara asked.

"We haven't found the suitcase she left home with on the Friday evening, her mobile phone nor traced the shoes she was wearing either," Janssen said, sounding frustrated. Eric figured that if they found any of those then they would be on to where she spent her last hours, who with and perhaps, how she wound up dead.

"I've been onto the phone company for her records. They should come through tomorrow." Eric was pleased he had something useful to contribute, to demonstrate his value. "The phone is switched off or out of signal. I tried yesterday and this morning. I also spoke with the tutor last night."

"Good," Janssen said. They had been unable to reach him throughout the day on Saturday. "What did he have to say?"

"Holly never showed up for her tutorial." The tutor was amenable and came across as very organised when they'd spoken on the phone. "He claims he called the parents at home in case there was a misunderstanding in the scheduling but only got the machine. Says he left a message."

"Marie said she was at choral practice on Friday night, dropping

Holly off at the bus stop." Janssen said aloud, presumably for Greave's benefit. "Neither of them mentioned an answerphone message. I guess they might not have picked it up."

Eric was pleased he could contribute again. "I also spoke with the bus driver on Friday's route and he didn't recall picking anyone up in Burnham Market, Friday evening. He said it was a quiet route at that time of the evening and he would have remembered if Holly got on. She makes that journey a couple of times a week and he was confident he would recognise her."

Tamara turned to him, concentrating hard. "I read in your notes that the Bettanys planned for Holly to go to medical school, follow in their footsteps. Is that right?" She looked to both of them in turn, they both nodded. "What was the tutor's assessment of Holly? I take it you asked the question?"

Eric blew an internal, silent sigh of relief. He had asked. "Curiously, the tutor didn't think Holly's heart was in her academic studies." Tamara's eyes narrowed, focussing on him intently. "He said she seemed…" He thought hard to remember. "Distracted recently. Yes, that was how he put it, distracted."

"Did he say by what?" Janssen asked. The tutor had been reluctant to speculate, so Eric didn't know. He shook his head.

"Sounds to me like we still don't really have a handle on who the real Holly Bettany is," Tamara said, stepping back from the desk and pacing away. Eric considered she was momentarily lost in thought and he exchanged glances with Janssen. His DI giving little away as usual. He could be a hard man to read sometimes and that made him intimidating. At least, it did to Eric. Tamara turned, perching herself on the edge of a desk. "I want us to revisit Holly's friends and we really need to locate Mark McCall. According to this friend of hers, Amelia, she was dating Mark in some sense of the word. I want to know the extent of their relationship as well as why they kept it so quiet. It seems to me that their peer group were aware but only the parents were in the dark. If so, we should have no shortage of people who can shed some light on them as a couple. Eric, you go into the sixth form tomorrow, if you have to."

"In the meantime," Janssen said once she appeared to have finished handing out assignments, "I'll head back out to speak with Ken Francis, see if he can direct us to some art classes Holly may have attended. You never know, he may have been there himself." Janssen looked to her, seeking approval or was he looking to call the shots? It was hard to tell. After a moment, she nodded. "I can drop you at your B&B if you like. Give you a chance to freshen up."

"Do I look tired or something?" she replied. The words sounded sharp, accusatory, as if coming from someone suffering from a lack of sleep. Eric felt awkward. As if he was standing between two parents gearing up to have a mild disagreement. Janssen smiled and the tension Eric perceived was there, evaporated. He was often prone to interpreting things that just weren't there. Paranoia, his mother always said.

"Not at all. You can always come along if you like?"

"I will. You can drop me off on the way back, though." She glanced at Eric's desk. He wasn't sure if she was assessing the damage to his paperwork or revisiting his clumsiness. "And if you know of somewhere where we can have lunch on the way, that'd be grand too." Eric followed her gaze and his eyes fell on his sandwich. His stomach rumbled. He was also hungry.

CHAPTER TWELVE

TAMARA LOOKED FORWARD to seeing the names on the road signs as they flashed by. *Burnham Overy Staithe* was the next to catch her eye. She hadn't spent much time in this part of the county. Since the move east her time was dominated by finding her feet in Norwich. The personal requirement to prove her ability in the role was almost all-consuming. Taking on the mantle she set herself was already impacting on the rest of her life, that being Richard and their impending marriage. Not that they'd set a date, much to her future mother-in-law's chagrin. *Wait until she finds out we're not getting married in a church.*

Another road sign. This one was *Egmere*. Trying to remember her history, she thought all the *hams* and the *thorpes* derived from *Old English* but then again, the impact of *Norse* on the region was well known and documented. She glanced across at Janssen, concentrating on driving the car, and considered asking him. He was local and would probably know. She thought better of it. Tom Janssen was an intriguing man. Her initial assessment of him now appeared way off the mark. Not once did she have the impression he was irritated by her arrival or her taking over of the investigation. He was diligent, courteous and focussed. Definitely focussed.

Glancing over her shoulder at the child's seat in the rear, she found it curious he didn't speak of his family. Nor had he made any reference to working over the weekend and therefore being away from them. It did come with the job, after all. Then again, maybe he silently celebrated not being around the child. Kids weren't everyone's cup of tea.

Richard was keen. So keen, in fact, he was already asking about maternity leave, pay and whether she would want to go back to work at all. They weren't quite on the same page. It wasn't that she hadn't necessarily been truthful with him, more that she'd ducked out of voicing what she was thinking. It was often easier to keep quiet and let others do the talking, particularly if they might not take to your opinion. *Got to think about these things,* he would often say. Presumably, that was his way of pointing out her age. She didn't see the issue. It was commonplace for women to have children in their late thirties, perhaps even into their early forties…

Turning her thoughts away from her relationship and towards Holly, she considered what they knew. The girl was an enigma to them, once you stripped away the veneer of presentation projected to the world. Through her parents' eyes, she was off to medical school. Perhaps struggling a little academically but with their resources they could pay for the extra she needed to get through. Then she would follow them into their profession, pursuing the same career and lifestyle. She found herself wondering if the younger sibling was being funnelled in the same direction. That was one to check.

Whatever Colin and Marie Bettany thought, they didn't appear to know their eldest very well. Listening to Eric's description of her bedroom along with the results of the detailed search, she saw similarities of her own experience as a teenager. Eric documented the lack of cosmetics found in her room, assuming Holly took them with her to prepare for the night ahead. Judging from the impression she had of the Bettanys, it was more likely Holly kept much of her make-up secreted somewhere. Most likely applying the more striking elements to her appearance elsewhere, away from the home if it was a regular theme. The image of Holly's appearance on the path came to mind. The black eye-liner, pale foundation and the bright red lipstick. Instinct suggested she was masking herself, desperate to present an image to the world other than the one she usually offered. Or perhaps not the world, maybe just one person. One special person.

Janssen applied the brakes. They snatched so fiercely that Tamara grasped the handle of the door alongside her seeking to brace against the force of the manoeuvre. Caught by surprise, she glared at Janssen. He released the brakes, looking up the road before turning the car and setting off back in the direction they'd just come from.

"Sorry."

She didn't acknowledge the apology but had no time to ask what he was up to as the car pulled off the main road at the next intersection. Janssen stopped the car, switching off the engine and releasing his seatbelt. "Are we going somewhere?" The words were angry, a result of shock and surprise.

"We just drove past Mark."

Tamara unfastened her own belt and hopped out of the car, rushing to catch up with the tall detective as his long legs strode back towards the main carriageway. As they approached the junction, a young man came into view from their right. He appeared startled to see the two of them squaring off his path in front of him. He stopped, looking to both left and right before glancing back over his shoulder.

"We just want to have a word, Mark. There's no need to think about running." Janssen was authoritative but at the same time his demeanour was reassuring. She was impressed. Mark visibly appeared to relax, his shoulders dropping and any suggestion he was preparing to run dissipated. The boy still looked like a rabbit caught in the headlights, though, and she stepped forward, smiling, seeking to put him at ease.

"Mark. My name's Tamara and this is Tom Janssen. We're police officers. It is true, we only want to speak with you about Holly. We're trying to get to the bottom of what happened to her. That's all." He fixed her with a stare. When she first spoke, his eyes conveyed fear but now, glancing between the two of them, perhaps as the initial surprise faded, he seemed calmer, more agreeable. "We were just going to grab a bite to eat. Are you hungry?" Mark's lips parted and she saw his tongue pressed against the lower lip. He appeared thoughtful, assessing her just as much as he was her offer. Then, he nodded.

The officers parted, turning side on and Mark came forward to stand between them. Janssen smiled. She knew it was forced. A gesture to put the boy at ease but even so, he managed to make it seem natural. She had the impression Tom Janssen smiled a lot. Only, perhaps, not so much while at work.

They found a small café still open after the lunchtime rush. The sign listing the opening hours stated the business should be closed. Full trade would take effect at the end of the month, coinciding with the fall of Easter this year, if Tamara had worked the dates out correctly. She always struggled with the fluctuations of the religious calendar not having been raised among it. She presupposed the onset of the fine weather, so early in spring, saw an influx of customers and made it sensible to throw open the doors.

She was sitting outside with Mark at a picnic table painted blue and white. There was space for only a handful of patrons and she was thankful that the busy period had passed prior to their arrival. A small group of ramblers funnelled past the table, clutching takeaway coffees and some home-made cakes and biscuits. It was a fine afternoon for a walk. Janssen appeared from the interior carrying a tray. On it were two coffees, one for each of them and a bottle of coke for Mark. Setting the tray down, he lifted a pint glass off it containing a wooden spoon, a large number four was written on it in black marker. She looked around them at the empty tables and then past him, into the interior. It was devoid of customers now.

"You think they'll struggle to know who the rolls are for?" She nodded towards the spoon, the marker to guide the staff to the correct table with their order. Janssen smiled but said nothing, placing her coffee before her. She thanked him.

"I ordered you a fried egg in yours. That was right, wasn't it?" Janssen asked her, she nodded. She didn't eat meat, having been raised a vegetarian but she still wasn't prepared to go vegan. Not yet. Although, every trip to visit her family imposed it. Mark sipped at his coke. She watched him for a second before speaking.

"You were with Holly on Friday night." She could have tested the boy's honesty by asking but was keen to progress the conversation. At this stage, she didn't see him as the most probable killer. Never in her experience had she come across a killer who disposed of a victim, only to return to it the following morning carrying his breakfast. Sociopathic narcissists could do such a thing, those devoid of all empathy, but they kept their victims secreted in their homes, not on public display. "One of your friends at the party told us."

Mark looked her in the eye. "None of them are my friends. Only Holly." The animosity in his tone was obvious.

She acknowledged the correction, making a mental note. "What time did you and Holly leave the party?" He shook his head, offering an accompanying shrug. "Where did you go?" He seemed reluctant to answer but she didn't sense he was trying to conceal something or fabricate an answer. "It's important, Mark."

"There's a place. I go there when... when I need to be alone."

"And you went there with Holly?" Again, he paused, looking down. She was about to push when the waitress arrived with their food. She was an upbeat, enthusiastic woman, passing round their orders, cutlery, and offering them sauces. The interruption passed and the three were alone again. Tearing open a tiny packet of salt, she sprinkled it over her egg and then secured the top of the roll in place. Mark struggled to open a ketchup packet for his bacon roll and Janssen assisted him.

They began to eat, allowing the boy a moment of peace. He set about the food with such gusto, she wondered when he last ate. "Mark. You took Holly to your place. Is it special to you?" He looked up at her, bobbing his head in answer as he chewed a mouthful. Wiping ketchup from the corner of his mouth with the back of his hand, he smiled.

"She was keen. I always told her I would take her one day."

"And did she like it?" Biting down on her roll, she tried to keep the conversation low-key and relaxed. The yoke split and ran from the bread, over the back of her hand. Placing it down, she dabbed at the corner of her mouth with a paper napkin and then cleaned her hand. "Did she?"

Mark shook his head. "We never made it."

"Why? What happened?" she asked him, glancing at Janssen. He wasn't contributing. To the uninitiated, he was paying little attention, merely eating his food and sipping at his coffee. She knew better. He was absorbing every detail, every nuance, no matter how slight.

"She changed her mind."

Tamara waited for him to elaborate but nothing was forthcoming. "Just like that?" Mark nodded, crestfallen. "Was that unusual for her. To behave like that, I mean?"

"No, not really," he replied. His tone was melancholic now, disappointed. "She would blow hot and cold. Some days I think she would be so excited around me and others... well... she was changeable as the weather, that's what my mum used to say."

"About Holly?" she asked.

"No. People in general. Fitted with Holly, though."

"And where did she go, then?" Mark shook his head to indicate he didn't know. "When did you next see her?"

"Saturday morning, on the path... when I..." He fell silent, probably reliving the memory, she suspected. Looking to Janssen, he met her eye with a flick of one eyebrow.

"Why did you run, Mark?" she asked him, applying a stern tone to her voice in order to convey the seriousness of the question.

"Because of her. *That woman*." He spoke with such venom that it threw her off guard, albeit for a second.

"Jane Francis?" Janssen asked softly. Mark looked to him, his eyes narrowing. "What is it about her you don't like?"

The answer was almost spat with anger. "*She's evil*, that's what."

CHAPTER THIRTEEN

TOM JANSSEN PONDERED their discussion with Mark McCall. For a young man of seventeen, he seemed awfully naïve about the ways of the world. That assessment was exacerbated by the family he sprung from. If there were a family whom you could rely on to be cynically manipulating people or the system for their own benefit, it was the McCalls. However, Mark fell short of what he expected and that threw him. He'd be lying if he denied slotting the lad into the frame almost as soon as they heard Mark and Holly were involved with one another. That's not the same as believing him guilty, but their family reputation was well earned. He wondered whether Tamara was thinking the same.

She hadn't said much since they dropped Mark off at the end of the track running up to his home. The boy didn't seem in much of a hurry to walk away. Perhaps that was to do with the bruising that he noticed just visible beneath the neckline of his t-shirt. Without any visible defensive wounds to Holly, he was confident they weren't caused by an altercation with her. Besides, the yellow tinge indicated they were older, developing for a week or maybe more.

The children must have heard their car approaching, dropping whatever they were doing and running to the gate to inspect the arrivals. Rosie, the younger one, probably six or seven years old, and a similar age to Saffy, climbed the gate as they took the turn from the track into the yard. Her feet planted on the bottom bar, Janssen was pleased to see the gate tethered in place as the little girl swung backwards and forwards. The boy, *William* if he remembered rightly, stood off to one side. He watched them with a fixed expression, bordering on regretful and far more serious than any ten-year-old should bear, in Janssen's mind, anyway.

Coming to the rear, where the Francis's parked their vehicles, he was intrigued to see Ken having something of a clear out. Coming out of his studio with bundles of wood and what appeared to be canvas in his arms he was heading towards a skip, sited at the far end of the yard, adjacent to the former barn. There was a great deal of builder's residue stacked up nearby, presumably leftover from the renovation works, waiting to be either reused or hauled away. Ken eyed them as he walked past, tossing his load into the skip before returning to them. His expression was stern. Janssen thought he looked uptight, emotional.

"I wonder what he's up to," Tamara said under her breath. The best lip readers in the world would have struggled to interpret her words, Janssen was sure.

"Just what I was thinking."

"You take Ken. You've met him already. I imagine he'll more likely speak to you, than me. I'll pull Jane aside and sound her out, see if I can get a steer on what Mark was talking about."

He agreed and they both got out of the car. Rosie was still perched on the gate, although she now sat on the top bar, legs dangling over the side watching them, fascinated. William was nowhere to be seen. Janssen greeted Ken while Tamara looked towards the main house. "I wanted to pick your brains about the artist community, if you can spare me a few minutes?" Ken stopped, an almost unreadable expression crossing his face. *Was it irritation?* Whatever the motivation, it passed swiftly enough.

"If you don't mind me cracking on as we talk," Ken replied, setting off towards the studio.

"Is your wife about?" Tamara called after him and he responded over his shoulder without looking at her.

"In the house. The door's open."

Janssen was surprised. If Ken was curious as to who she was, he didn't seem bothered about asking. She was with Janssen and must therefore be a police officer but the offhand nature of the response was interesting. He glanced at Tamara and she appeared to find it just as odd. The two parted, with Tamara heading for the house while he followed Ken into the studio.

Entering, he failed to mask his shock at what he found inside. His mouth fell open as he scanned the studio. The place was trashed. An effort had been made to pull things together, a partial attempt at tidying up. Piles of rubbish lay sporadically around the space. Ripped canvases were neatly stacked against one another and nearby, a pile of shattered ceramics was swept into a corner. A fine dust hung in the air, catching in his throat as he breathed in. Paint had been thrown around the interior and someone had obviously had a go at cleaning something off the walls. Two of them were damp. The contrast to the dry surface alongside was stark. A bucket of water stood beside one wall, still soapy with a sponge floating near the surface. The residue of purple paint remained visible on the wall above, smeared over the white of the base colour.

"I dread to ask," he said softly, Ken watching him with a wary eye as he gathered another armful of his work, now resembling more junk than art.

"We had a break-in last night." His tone was bitter, angry.

"Did you report it?" In his head, he sounded accusatory. It wasn't his intent.

"What's the point? They didn't take anything, just smashed up my work. Only my finished pieces are insured and they're not kept here." Ken was dismissive. Disappearing back outside, Janssen chose to wait for him to return rather than follow him like a puppy. Looking around, he saw none of the windows were broken and he casually inspected the door to see if it was forced. There was no damage. It was strange. The man had no reason to lie, though, as far as Janssen knew.

Ken reappeared to find him eyeing the lock. He must have clicked what he was thinking. "I don't bother locking the studio at night. Who would want to nick a load of half-finished paintings? Utter madness."

"I bet you'll start now." The response was instant, perhaps coming across as flippant.

"Probably just kids pissing about anyway." Janssen flicked his eyebrows at the suggestion but didn't comment. He hadn't come across bored youngsters doing anything on this scale before. The odd bus shelter or estate agent's *For Sale* board, maybe, but this was a different level of vandalism altogether.

"Anyone express any dissatisfaction with you recently?"

"No, of course not!" Ken replied, irritated. "Look, I don't wish to be rude, Inspector, but you can see I have rather a lot on. Perhaps you could get to the point of your visit?"

"Fair enough, Mr Francis." He adopted a commanding, professional tone. "We're following a line of inquiry that relates to art and seeing as you're the foremost artist in this area, and also the only one I happen to know, I was wondering if you could tell me of any amateur classes, workshops or the like going on around here?"

Ken was kneeling pulling together broken frames, some still with the remnants of canvas stretched across them. He stopped, looking up at him. "What style? Painting or ceramics?"

"Sketching, I would say. Using charcoal maybe," he replied, pointing towards a piece offset nearby, leaning against the wall. One of the few works that appeared to have been spared.

"Yes, that's charcoal. Not many use it around here as far as I know. Not any of those who claim to be teachers anyway."

"But you do."

Ken met his eye, before resuming his selection of pieces to carry. "Yes. I do but no, sorry. I'm not aware of any classes. You've no idea how annoying these provincial amateurs are. I tend to steer clear of them. Once they know you've sold a few pieces, they are all over you to come and join their sessions. Keen to bask in the light of your name and develop their own kudos. I don't mix with the *artistic community*." The last was said with derision which was a surprising take on a group of people who held mutual interests. Ken gathered up his next load and set off.

Janssen took a deep breath. For the life of him, he couldn't figure out why someone may have taken offence to this man and his attitude. The previous day, Ken couldn't have been more pleasant but he'd been playing the perfect host then. Somehow, this revelation of an angry man, albeit with an arguably justifiable reason for his mood, seemed closer to the real Ken Francis than the one seen yesterday. The man who usually kept himself veiled behind a successful, creative persona harboured a darker edge.

This time, he followed Ken out into the yard. The man was rattled and therefore, he judged, more likely to give something away with an angry response or an ill-thought out comment. Perhaps he would be honest. Emerging into the sunlight, Janssen shielded his eyes. The interior of the studio was somewhat gloomy. The thought occurred that the windows faced north. An obscure fact popped into his head how artists often angled studios to the north as the light remained constant, unchanging with the passage of the sun through the day and the year.

Ken was walking back towards him. Janssen looked around. The children were nowhere to be seen. "How well do you know Holly?" The question came out of the blue and Ken Francis stopped dead in his tracks.

"I don't!" He was emphatic. "I mean, I've come across her parents socially. Her name came up."

"So, you do know her then. At least, a little."

"I guess. Why do you ask?"

"What about your wife?" Janssen glanced towards the house, remembering Mark's outburst regarding Jane. He could see figures moving in the kitchen through the window. Ken's mouth partially opened. He appeared ready to speak but didn't. "Would she know Holly any better than you?"

"I… don't know what you're inferring."

"I'm not *inferring* anything, Mr Francis. It's a question." He watched the man intently, gauging his reaction, for there was one. It was just that right now, he couldn't interpret it.

"I don't know. You should ask her."

Ken walked past Janssen and back into his studio. Janssen watched the man go until he disappeared from view. He then crossed the yard, heading for the main house, wondering what was scrawled on the walls that needed cleaning off before anything else was attended to?

CHAPTER FOURTEEN

JANE SAW the woman walking towards the house while Janssen addressed her husband. Why couldn't they do it the other way around? Janssen was sharp but she could read him, well enough at least. He was also quiet, no doubt very observant but she figured he was malleable, of an age where she could still deploy her charm successfully if needed. The thought of spending more time with him was agreeable. Hurrying back into the preparation area, she busied herself. Hearing the back door click open, she took a deep breath and steadied herself.

"Hello!"

The voice was light, coming from the boot room and attempting to sound familiar. "Hello! I'm in here," she called back, trying to sound breezy. "Come on through." Loading the last of the lunchtime crockery into the dishwasher, she closed the door just as the woman entered the kitchen. By the way she spoke with Janssen, it was likely that she was his senior. A bit young for that role, in her opinion.

"Hi. I'm DCI Tamara Greave. I'm the senior investigating officer on the Bettany case. Your husband said I could come in."

Jane glanced towards the open window. He'd said no such thing but there was the tacit suggestion for her to enter. She didn't like this woman. Her fake smile and amicable approach were merely a mask to put her at ease, or off her guard. She took her measure whilst reaching for the kettle. "Would you like tea or coffee?" She was attractive, if you were into that sort of ordinary look. Quite plain, terrible hair and a dress sense taken from a horrible seventies television sitcom by the look of it. She mustn't care much about what people think about her, style-wise.

"Tea would be lovely, thanks."

There was that smile again. Although, she had her natural teeth taken care of. No one's smile came out like that without significant dental work. "What brings you back so soon? I'm not sure I can tell you anything more than I told your colleagues, yesterday." Jane set down two cups and put a bag in each. "These are okay, aren't they? I'm not really one for using a pot."

"Me neither, unless my mum's visiting. That'll be fine," Tamara replied, pulling out a chair and sitting down. Jane glanced towards her but said nothing. *Make yourself at home.* "Don't worry. I've read the report and you're right. It is comprehensive. We're actually here following a different angle of the investigation."

"Oh, that sounds intriguing." *You're trying to sound disinterested,* she told herself. *Trying too hard.*

"How well did you know Holly?"

That was it. That's why they were back here so soon. They know. The kettle boiled and she poured the water, furrowing her brow as if she was concentrating on the question. Replacing the kettle, she turned towards the detective. "Reasonably well, I guess. We know her parents, you see."

"Well?"

Jane shrugged. "We've had dinner a couple of times. Once here and another at theirs. We were quite the local additions when we first arrived, what with Ken's name and everything. I think the *Sunday Times* did a write up of one of his exhibitions last year and that tickled the interest of some of the locals."

"Right. I see."

She's fishing. Be careful. "And of course, Holly has been here to sit."

She made certain the comment would be delivered as casually as possible.

"Babysitting the children?"

Jane shook her head, smiling. "No! Sitting for Ken, as one of his models." She finished making the tea and crossed the kitchen, passing one of the cups over. Returning for the other, she cupped it in both hands and leaned against the worktop blowing the steam from the top of the liquid. Reading the quizzical look on the detective's face, she smiled again. "It's quite above board, you know. Ken is known for his contemporary interpretation of still-life paintings. They are his bestselling pieces to date. You've seen Holly. She had a lovely bone structure, perfect for Ken's style."

"I see. You didn't mention that to my officers."

The friendly, reassuring smile wasn't there anymore. Now she was picking away at the details, trying to reveal a loose thread to tug on. "I'm sorry. I didn't see it as relevant, I guess."

"Let us be the judge of what is or isn't relevant in future, please."

"I suppose I should have thought of that. I'm sorry. I will in future." She was angered by this upstart with her frizzy hair and an off the rack blouse. *How dare she speak to her like this.* Telling herself to keep calm, she sipped at her tea. It was far too hot to drink and burned the tip of her tongue.

"And how did you get on with Holly?"

"Okay, I suppose." On this, she felt comfortable. They rarely interacted. It was Ken who would feel the awkwardness of such questioning. "As I said, I knew her reasonably well. Well enough to speak to but to be honest, she wasn't sitting for me." Her thoughts turned to Ken and his studio. *His rules. His choices.* Pushing the thoughts aside, it wasn't the time for her to think of them.

"And the models. How many are we talking?" Jane looked over at her, reading her expression. *Why was she asking? What did she think she already knew?* "Was it a regular event with girls visiting your husband's studio?"

"Women!" she snapped. Unable to help herself.

"Holly was barely seventeen, wasn't she?"

The detective was seeking to provoke a response for some reason, negative or otherwise. Jane looked out of the window, towards the studio and nodded. "I believe so. She studies at the local sixth form."

"Barely a woman, then." The woman was pointed. Jane's gaze drifted to her. Neither of them said anything for a few moments, merely looking at each other.

"I'm sorry. Is there a question in there somewhere?" This woman wasn't going to be a pushover but Jane knew she had to hold her nerve.

"I was just wondering." The officer stood up, glanced briefly out of the window towards the studio and then back towards her, raising the cup to her lips. "How a wife might feel about her husband spending so much time with other women, particularly young girls?" Jane looked towards the studio. The two men were standing outside, conversing. Ken went back into the studio and Janssen turned and began making his way across the yard towards the house.

"I think you should leave now."

Tamara put her cup down on the table. "Thank you for the tea."

Crossing the kitchen and staring out of the window, Jane watched her leave. She met with Janssen outside and he looked briefly in her direction. His phone rang and he answered it whilst walking back to the car. He was talking to someone as he got into the driver's seat. The conversation continued for a moment before she saw him put the phone down. Looking to his boss, sitting next to him, they conversed briefly and she appeared shocked. Jane could only guess at what that was about. For a moment, she felt a stab of fear in her chest as she thought they might get out of the car and come back inside. The concern subsided when she heard the engine start up.

William appeared from upstairs. She smiled at him, feeling it was half-hearted. "Will the police be coming back again?" He sounded worried, as he was prone to do at times of stress.

"Only if they think we can help them." The answer was clearly inadequate to the boy but it was the best she could manage. He turned around and stomped back upstairs. He was prone to picking up on the anxiety within the house. He was much like his father in that respect. How much had he heard? Was he listening to the whole of their conversation? She hoped not.

Stepping out into the yard, the police were gone and she trotted over to the studio. Ken appeared carrying a black bin liner, the plastic straining under the weight of broken pottery. He must have read the look on her face for he put the bag down.

"What is it?" he asked, looking concerned.

"What did you tell them about Holly?"

"Nothing! I said I barely knew her."

A flash of anger shot through her. For a supposedly intelligent man, he could demonstrate limited ability at times. "Honestly, Ken. Why do you think they were asking? You should always tell them anything they can easily find out *any other way*. They probably knew full well she was here before they came out and now you've just dropped us right in it. You can be such a fool sometimes!"

"I'm sorry." His tone was feeble, bordering on pathetic.

"What has got into you?" She saw her words cut him deeply. He looked ready to cry again.

"She's dead, Jane. Holly's dead."

"And what makes her *any more special* than all of those who came before? Nothing!" When he was struggling like this, she would usually choose her words carefully but now, after the events of the past few weeks, she couldn't muster the energy to spare his feelings any further. His head dropped and tears welled. Turning on her heel, she stalked back towards the house "Get a grip and sort yourself out, Ken. You can't leave it all to me this time!"

CHAPTER FIFTEEN

JANSSEN ACKNOWLEDGED Tamara as she came out of the house. Catching sight of Jane Francis standing at the window, he read her expression. Whatever the nature of their exchange, Tamara certainly made an impression. Hopefully, Jane was more forthcoming than her husband. Ken was withholding. That much was obvious to him but where it would lead, he didn't know. The look on the DCI's face indicated he'd missed something between them and he was keen to know what. His phone rang and he answered it. It was James Collins, the pathologist in Norwich. He was a man approaching retirement and his voice carried like a narrator in the old black and white news reels.

"I have something for you." No real greeting. He was always direct. "I'm sorry to call you with partial information, Tom, but I thought you would want to know. The cause of death was certainly a result of manual strangulation. Another thing, the primary reason I'm calling, really, your victim was pregnant. Latter stages of the first trimester, if I'm correct although, it's challenging to be accurate. Perhaps eight to ten weeks."

"Are you sure?" Janssen turned and made his way back to the car. Unlocking it, Tamara got into the passenger seat. She glanced at him, interested. He closed the door and put the call onto speaker, indicating to her that it was important. "I'm not doubting you, James, obviously. I couldn't tell, though."

"Well, she's a slight little thing to be fair."

"Would she have known?" His knowledge of pregnancy was limited. If she knew, that could certainly motivate a change in her behaviour. Tamara's eyes narrowed.

"Oh, without a doubt. She will have been susceptible to morning sickness and wouldn't have been ovulating. I would be amazed if a girl of her age was unaware. Anyway, I'll let you get on. I'll be in touch with my full report tomorrow. Perhaps then, you can let me know how you're getting on with your new DCI. Rumour has it she's a bit of a ball-breaker!"

"We're getting on just fine!" Tamara spoke up, loud and clear. Silence followed. Janssen looked across. Her face was set and he found it hard to judge whether she was offended and if so, how deeply it ran. Internally, he was grinning.

"Splendid… splendid. I'll speak with you… both, tomorrow."

The call ended. Janssen thought best to ignore the comment and was relieved when she didn't raise it either. Starting the car, he looked around them to make sure they were clear and set off. The call from the pathologist was something of a bombshell. The added dimension of a pregnancy brought all manner of different motivations for the murder into play. Looking across at Tamara once again while he drove, she appeared preoccupied. Most likely working through her own thoughts on the case. Usually, it was him who suffered from being overtly introspective. A habit that often irritated his colleagues. She must be similar. Either that or she was able to switch off from a case and drift away with thoughts to better things. He doubted that was the case. She wasn't an acting DCI for nothing.

"So, who's the father?" Her question followed the prolonged period of silence, confirming his thoughts. In truth, he hadn't stopped churning over the possibilities in his mind since the moment they left the Francis residence.

"Mark's the obvious candidate." Even he found the suggestion unconvincing. Tamara nodded. He saw it in the corner of his eye, at the same time recognising her lack of belief in the theory.

"He came across as..." She seemed to struggle to find the right word. "Young?" Janssen could agree. Mark McCall appeared excited at the mere prospect of Holly spending time with him. Was that because they had sexual relations? It was possible.

"Their relationship strikes me as complicated," he said, negotiating a T-junction and pulling out behind a passing van. "But, as to whether that's complicated by a physical relationship, I'm not so sure."

"They wouldn't be the first kids to get themselves into trouble." Her tone was regretful, sympathetic. Janssen found himself wondering if she was referring to personal experience or that of the job but he didn't ask. "Her father's a GP, isn't he?"

"The mother is too. They are the senior partners in a local practice," he confirmed. "You'd think one of them may have spotted the signs."

"Unless she was adept at hiding stuff from her parents. Teenage girls are good at that!" On this occasion, he was certain she spoke from experience. They would need to speak to Colin and Marie Bettany, as well as revisit Mark and Holly's friends. The pregnancy may well turn out to be unrelated to her murder but at the same time, if it was a secret, then it could equally be a contributory factor. In the absence of any other major event in her life, if she confided in anyone about the baby, her chosen course of action could be enough to lead them to her killer and explain how she wound up dead. "I want us to speak with the teachers at the sixth form."

Janssen figured that would be astute. "Find out how Holly was getting on? If her parents felt she needed extra tuition, was it an attainment issue or one of attitude?"

"Sure." Her reply was a confirmation but he figured there was more. He waited. "I want to hear more about Mark as well. How does he fit in with the class dynamic? He seems an odd choice for Holly to buddy up with."

Janssen considered that. "Maybe it's the opposite." She looked over at him, encouraging him to continue. "Mark's on the outside of the group by all accounts, doesn't fit in. With his home life, that's not a shock but it's more than that. There's something about him. Everyone seems to think he's..."

"Weird?"

"Yeah. A bit of an oddball but the way he spoke with us... He was so adamant about things, giving other people's opinions as if they were facts. Like he couldn't distinguish between the two."

"What are you saying?" She sounded inquisitive, not sceptical. He thought about it a bit more, trying to find the best way to articulate his theory.

"I don't know exactly. I just think there's more going on with him. As I understand it, he's the least problematic of the McCalls. From a policing point of view, certainly. It's not that I think he's withholding as such, unlike Ken Francis, but... maybe Holly and he shared an affinity of sorts. Their being outsiders. Her parents were expecting her to make it through medical school and she wasn't achieving the grades and let's not forget, a baby would certainly put the pre-planned route in jeopardy."

Tamara nodded solemnly as if taking onboard his point. Not that he was sure he had actually managed to make it very clearly. Conversation fell away as Janssen picked their way back through the villages. They made good time. Once they approached the Easter Bank Holiday weekend, the A149 and the surrounding roads would be jammed with vehicles. Likewise, accommodation would become scarce. Most would be booked up well in advance. He had lined up a hotel for her that lay between Deepdale and Brancaster. Convenient as well as reputable, he figured she would be okay with it.

"Manual strangulation is interesting," Tamara said after a few minutes, staring straight ahead. "That implies personal, highly motivated."

He had to agree. Choking someone to death with your bare hands took time. It wasn't like in films or television shows. The process could take five minutes or more. The neck muscles don't just collapse during the squeeze, they push back. "Personal could indicate a crime of passion."

"I doubt she stumbled across a passing serial killer, although we could never rule that out. Statistically, we're looking for someone local, probably within her circle and the baby throws up all manner of possibilities."

His thoughts drifted to Alice and Saffy. Imagining the little girl as a baby made him feel sorry for Holly and her unborn child. Neither of them would get the chance to see what life could have been like. Alice managed well as a single parent. If that would have been Holly's situation, would she have gone it alone if required? He was only theorising. She would have had wealthy parents nearby as well which was something Alice didn't. Juggling shifts at the hospital along with childcare must have been a nightmare, hence the move back to Norfolk and a job as a practice nurse with the Bettanys. Half-tempted to call and pick her brains about her employers, he realised it would be better to do so in private. The last thing he wanted was to make her life awkward and run the risk of straining their relationship. He smiled, pleased to have her back in his life.

"What's caught you?" Tamara asked, obviously interpreting his expression. He felt himself reddening, shaking his head.

"I'll take you to your digs, if that's okay?"

"Sure. Do you fancy a working dinner? We can map out a course of action." She must have read an involuntary micro-expression for she quickly cancelled the idea. "If you have plans, it doesn't matter. I forgot you actually live here."

Alice came to mind again. Only this time, he ensured the accompanying smile was directed inwardly.

CHAPTER SIXTEEN

TAMARA WOKE EARLY. Whether it was the strange bed, room, or simply the lack of Richard's presence, she was unsure. The time on the digital clock on the bedside table was wrong. She noticed before going to sleep but hadn't been able to figure out how to work it and gave up, turning in. Richard called the previous night. The conversation was short, tense, with him obviously still aggrieved at her returning to work early. Not that he would say so unless intensely pushed. Instead, their conversation was stilted, bland. Each of them offering up a succession of anecdotes from their day with the other feigning interest as best they could, both failing miserably to convey genuine enthusiasm. There wasn't any. She was preoccupied with the case and Richard with his family, subjects not mutually interchangeable.

Slipping out from beneath the sheets, she crossed the room and looked out over the wetlands of Brancaster Bay to the sea beyond. An orange glow was building on the horizon, a cloudless start to the day. Throwing open the doors to the Juliet balcony, the cool breeze felt wonderful against her skin. The cold snap appeared to be over with a change of wind direction drawing up warmth from continental Europe. Gulls could be heard calling overhead. Boats lay at anchor in both directions, ranging from yachts down to little skiffs. The low-lying land and tidal creeks must be good for safe harbouring. The sight of the boats and the sounds all reminded her of home, back in the west, but it was different here. The coastline was calmer, somehow less brutal. It was certainly quiet. Norfolk seemed to offer a respectful peace. A place where she could concentrate, be alone with her thoughts. She wondered whether Richard would feel it too, if he were here. More likely, he would bemoan the lack of facilities. *That's harsh.* She told herself off. He was intelligent, charming and fun to be around as well as devilishly sexy.

Showering and throwing on a clean set of clothes, her last, she left her room and wandered downstairs. According to the hotel's information pack, breakfast wouldn't be served until seven but she saw no harm in waiting. At the back of the building the proprietors had built a dining space, all glass and steel, with which to maximise the views over the marshland. The exterior terrace offered outdoor seating but even she thought that a step too far this morning. Instead, she stood at the floor to ceiling glass taking in the vista. The sun was cresting the horizon now. More used to coastal sunsets this made a nice change.

A sound came from behind and a member of staff appeared, startled to find a guest already present. Tamara smiled at her. They exchanged pleasantries and the lady offered to get her a coffee while she set about laying out a selection of fresh breads, pastries, and what Tamara hoped would be fresh local produce. Another employee appeared and before the laying out was complete, Tamara descended upon the offering. Not a big fan of eating a large breakfast first thing in the morning, though, she selected a seeded roll and some cheese. No one appeared to mind as she found herself a knife, plate and a packet of butter and retreated to the far end of the room, taking a table by the window. Coffee arrived shortly and she was grateful.

Absently buttering her bread, her eyes drifting over the view, she heard her phone beep. It was a text from Janssen asking what time he should pick her up. He must be an early riser too. Perhaps it was the child. She replied to say she was ready. Barely had she sent it when he responded. *Pick you up in ten minutes.* A very early riser, she thought.

She was outside waiting for him as Janssen pulled into the car park.

He acknowledged her with a wave and she crossed the distance between them quickly, climbing into the passenger seat. They exchanged morning greetings but then she was straight onto the case. "I want to speak to the parents this morning. The Bettanys. We should call ahead. I don't want them to feel ambushed."

"I figured as much," Janssen replied with a half-smile. "I called them last night and arranged for us to drop by first thing. They're expecting us. How is the hotel?"

"Good. The coffee was lousy but everything else is grand," she replied. He laughed. It appeared to come naturally to him, reinforcing her impression that when off-duty, Janssen laughed a lot.

"I know somewhere we can call in on the way. They won't be open but I know the owner and he'll be there." She checked the time and then looked across at him. A decent cup of coffee was appealing but she wanted to speak to the Bettanys while they were still processing what she referred to as the morning fug. That period of the day when you exist almost on auto pilot. It was true she didn't want them to feel ambushed but, at the same time, if there was something they were reluctant to share then she didn't want to give them the opportunity to plan what they would and wouldn't say.

Janssen appeared to see her mulling over the timings. "I said first thing but not the crack of dawn. They'll not be expecting us right now, unless you want to catch them in their pyjamas? We have time."

She relented with a smile. "Who is this friend of yours, then?"

The place was nearby. It was a little seafood restaurant near to Burnham Norton. The sign positioned outside, handwritten in chalk, advertised their focus on the best that Norfolk could produce, oysters collected from the creeks running into Brancaster Bay, crab and fresh fish from the market, supplied by local trawlers. Janssen walked towards the rear of the building. It appeared deserted, closed up, but he hammered on a side door. Sure enough, soon after, it cracked open and a face appeared from within. The newcomer was short and muscular, greeting Janssen with a firm handshake. He really did stand out. Callum McCall was right, Janssen didn't look like the other locals, towering above most.

Watching from her vantage point in the car, she looked at her watch. Everyone knew everyone else. The benefit of an enclosed community but also its curse. He was only out of view for around five minutes. It felt like longer. Enough time to test her patience, at least. Reappearing with two coffees in brown takeaway cups, lids securely fastened, Janssen crossed to the car. She leaned over and popped the door for him. He angled it open the rest of the way with his knee, reaching in and passing her one of the cups. It was hot to the touch and she set it down.

What passed for rush hour traffic in this area was steadily building. Janssen drove them back towards Burnham Market, turning off the main arterial route. Most of the traffic was heading in the opposite direction but as they approached the village itself, roadworks and temporary traffic lights ensured they had time to enjoy their coffee before arriving at Brancaster House, the Bettany family home.

Marie Bettany was ready for them, inviting the two of them through to the sitting room. She already had a tray set out with a teapot and biscuits, apparently hosting manners were still observed under any circumstances. Tamara found it a little odd but made appreciative noises nonetheless. Their host encouraged them to sit down, taking up a seat opposite and pouring out the tea.

"Will your husband be joining us?" she asked. Marie's expression altered but only for a second, before the friendly smile returned albeit nervously. At least, that's how she read it.

"No, I'm terribly sorry. We were only able to call on one locum at such short notice. You'll appreciate we still have a number of patients to see. It would be awful to let so many people down. Colin had to go in early to arrange some more cover and he will be working today."

Tamara noticed Janssen looking at her. He seemed surprised Colin had gone into work. So was she. "No matter. We can catch him later at the surgery."

"I'm afraid he will be very busy," Marie Bettany said with a shake of the head.

"I'm sure he'll make time for us," she replied, accepting the tea, served in a floral china cup with a saucer. "We really wanted to speak with both of you regarding this, Dr Bettany, so please forgive me for being blunt with my next question." The comment made Marie sit up and take note. Her expression suddenly changed, revealing the depth of the pain she felt, presumably over the past couple of days. "Were you aware that your daughter was pregnant?"

The question came like a hammer blow. That was intentional. Marie's face dropped. Her mouth fell open. "*Pregnant?*" Her response seemed to be one of genuine surprise. "I... don't..." She was stammering, failing to complete the sentence. "How can that be? I mean, obviously I understand the biology but..."

"Was Holly in a relationship with anyone that you know of?" Tamara asked. She knew Janssen had already asked the question on his previous visit and Colin was quiet emphatic about there being no boyfriend but he wasn't here. Marie looked up, meeting her eye before glancing to Janssen. "It is important, Marie." She switched to addressing her by her first name seeking to build a rapport.

"There was one boy." Marie's reply was hushed almost as if fearful of being overheard. "One of the McCall boys. The youngest, Mark, I think his name is."

"Why didn't you mention this to my officers on Saturday?" Marie shot her a look. She was uncomfortable. That was obvious. Was she betraying a confidence?

"Colin didn't approve. When he found out, he did what he would always do when Holly befriended a boy."

"Which was?" she asked, keen to hear.

"Put a stop to it, of course!" Marie shook her head, a sign of her disapproval of her husband's actions. "He thought Mark wasn't good enough for Holly. Don't get me wrong, I shared his concerns what with the family's reputation and everything."

"There's more, though, Marie. Isn't there?" She framed it as a question but in reality, it was more of a statement she sought confirmation of. Marie nodded. "Please, go on."

"No one was ever good enough for Holly. It didn't matter who she chose. She could have brought home one of the royals from Sandringham and he wouldn't have made the grade for Colin. He stifled her at every turn."

"So, your husband put an end to the relationship?" There was movement behind Marie. The door to the sitting room wobbled slightly, too much to have been the result of a draught from an open window.

"With good reason, so it would seem!" Marie snapped, her frustration coming to the fore. She immediately apologised to both detectives. She waved it away.

"I know you covered this before but neither you nor your husband knew where Holly was intending to go on Friday night. Is that correct? Nothing has come to mind since you spoke with my officers this past Saturday?"

Marie shook her head. "No. We both thought she was going to Norwich. As we said."

"And you didn't think to check that she got there okay?"

"I don't like what I think you are insinuating. We are caring parents and Holly is… was… seventeen."

The door moved again, drawing her attention. No one else seemed aware of it. "I see. You didn't know where she would be. May I borrow your lavatory?" Marie was thrown by the sudden shift but gathered herself, offering directions. Janssen looked at her as she stood up, puzzled. "I won't be a moment."

CHAPTER SEVENTEEN

TAMARA SWIFTLY CROSSED the room and stepped out into the hall just in time to see the back of a young girl disappearing into the kitchen. She set off after her, passing the door to the cloakroom and entering the kitchen. The girl was already seated on an occasional sofa overlooking the neatly manicured gardens. She absently flicked through a magazine, a vain attempt at indicating she'd been there for some time.

"Hello. My name's Tamara. I'm a police officer," she said, approaching the girl. She must have been twelve, thirteen at the most. Her long brown hair was pulled back into a pony tail, a tidy fringe fell across her forehead to just above her eyebrows. "You must be Madeleine." The girl glanced up, offering a brief smile.

"People call me Maddie. I don't like Madeleine."

"In that case, please accept my apologies. May I sit down?" Maddie indicated that would be okay and she took a seat alongside her.

"Are you going to find out who hurt Holly?"

"I am, yes." The girl had a bone structure similar to Holly's, albeit she was fuller in face, possibly due to being younger and still with some height to reach but when she did, the two of them would be a spit of one another. "Did you hear what we were talking about in there?" She indicated back towards the sitting room with her eyes.

Maddie nodded but said nothing, casting her eyes down. "Don't worry, I won't tell anyone."

"They don't tell me anything, Mummy and Daddy." Tamara tried not to judge her reaction as childish.

"They are probably looking out for you."

The girl's expression conveyed disdain for that point of view. "Holly was the only one who looked out for me. She wouldn't back down from anyone!"

"Did your sister talk to you about Mark at all?"

Maddie shrugged. "A little. She liked him a lot. He was nice. To her and to me, but he was never her boyfriend, not really."

"Did she have a boyfriend? Someone that you knew of but maybe your mum and dad didn't?" She knew she was pushing her luck speaking to a minor without consent but it was hardly a formal interview. Besides, if the girl knew anything of note, they could always get it on the record later. Maddie shook her head. She was disappointed. "What about the pregnancy, did you know about that?" Again, she shook her head. "When you said she was protective, what did you mean?"

Maddie looked her in the eye. "Exactly that. She wouldn't let anyone hurt me. Not at school, not… not anywhere." She said the last in a barely audible whisper. Before Tamara could follow up, she spoke again, unprompted. "It was the same with Mark. People have a go at him at school all the time because he's so different but Holly wouldn't let them get away with it. She made sure everyone left him alone. I think that's why he is so infatuated with her."

"Who described him as *infatuated*, Maddie? Was it Holly?"

She shook her head. "No! Although, she agreed but it was Daddy who said that. That's why he banned her from seeing him. He even went around to speak with his father."

"Your father went to see Callum McCall?" She was surprised by that, imagining a man such as Colin Bettany would feel confident enough to pay the McCalls a visit. Particularly in light of the fact he was insinuating Mark wasn't good enough to mix with his daughter. "He must be a brave man, your father. I've met Callum and he's quite fearsome."

Maddie nodded furiously. "Me too. He's scary. Mark was terrified of him as well."

"When did he scare you?" she asked, puzzled as to how the two would come across one another, even in a community such as this one.

"I was with Holly a few weeks ago and we ran into McCall... sorry, Mr McCall, and he was ranting and raving at her. It was really scary. No one said anything or tried to help but Holly didn't care. She stood up to him and told him where to get off."

That was very interesting. She was aware of the altercation, Janssen told her about it but as far as she knew, no one realised Maddie was present at the time. "What was it about?"

"No idea. I did ask. Holly told me I should mind my own business. She was great, my sister, but she had a frightful temper. She could fight with anyone, even Mummy and Daddy."

"Did she? Fight with your parents, I mean?"

"With Mummy mostly but Daddy as well, sometimes. Like when he insisted on knowing where we were all the time. Holly didn't like that one bit! He bought us new mobiles and insisted we should check in if ever we were going to be late home or something."

"And did you? You and Holly?"

Maddie looked at her sideways from the corner of her eye. "*Sometimes*. Holly refused."

A noise came from the direction of the sitting room and Maddie became agitated. "What is it?" Tamara asked her.

"Mummy told me to keep out of the way. She won't be happy if she sees me talking to you."

She reached across and patted her on the knee, smiling warmly. "Don't worry. I'll not say a word." Standing up, she took out one of her contact cards and passed it to the girl. "Keep that safe and if you fancy a chat about *anything at all*, just give me a call. Okay?" Maddie smiled, nervous eyes flitting between her and the doorway. They could hear muffled voices. Tamara whispered a farewell and trotted across the kitchen trying her best to ensure her heels made as little noise on the floor tiles as possible.

She met Janssen and Marie as they were coming down the hall. "We thought you'd got lost," Janssen said, his tone was one of relief edged with concern and he was amplifying the usual pitch. He must have known she was up to something and feared her being rumbled.

"Well, you know how it is. If you have to go..." she replied, smiling. "Sorry about that."

"That's okay," Marie Bettany replied without feeling, eyeing her with what she thought was a wary look, if not outright suspicion. She seemed to peer past her into the kitchen beyond. Looking back over her shoulder, the sofa was empty. Maddie was nowhere to be seen.

"Thank you for your time, Dr Bettany." Tamara addressed her by title, shifting back to the stance of keeping a professional distance. Between Marie and her youngest daughter, they'd given her plenty to think on but perhaps without realising it.

Marie escorted them to the front door and once clear, it was quickly closed on them. Neither spoke as they walked to the car. Janssen unlocked it and they got in. As soon as the engine started, he looked across at her. "Mind telling me what that was all about?" His tone was curious, not angry or accusatory. She looked back at the house spying Maddie's face watching them from an upper window. There must be a second staircase to the rear of the house. She smiled and the girl returned it. Pulling across her seatbelt, she glanced to him.

"Let's head over to the surgery and have a word with Colin. I'll fill you in on the way."

THE WAITING ROOM WAS QUIET, surprisingly. Tamara found herself wondering if these rural surgeries were immune from the waiting times and delays that so often afflicted the larger towns and cities. Janssen must have been thinking the same as he looked around. The receptionist noted their arrival as a patient stepped aside from the desk, offering them a wave. She also thought they were polite here as well.

"I know her," Janssen said. She wasn't surprised. "Margaret used to work with my mum years back." She let him take the lead, hanging back a step as he approached the desk. Janssen asked to see Colin Bettany.

"I'm afraid he's not here, Tom. You've missed him." Janssen glanced at the clock mounted high on the wall behind the desk. They'd left Marie barely ten minutes earlier. "He came in this morning, opening up before even I arrived but he's gone now."

"Is that unusual?" Janssen asked. "For him to open up, I mean?"

"Certainly. Admin and the nurses are always here before the Bettanys. Not that they're late. I wouldn't want to give that impression. Dr Colin, that's what we call him, as do the patients, otherwise we couldn't differentiate between the two Bettanys, came in early to arrange for a locum."

"Ah... that's what his wife said he was doing but we thought he was staying on to see his patients today."

Margaret looked puzzled. "Strange. Dr Colin left me a voicemail last night asking me to cancel all his appointments today and reschedule them for later in the week. I must admit I was surprised to see him this morning what with what happened to poor Holly."

That explains a lot, Tamara thought, as Janssen glanced over his shoulder at her. He turned back to the woman behind the desk. "No matter, we must have got the wrong end of the stick. We probably passed him on the way here. How long ago did he leave?" He was casual, charming but the question was searching, far more so than Margaret realised.

"Oh, he left by eight." That was long before they left the Bettany's. Had he been heading for home, then they would have seen him, met him even. Unless of course, he planned to avoid them all along. She found that prospect intriguing. A man with a controlling streak who didn't appear to accept challenge well. A man who steered clear of the police, even when they were investigating his daughter's murder.

"Had he sorted out cover? I believe he was looking for a second locum." Janssen was still seeking detail, doing so in a calm manner belying his professional interest.

"Not that he told me." Margaret lowered her voice, possibly conscious of people listening in. Tamara looked around at the people in the waiting room. There were three present and none appeared to be taking much of an interest in them. She had to strain in order to hear. "I'm not sure what he was doing here to be honest." Margaret took on a conspiratorial tone. "He achieved nothing, barely spoke to any of us. He's not an easy man to be around, you know, Dr Colin. Don't get me wrong, he's a wonderful practitioner but as a person... some of us struggle with him... on a personal level, and I know him better than most seeing as I've been here for years."

Janssen thanked the receptionist and came back to join her. The pair turned to leave. Approaching the exit, a side door opened and a nurse stepped out, almost colliding with them. Tamara apologised at the same time as the woman but her focus was on Janssen and not her.

"Hi Tom. Nice surprise! What are you doing here?" The nurse's eyes lit up, gleaming. Quickly finding herself something of a spare part in the conversation as Janssen replied, Tamara politely disengaged, leaving them to chat safe in the knowledge neither would have noticed her departure had she not mentioned it.

Janssen reappeared a few minutes later, meeting her at the car. He unlocked it and as she went to get in, noticing the child seat was no longer in the rear. "Friend of yours?" she asked playfully. Never one to pry, she did however want to get to know him a little better and felt confident she could prod him, if only slightly.

"Good friend." His tone was neutral, closing down the conversation. Janssen obviously wasn't one to share. She turned her thoughts to Colin Bettany, wondering how he was filling his time this morning.

CHAPTER EIGHTEEN

ERIC WOKE to the smell of frying bacon. Propping himself up on his elbow, he looked at the clock. It was only just past six o'clock in the morning. The sun was up, streaming through the gap in the curtains of the bedroom. He felt young again. As if he could ever describe himself as old at the age of twenty-four. Throwing on a t-shirt and some joggers, he made his way downstairs to find his mother in the kitchen over the hob.

"I thought you might like something to go to work on. I'll expect you're finding it hard to find time working these hours."

He smiled, kissing her on the cheek. Although she never said so directly, she was both immensely proud of him and at the same time concerned for his wellbeing. That's why she would go to such efforts providing him with lunch and now, apparently, with breakfast. She felt guilty. Only on the odd occasion, perhaps after one too many gins on a Saturday evening, his mother would let slip how she beats herself up. The sudden passing of her husband, Eric's father, and her own debilitating battle with cancer transferred the burden of supporting the family onto him at an early age. She knew the weight that placed on his teenage years. While his friends were out partying until late on the beach, Eric was at home, taking care of things and getting up early for work, whatever the day or the weather.

The police force was recruiting. It was a sensible job, stable, and he could stay near home and look after her. She wasn't to blame, though. Nor was his father for dying. The thought occurred as to what he would do once his role was no longer needed? Hopefully, a day long in the future. Stay in the police, probably. Catching sight of his lunchbox, set aside on the worktop, he smiled again, shaking his head.

His first stop was at the school, incorporating the sixth form college attended by both Holly Bettany and Mark McCall. Admittedly, meeting the headmaster filled him with anxiety. Driving through the gates and up to the entrance, pulling into a car parking space, seemed only to spur those feelings to new heights. It was an unsettling sensation. He'd walked through those gates hundreds of times but always as a pupil and he remembered doing so as if it was yesterday.

Not that school was a particularly difficult time for him either within his peer group, academically, or with his relationships with the teachers. Eric had sought to be, unwittingly at the time, the grey-man of his year group. Never one to draw attention to himself with the so-called *look at me gene*, he caused no trouble for staff or students alike. To be honest, his impact on the school must barely have left an imprint and yet here he was, sweating on setting foot inside and coming before the Head. Perhaps it was the knowledge that he never really applied himself to his studies, always feeling something of a fraud when he came home with an above average report card. Had he applied himself maybe he would have gone onto sixth form, university and a completely different career path. Unlikely, considering the domestic influences that shaped his life.

The headmaster hadn't changed much, albeit he was greyer and shorter than Eric remembered; his name was Carl Hendry, or *Demon Hendry* as they used to call him, a play on a book title they all read once as part of the early years' syllabus. Their interaction was interesting. He recalled Eric as a pupil which surprised him, commenting on how effective he was as a senior prefect. Eric didn't think he did anything remarkable in the role but accepted the compliment with good grace. Hendry spoke to him as an equal. Another strange experience for the young man.

"Awful what happened to Holly. She'll be greatly missed here at the school and our hearts go out to both Colin and Marie... and Madeleine, of course. We've set up counselling for any pupil who feels deeply affected. However, I'm not aware of how I can help with your investigation."

"I'm gathering a bit of background on her. How she mixed with her peer group for example?"

"Interesting girl, I must say. Not what we would refer to as a chequered record exactly. We have more difficult children here at the school, but far from the example we would expect for a student of her roots."

Eric found that comment irritating. Much more like the Demon Hendry he remembered, elitist, condescending. "Did she have any problems with teachers or classmates. Anything specific?" he asked, taking notes.

"With Holly, it was always a case of poor attitude and application. The girl was incredibly bright. Everyone thought so, but she couldn't channel that into her academic work. If she had, then her father's dream of her attending medical school would have been a foregone conclusion."

"Her father's dream, you say?" he asked. Hendry nodded. "But you think that was an... unrealistic goal to set for her?"

"I put Colin, her father, in touch with a former colleague of mine in Norwich, an exceptional educator, hoping to inspire her to fulfil her potential but... and I see no harm in saying this to you now, he didn't rate her very highly. Not her ability you understand, but again, her application. As for her interaction with fellow pupils, you are best to speak with our head of pastoral care. She is much closer to these things than I am."

———————

THE LADY HEADING up the pastoral team was also responsible for special educational needs, and she was prickly. They'd never met and Eric was unfamiliar with her role. He didn't recall a structure such as this during his schooling. Things must have changed since he left. *Very much for the better*, he thought. It made sense to him to have somebody responsible for overseeing the mental and social wellbeing of the pupils, a port of call for troubled children outside of the teaching structure. Eric had the impression she felt he was interviewing her in search of a sign she must have missed, something in Holly's time at the school that resulted in her winding up dead. Nothing could be further from the truth. Unless of course, she had let her down in some way and knew more than Eric expected. That thought spurred him along a different line of questioning.

"Why do you think Holly struggled to interact with her peers. After all, she had few friends."

"There was nothing to necessarily indicate she was struggling." The woman was defensive, looking to slide away from any blame. Why she felt this was required, Eric could only guess at.

"So, you think she *was* struggling?"

The question cut through the mirage of deflection. Eric wished all the criminals he came across were as quick to fold. "Well, academically she was, without question. The teaching staff were exasperated with her attitude. They looked for all manner of reasons as to why they couldn't get the best out of her. They were receiving pressure from…" She paused. Eric knew he'd sparked something. She wanted to get something off her chest but at the same time, wanted to avoid being quoted.

"You can speak freely," he said, symbolically putting his pen and pad down. He had a good memory and could record it later.

"Holly's parents were great contributors to the school. I know we're not an independent school but funding is tight. This is an affluent area and pupil premium places are low in comparison to the national average." Eric understood. State funding for schools with a higher than average number of pupils from low-income households stood to benefit from larger subsidies than those that didn't. Educational funding was a political hot topic, always so when spending cuts were deemed necessary. "The last round of budget cuts has been tough. The school asks for contributions and the parents are truly wonderful. The Bettanys, in particular, are very generous." Eric read between the lines.

"And in exchange for this, they wanted to see a return on their… investment?" He said the last in a suggestive manner, unsure of it being an appropriate choice of word. He needn't have worried.

"Absolutely right. As a result, Holly was repeatedly pushed in my direction. As if I could somehow sort her out."

"How did that go?" She scoffed at the question. An answer of sorts.

"She wouldn't open up to me, or anyone else for that matter. The girl was very closed off, defensive." To Eric, that behaviour should have set off alarm bells but he wasn't qualified to judge, not really. Casting his mind back, he could think of a half dozen school friends who fitted that description and none of those had diagnosable conditions as far as he was aware. Perhaps events beyond the confines of the school gates were affecting them. Perhaps, so it was with Holly as well. He had never experienced the *Tiger Parent* phenomena. He was grateful.

"Friends?" His tone was casual, seeking to put her at ease.

"Always on the periphery from what I could see, mixing with plenty but not with any one specific group."

"What about Mark McCall?" Eric watched her for a response. There was a hint of a flame at the mention of his name and he hoped to fan it.

"They were friends, certainly. Mark talks about her a lot." Eric encouraged her to elaborate by sitting in silence. Most people didn't like silence. It was a classic salesperson's technique. He had seen it on a fly on the wall documentary once. "I sometimes think he is a little obsessed with her. Not in a dangerous way, I must add, but he hangs on every word she says. I think it's a result of his condition."

"Condition?"

"Yes, his Asperger's. I'm not breaking any confidentiality policy in telling you for everyone knows." Eric found this enlightening.

"I didn't realise he had a disability."

"He doesn't! At least we don't see it that way and nor does he. Mark interprets information and processes it in a unique way that is different to the rest of us. This gives him both skills and talents that some of us would love to have. Some would see it as a strength rather than a hindrance." He felt a little embarrassed by his own ignorance. She appeared to notice his discomfort. It must have been obvious. "Please don't worry. There is a great deal of misunderstanding regarding those on the spectrum and I would be lying if I tried to push aside the negative aspects to his condition."

"And they are?" Eric asked, priming his pen once more. Any reticence from her had now passed.

"People on the spectrum are all different. In Mark's case, he sees the world as black and white. There are no grey areas. Almost everything is taken quite literally. If you were to tell Mark aliens exist, for example, he would believe you and not question it even for a second. He is a very trusting young man, far too much so in my opinion. We've had to work very hard to ensure the other pupils don't take advantage of him. They often did, which was deeply upsetting for Mark. If you're not in on the joke and don't understand, then it can be a painful experience. This often led to outbursts and on occasion, those outbursts turned violent. *Holly...* well, she used to look out for him in one respect but..." She failed to complete the sentence, her words tailing off.

"But?" Eric pressed, sensing this was significant.

"I don't know. I wonder what Holly got out of it. Sometimes... I got the impression her friendship with Mark was quite one-sided, that she was toying with him somehow. Leading him on may be overstating it but... yes, I think it fits." Eric sat back. That was quite an interesting turn of events. "I think she enjoyed the adoration he provided. I don't know if it's relevant but Mark didn't show up for classes this morning."

CHAPTER NINETEEN

JANE WOKE to the memory of the two bottles of wine the night before. Her mouth was dry. The bed next to her was empty, unslept in. Glancing at the clock, the kids should be up by now if they were to make it to school on time. Normality. That was required at this point. Her thoughts were plagued by that ordinary woman, the *senior detective,* or whatever she called herself. *The arrogant cow.* To come into their home and insinuate... who knows what? Ken hadn't helped. What he told the other one would undoubtedly put him at the top of the list of suspects. If not, then they were incompetent and she was certain they were far from it.

Slipping out from under the duvet, she pulled on some clothes and dragged a brush through her hair. Her senses were dulled by the alcohol but not greatly. Two bottles was standard these days, nothing exceptional. The curtains were open, she never closed them preferring to wake to the sun streaming in through the window. Ken must have slept in the studio again, although why he would want to was a mystery. *To be alone with his misery.*

Finding William's bedroom empty, she entered Rosie's. The children were nowhere to be seen. Heading downstairs, breakfast had already taken place. Cereal boxes were on the table, as were the cartons of fruit juice and a bottle of milk, but the dirty bowls and glasses were neatly stacked above the dishwasher waiting to be loaded. The children appeared from the boot room, coats and shoes on, school book bags in their hands. There was none of the usual squabbling that came along with preparation for the school run. Ken was a few steps behind. He smiled as he entered the kitchen.

"We're ready. Are you joining us?" he asked her. The children demanded that she did.

"I've not showered or had breakfast. What will people think?"

"Then you can stay in the car while I walk them in. No one will see. It won't matter." Usually so fastidious with her presentation, never one to appear in public without putting her face on, the thought of doing so was anxiety inducing. She relented.

Pulling up as near to the school gates as they could, Ken and the children climbed out. Despite their protestations there was no way she was going to enter the bear pit of the playground looking as she did. A group of the usual parents were huddled at the gates. A couple of them glanced in her direction, at least, she thought they were. *Could word have got around about Holly?* The handsome local detective didn't seem the type to speak loosely and the other one, the haughty mare, wasn't local. Her accent, the way she carried herself, she wouldn't know anyone.

The group at the gates began to disperse taking the children inside. They'd carry on their conversations as they always did, gossiping about whoever took their fancy. She pictured them as vultures, picking over the carrion they found lying around. They hadn't taken to her at all. She had tried to speak to some of them during the course of the last year and, one on one, they could be friendly enough but once in their familiar clique, they were closed to outsiders. Then they would act as if they'd never spoken with her, as if they didn't want to.

Ken didn't help. He was antisocial, preferring to spend time alone. Casting her mind back it was an absolute miracle he asked her out on their first date. She should have realised what he was like back then. Working as an event coordinator, a grandiose title for organising and laying out rooms for companies to showcase their products, they'd met when she was readying one such place. The exhibition was to coincide with a week-long celebration of cultural art. Ken's work was selling well at the time and attracting a great deal of interest. The artist himself, however, didn't care for the spotlight and having made the required number of introductions on the opening evening, retreated to the back rooms away from the glare of the media and those thirsty to bask in his perceived social status. That was where they'd first met and struck up a conversation.

Their time together had been comforting, relaxed, if not exciting but she'd had plenty of excitement in the years running up to that meeting. Stable, refined and comfortable appealed at the time. It still did. Although, a hankering for the devilment of her youth was apparent. The desire more prevalent now than at any time she could remember since they were married. She thought those days were behind her but, recently, what with everything else they'd faced, the sense of freedom she used to derive from passing over all responsibility and commitment felt somehow appealing once again.

Ken returned, getting into the car. He was different today. Half expecting his collapse of the previous day, after finding his studio trashed, to descend into a spiral of depression, she was warmed by his reaction. It was as if the weight on his shoulders had somehow been lifted. Perhaps this was the culmination of the past year coming to a point and either he would implode or grow in strength and move on. Fragile as Ken could be, somehow, he'd found an inner strength to draw on much as he used to.

"I was thinking, last night," he began, starting the car. His tone was upbeat, although there was something else there behind the easy smile. "Maybe we could go out for the day, take a walk together or something? The weather's been good. I think we could both do with a break from the house, me from the studio. What do you think?" The question was genuine. He sounded nervous, worried she would dismiss him.

"Yes. I'd like that." She smiled and his own broadened. "I want to go home and shower first, though."

"And have breakfast."

"*And* have breakfast," she repeated. This was something of a milestone, Ken suggesting they spend time together. She used to be the one to make those suggestions but it was a long time ago before everything became so complicated.

"I want to talk to you about something as well," Ken said. He sounded nervous again. "I think we need to clear up a few things." That was mildly alarming. She knew Ken was secretive. This was nothing new. *But why would he be sharing now of all times?* She looked across and he must have felt her eyes upon him. "Not now. Later."

HAVING RETURNED TO THE HOUSE, Jane grabbed a quick breakfast of toast and cereal before heading off to shower and change. When she came back down, Ken had prepared a picnic for their lunch. Nothing fancy, just a selection of fruit, some sandwiches and a flask of either coffee or tea. She didn't mind either. They exchanged small talk on the short drive to Holkham where they parked up and headed for the beach. The wind, whipping in off the North Sea for the previous few days, dropped and the sky cleared to reveal warm spring sunshine. The miles of open sand were shared with only a handful of dog walkers and a few tourists getting in ahead of the annual influx of people as holiday season began.

Conversation between them tailed away and Jane sensed her husband was mulling something over, perhaps building up to what this outing was really about. Part of her wanted him to let it go, keep it inside and allow them to enjoy the moment. A brief occasion not dominated by marital issues, demanding children or… she didn't want to think about *her*.

"I need to tell you something," Ken said, staring straight ahead. Whatever it was, he couldn't look her in the eye as he spoke, or wouldn't. A sideways glance revealed a pained expression on his face. She was suddenly fearful. "It's about Holly." They never discussed his models. There was an agreement. She wouldn't ask and he wouldn't say. That was their covenant. For some reason, he was breaking it now. She wanted to reach out and touch him, tell him she didn't want to hear a confession, that it wasn't necessary but she didn't. He stopped, turning to face her. "She came to see me."

"When?" Fearing the answer now.

"Friday. The night she... the night she died." This wasn't a revelation, she already suspected but she was still annoyed. He often spent the night in the studio after a modelling session. Those sessions were prearranged. Agreed. Scheduled so the children were not at risk of stumbling in on something as William once had when he was all but three years old. Holly wasn't supposed to be there that night.

"You asked her to come?" She failed to hold her accusatory tone in check. She was angry, hurt.

"No! Of course not!" he protested, turning away from her and setting off again. She hesitated before joining him. *You slept with her, didn't you?* She could cope with his desires, with his needs, his demands for freedom provided they were in the manner they'd agreed. *Not like this. She was too young for this sort of relationship, that was obvious, but you couldn't see past your own lust.* "She arrived around eleven o'clock. You fell asleep putting the kids to bed." *As I usually do,* she thought. *Here it comes, the act of betrayal.*

"What did she want?" The question was framed innocently but she was terrified of the possible answer.

"She wanted to leave."

"And?" she said, narrowing her eyes and placing a restraining hand on Ken's forearm. He stopped, looking to the sand at their feet.

"She wanted me to go with her."

That was it! The proof of what she had thought all along. "Ken! You're a fool. How could you let her get so close to you?" She felt the rage building. This little girl certainly wasn't the first to become infatuated with him but she thought he should have learned by now, particularly after the last time.

"I know, I know!" he replied, casting his eyes to the heavens. Knowing him as she did, she sensed there was more to it. *He wanted to go.* Ken must have read her expression and immediately went on the defensive. "You have to understand; it's been difficult recently—"

"Oh, I *understand Kenneth.* I've been living it too."

"The idea of running, leaving it all behind was... appealing. She was... different."

"She was more than half your age! Do you think you could keep up for more than a couple of weeks?" She was cutting, trying her best to hurt him like he was hurting her.

"I said no!" he protested. "When it came down to it, I couldn't countenance leaving you and the kids for—"

"A child?"

"For someone I *thought* I was in love with."

"You thought? You're a weak, pathetic man, Ken," she barked at him, taking pleasure in the way her words stung him. "Why didn't you go? The last thing you seem to want is to be with us anyway."

"I want that to change. Those girls… they don't mean anything, they never have. I believed she was different, Holly. For a time, I felt towards her as I did when we first met. She was a breath of fresh air to my stale life, something to provide new inspiration and reinvigorate me. I was wrong."

Jane resumed walking, this time it was Ken who had to catch up. She was done tailing around after him. She would need to fix this situation. Somehow. "Come on Ken," she called over her shoulder, "I know there's more."

"She was pregnant."

Jane stopped in her tracks, turning on him so abruptly he nearly walked into her. Ken brought himself upright just as she drew her hand across his face. He didn't react.

PLACING the sandwich down on the blanket, Jane wiped her hands with a tissue. She'd barely taken a bite, just nibbled at the edge. Her appetite was absent. The tide was coming back in. The roar of the breakers crashing against the beach carried to them. They sat amongst the dunes. They could have been anywhere, alone on a deserted island. Ken sat alongside her, his legs brought up, hugging his knees.

"She thought you would go with her, didn't she?" she asked without looking at him, instead maintaining her focus on the sea.

"Probably."

"What was she like?" Jane had a strange need to know about the dead girl, to understand why her husband seemed so enthralled by her.

"Captivating. She could make me feel alive." That description stung but she hid her reaction as Ken continued on unabated. "She would talk about leaving sometimes. Others, about attending art school. There's no way her parents would have allowed it and she knew that."

Is that why she wanted you around? I get what you saw in her – youth, passion, sexual appetite, but what did you have for her in exchange?

"She wanted me to open doors, I think," Ken said with regret. Meeting her eye, it was as if he could read her mind. "I couldn't obviously, not now anyway."

That brought her mind back to their most pressing problem. He had lied about how well he knew Holly. The police would investigate and learn what made them move here in the first place. *And now this.* She could cope. Every problem had a solution and she would find it. She was back in control now. "What time did Holly leave you that night? She *did* leave, didn't she?" Jane asked the question without looking into her husband's eyes. She would know if he was lying. She was too frightened to see.

"Of course, she did! What do you take me for?" Ken sounded hurt, desperate to be believed. "I don't know… perhaps a bit after midnight. Maybe later. I didn't really look. She was angry, upset."

Holly was there for over an hour. A request for him to leave wouldn't have taken that long and she didn't want to know the details of what went on prior to that part of the conversation. She could imagine. *I don't blame her for being angry. She must have felt used. Treated like an object to be discarded.*

Jane was about to unleash a scathing assault on her husband's naivety but the words were checked by a figure appearing over them, a silhouette backlit by the sun. Fists clenched at his side and barely controlled fury on his face, it was evident that someone else also knew about Ken and Holly.

CHAPTER TWENTY

TOM JANSSEN PARKED the car in front of the police station. Getting out of the car, he spied a lone figure hovering at the nearby bus stop. It was Mark McCall, and he seemed far more interested in them than the timetable he was supposedly reading. Acting on a hunch, he indicated to Greave. She followed his eyes and nodded.

"I'll head up to the ops room and see if Eric is back from the school," she said.

Janssen approached. Mark shifted his weight between his feet, glancing sideways at the detective. His face was drawn, eyes sunken. The lad appeared not to have slept well. "Hello Mark. Shouldn't you be in school today?"

"I didn't fancy it today. Everyone will be talking, pointing at me."

Janssen understood. He was an awkward boy with few friends and a difficult homelife. Holly was the rock Mark anchored himself to. Now she was gone and most of those present at the party would know she left with him. Despite the discreet nature of their investigation rumours would manifest, it was inevitable. "You going somewhere?" he asked, glancing at the timetable. Mark looked confused, confirming his suspicion. The boy was waiting to see one of the detectives. "Is there something you want to tell me?"

"No. Not really." Mark glanced around and then he sat down on the grass verge alongside the road. Janssen reluctantly followed suit, keen to put the boy at ease. "I miss her." His words were heartfelt.

"Your relationship with Holly was important to you." Janssen appreciated Mark's sense of loss. "Do you feel a bit lost without her?"

"Yes," Mark replied quietly. "It was always going to happen, I guess." That threw Janssen slightly, for a moment he was concerned. "She was always going to leave me at some point."

"Did she talk about it, leaving?"

"She didn't want to be a doctor, I know that!" Mark almost spat the words out, a flash of anger crossing his face but it soon dissipated to be replaced by one of resignation. "She wanted to be a creator. An artist."

"I've seen some of her pictures," Janssen said, remembering the drawings taken from Holly's bedroom. "She kept them hidden. Was that from her parents?"

Mark nodded.

"They wouldn't approve."

"They thought art was a waste of time," he said. "Something others did, for them to enjoy, but nothing more than a time-consuming hobby."

"Did she ever draw you?" Janssen asked, remembering the different images, wondering if one of them was Mark.

"Once," he said, his face splitting into a broad grin which faded rapidly. "It didn't look much like me, though. Holly loved drawing but… she wasn't the best."

Janssen held the sketches they found in his mind. Some were great, others less so. If Holly didn't draw them, then who did? "Did she show you the sketches she had? The ones in her bedroom?" Mark went quiet, looking down to the ground between his feet as a lorry rumbled past, the only noise to disrupt their conversation. "Were you ever in her room?"

"A few times," Mark replied, chewing on his lower lip. "If her parents were out or it was late. They were heavy sleepers and their bedroom was on the other side of the house. The way the bricks meet at the junction between the walls outside Holly's bedroom make it easy to climb up. They're pretty much footholds. You can get in through her bedroom window without ever setting foot inside the rest of the house."

"Holly encouraged this?"

"Sometimes, yes." Mark appeared lost. As if the memory was too painful to picture. "I would stay the night on the floor, leave before anyone got up."

"You wouldn't sleep with her? In her bed, I mean?" He was attempting to figure out how far their intimacy went without scaring the boy back into his shell. Mark shook his head in response to the question.

"Holly wouldn't. Sometimes she would kiss me... let me kiss her... even touch her occasionally but we never did much else. I'm not daft. I think she felt sorry for me. That's why she let me stay over. It was on nights when my dad was at his worst. Since my brothers left, he's worse than ever." Mark's gaze drifted towards some far away point in the distance.

They sat together in silence for a few minutes, Janssen thinking through Mark's portrayal of their relationship. His description of their interactions came across as honest, very matter of fact. He pondered whether he should ask the next question. If it was fair to. "Did you know Holly was pregnant?" Mark was visibly shocked. Too strong a reaction to be faked, he was almost certain. "Have you any idea who the father might have been?"

"No, sorry." Janssen scrutinised the boy. Apart from fleeting facial expressions and occasional outbursts that quickly subsided, he gave away little in regards to his emotions. Each response was measured, dead pan. The outbursts, however, gave Janssen pause for thought. Although, they appeared to pass quickly, were he to be in a fit of pique how quickly would they subside then? *Two minutes? Three?* Perhaps enough time to strangle a petite girl like Holly Bettany for sure. "It doesn't surprise me that she was seeing someone else," Mark said, speaking softly and without judgement. "Holly was aware of how attractive she was to all the boys. I always thought I was lucky she wanted to spend as much time with me as she did."

"When you were in her room did Holly ever show you her

laptop?" he asked. Mark nodded. "Do you know where she got it? Her parents said it wasn't hers."

"She never mentioned it. I assumed they bought it for her. They're loaded."

"What about a mobile phone. Does she have one?"

"Yes. Her dad bought both her and Maddie new ones recently. Holly moaned about it. It was an iPhone and *she hated it*." Janssen was surprised by that, believing most kids wanted the top of the range accessory. Mark seemed to notice his bemusement. "She said her dad had an iPhone and that's why he got them. She couldn't figure out the operating system, plus he'd configured it somehow and she didn't like it. He cancelled the contract on her other phone to force her to use it. The man's a control freak." Mark turned to face him, marking a shift in his focus. Suddenly, he was attentive, sitting forward and crossing his legs beneath him, resting elbows on knees. "Will you catch the person who killed her, Holly?"

Janssen usually preferred not to answer such a question. To give loved ones, friends or relatives false hope was something he generally frowned upon. However, on this occasion, there was something about the boy's expression that made him want to behave differently. Besides, he was confident. "I believe we will, yes."

"And what will happen then?"

"Well, there will be a trial and, provided we do our jobs properly, the killer will be convicted and sent to prison." Mark's brow furrowed as he processed the events. "For a very long time," he added, as if that wasn't obvious to the boy. Mark inclined his head.

"My dad has been to prison many times." Janssen knew that to be true. "He says you can't trust the police." The statement was unsurprising. There wasn't a convicted criminal who hadn't either been fitted up by the police or poorly treated by both judge and jury. "He says it's only people like us who go to prison."

"People like you?" Janssen queried, presuming Callum McCall was inferring those at the lower end of the economic scale or with criminal pasts.

"Yeah. Those of us doing what we can just to get by." Janssen thought those were the words of his father, issued from the offspring's mouth. "I know what you must be thinking. I've watched cop shows on the TV. I was the last one to be seen with Holly and I'm... me."

Janssen drew breath. Mark was still intently focussed on him, watching for the merest hint of dishonesty but there was something else, beyond that, something more but Janssen couldn't put his finger on it. "Did you kill Holly?" he asked. Mark shook his head. "Then, you *can* trust me. You have nothing to fear from the police." The boy seemed to accept that response, or, at least, he didn't comment further, looking away. "I know you should be in school but is there somewhere I can take you? Home perhaps?"

Mark stood, brushing off his trousers and wiping his hands against one another. "No thanks. I've got somewhere I need to be."

Without another word or a backward glance, he strode away. Janssen looked on for a moment, watching him leave, feeling empathy for the boy and considering his role in all of this. He was a much-troubled soul. Then he turned away and headed inside.

CHAPTER TWENTY-ONE

JANSSEN ENTERED THE OPS ROOM. Eric had a phone clasped to his ear, concentrating hard. Crossing into the adjoining room where they had the tea and coffee, he was pleased to find the kettle was hot. His fingers recoiled from touching the side but he flicked it on anyway, just to ensure the water boiled. Never one for instant coffee except in an emergency, his father wouldn't have it in the house, he chose one of the flavoured green teas. They were a new addition. It must be Tamara's influence. Eric would never have bought them.

Returning to ops, Eric was off the phone and out of his seat. "I've just spoken with a DC in Canning Town." He was excited, keen to share. "You know, in Newham, where the Olympic Stadium is." Janssen frowned at the irrelevance. He knew the area. Eric continued. "Turns out there were allegations made against Ken Francis two years ago. The subsequent investigation led to the CPS charging him."

"What with?" Tamara Greave's voice came from behind, entering the room.

"Three counts of sexual assault and one of false imprisonment," Eric replied, turning to her. "Now, the case fell apart before it reached the courtroom because the primary witness recanted her statement but the guy I spoke with thought Francis got away with one."

Janssen perched himself on the edge of one of the desks, cupping his tea with both hands. "Who was the complainant?"

Eric returned to the notes he made during the call. "Rebecca Martins. She's very much a part of the gig economy with her goal of making it in modelling as I understand."

"And her connection with Francis?" Janssen asked, sipping at his tea. It was too hot to drink but the aroma was pleasant.

"Apparently, she modelled for him and… it all got a little bit touchy-feely, if you know what I mean." Janssen suppressed a smile at the young man's obvious embarrassment. There was a tinge of red growing on Eric's neck. "When she tried to leave, she alleged Francis refused, blocking her path and locking her in his studio. Obviously, he denied it, writing it off as a misunderstanding."

"You said three counts?" Tamara came to stand alongside Janssen. He thought she looked tired. Her face was lined.

"Yes, they followed up with other models and two more women came forward offering similar stories. The CPS didn't feel they were strong enough to warrant prosecution, so those cases were dropped and it fell on the one woman." Eric looked expectantly between the two senior officers. Janssen thought that cast a different light on Ken Francis and his potential involvement in the case. By his wife's admission, Holly modelled for him and he'd lied about how well he knew the girl. A past history of this nature certainly warranted his inclusion on the list of suspects.

"I wonder if this is what fuelled their move out of London and into the countryside?" Tamara asked. "Perhaps his reputation took something of a hit and they left under a cloud. Eric, can you follow up on this. See if there was damage to his career. Jane Francis says he sells most of his work to clients abroad these days. In which case, there's every possibility that isn't necessarily through choice."

"Should we bring him in?" Eric's eyes flitted between them, sensing he'd uncovered something hugely significant.

Janssen looked to Tamara, chewing his lower lip. Eric was ahead of himself. On the right lines but grasping nonetheless. There was a broad gap to bridge between an allegation of sexual assault and murder, although, new possibilities were opening up for consideration. His suspicion leant towards Francis being the source of the sketches they found in Holly's possession. Everything was far too circumstantial at this time to warrant a formal interview. "We need to speak with him again, certainly." Judging by the expression on her face, he figured she must be thinking similarly.

"We'll head out and speak to him now, apply a bit of pressure about why he lied to us. I'm sure he will have spoken with his wife about it, so we'll not be overplaying our hand." Janssen agreed with the plan. "We can always make it formal at a later date, depending on anything that comes back from the lab or a witness to tie him in further."

"He may incriminate himself," Janssen added. "Eric, can you try and get a hold of the original complainant. Perhaps she can shed more light on what happened than you got from the officer in Canning Town."

"I'm not sure how keen she'll be to talk to me," Eric said, sounding worried. "From what I gather she was threatened with prosecution for wasting police time after she recanted. There'll be no love lost there."

THE DAY WAS PREDOMINANTLY overcast but every so often the clouds would break and the warmth of the spring sun would cut through reminding them of the promise of the forthcoming summer. Janssen loved Norfolk in the summertime. Sheltered on the east coast, the prevailing wind kept the edge off the North Sea and the Atlantic storms would usually dissipate over land leaving the region blessed with more sun and less rain than the rest of the country. The downside came when the prevailing winds were knocked off course from the east. On those days fog could hug the coastline for the daylight hours and whereas inland people were treated by blue skies and hot sun, those unfortunates on the coast could barely see a hundred paces in front of them. Today, spring seemed in touching distance.

"Do you think Ken Francis could have been Holly's benefactor?" Tamara asked him, following a long pause in conversation. She had seemed lost in thought since they left the station and Janssen hadn't wanted to intrude. Perhaps she'd been puzzling over the case. She must have been thinking along the same lines as him.

"The source of where she got the laptop?" he asked, just to clarify. She nodded. "Do you think it could be a present? Ken certainly has the money and if she didn't buy it out of her allowance, how else could she have got it?"

She retreated into herself once more, falling silent and so he didn't comment further, allowing her space to think. "There's another possibility. The laptop is neither Holly's nor a gift."

"She borrowed it… *or stole it*?" He was thinking aloud now. They had no proof for any of their ideas, it was all merely supposition.

Tamara laughed but it was a sound without genuine humour. "For all we know, we're looking at Holly as a pure innocent here. How often does it turn out the victim was somehow culpable in their own murder?" He looked over at her, feeling himself frowning at what was rather an odd comment. Regardless of how Holly may or may not behave, her baby was certainly innocent. She must have read his reaction and sought to explain. "I'm just saying Holly comes across as something of a mixed-up kid, not that that would necessarily make her responsible for what happened to her. All I'm saying is she seems to have a lot of secrets. No one really knows her, least of all us. For all we know, she could have been blackmailing Ken Francis, extorting money from him. Who knows."

"He could just as easily be her sugar-daddy," he bit back, possibly harsher than was necessary. "Hell, if he has a tendency towards young girls then, regardless of her being over age, we could have found a motive."

"The model in Canning Town was in her twenties."

"Still over half his age!"

"If that's a pre-requisite for suspicion we will have to investigate most of the divorcees who holiday in Thailand… for the diving, obviously."

He found himself smiling. His interpretation of what she meant may have been off target and he sensed she was prone to the darker end of the scale when it came to her sense of humour. "You know a fair bit yourself about keeping secrets, as a teenager, I mean?" She glanced across and smiled, remaining tight-lipped.

Flashing lights appeared in the rear-view mirror and he pulled to the side of the road. A fire engine flew past at speed, blasting the sirens as it approached the next junction before disappearing from view. Janssen moved off and around the next bend they came upon the turn for the unmade track leading up to the Francis house. Moments later they came upon the house itself. Smoke billowed from the rear, dark grey clouds churning into the sky that were then carried away on the breeze. The firemen were already hard at work, unfurling hoses and the appliance blocked the approach. Unable to enter the rear yard it was parked alongside the gable end on the east side of the house.

"Is that the house itself?" Tamara asked.

"No, I reckon it's the studio," Janssen replied as he clambered out. The wind momentarily altered direction and a gust carried smoke and embers towards them. Even the slight exposure to the fumes left an acrid taste in his mouth. They moved closer only to find their path blocked by a fireman. He took out his warrant card, identifying himself but was still asked to remain well clear. "Is there anyone inside?"

"Not as far as we know. The owners are in the main part of the house."

Turning, they made their way to the front door. The little used approach path was overgrown, foliage growing between the slabs and encroaching from either side. Reaching the front door, he rapped the knocker loudly several times. The noise from the appliance crew at work in the yard carried around the house to them and Janssen found he had to repeat the process before they got a response.

Jane Francis opened the door. Her expression was one of intense shock, wide-eyed and fearful, and if she was surprised to see them, she didn't show it. Stepping back, she beckoned them in. They followed her into the main living area. Ken stood with his back to them at the French doors, overlooking the yard, staring at the studio opposite. Upon hearing them enter, he turned. One hand was drawn across his mouth and nose, his skin was pale, colourless, and he was breathing heavily. Janssen wondered if he was having some kind of anxiety attack. Coming closer, he was surprised to see Ken was developing some swelling around the left eye. He wondered if he'd tried to attack the flames himself and fallen. His wife looked nervous now, unwilling to meet Janssen's eye. She immediately offered to make coffee, an opportunity to busy herself and avoid attention, Janssen thought.

Tamara cleared her throat, coming to stand alongside Ken. "You're having a rough few days, aren't you," she said quietly.

CHAPTER TWENTY-TWO

KEN FRANCIS TURNED AWAY from the sight of the firefighters marshalling powerful jets of water as they wrestled to bring the blaze under control. Tamara Greave paid close attention to his demeanour. On previous visits he came across as an amiable man, trying too hard to appear so but nevertheless, pleasant enough. He reminded her of an uncle, long since passed away, who was quite similar. On the surface, when required, he could portray a persona that was expected of him knowing what he should say and how to act. Most of the time, however, with no one else around, the façade would drop away and on those occasions, the real personality would appear. Usually that was in private or in front of immediate family or close friends. She witnessed it only a few times, or at least, she only noticed it then for she was very young.

Now, Ken struck her in the same way. Even making allowances for the brutal destruction of his works of art, not least his livelihood, there was precious little of the man she'd first met. His face was drawn, settling in to what looked very much like his natural resting state. Whereas before he took care to acknowledge their presence, now he appeared disinterested. More so than merely preoccupied with the events unfolding before him.

"How did the fire start?" she asked casually, floating the question. Either the couple were hitting an unfortunate patch of misfortune with the vandalism of the studio and now the fire, or something more sinister was at play. Ken shook his head, pulling out a chair at the breakfast table and sitting down.

"We were out." It was his wife, Jane, who replied. Tamara glanced in her direction. She was cleaning the coffee machine, preparing it for use but much too fastidiously, in her opinion. Perhaps it was her cynicism, drummed into her by experience, that led her to cast an eye over both of them for signs of anything out of the ordinary.

Their relationship was somewhat strained, that was obvious, but neither were behaving as she might expect in this scenario. Jane was fussing in the kitchen making a show of being a courteous host while her husband's studio, part of their fabulously renovated home, burned nearby. Ken, on the other hand, sat expressionless, a vacuous shell of a human being. Arguably numb from shock but even so, no emotion, no anger, it was bordering on acceptance.

Jane seemed to notice her interest, appearing flustered and overfilling the filter head with freshly ground coffee. She cursed under her breath, cutting the utterance short almost as soon as she said it. Tamara moved closer to her, noting Janssen following with his eyes. "You were out when it started? Together?" Jane nodded, picking up a cloth from the nearby sink and wiping up the spillage. "Do you mind if I ask where?" Jane Francis glared at her. It seemed a particularly venomous look and she was reminded of Mark McCall's statement about her being *evil*. With that one look, she understood why he might get that impression, especially seeing as Jane was clearly intimidated by the police presence.

"Ken thought it might be nice for us to spend the day out, make the most of the weather and the time we have while the kids aren't around."

She glanced at her watch; it was barely midday. Jane looked nervous, agitated. "Home early?" The question went unanswered or ignored. She couldn't decide which. Ken's head lowered and she saw Janssen incline his own. He was thinking something, she could tell.

"What happened to your face, Mr Francis?" Janssen asked. So

focussed was she on their behaviour patterns that she hadn't noticed. Now she paid closer attention. The redness and minor swelling around the eye on the left side of his face looked sore. Ken didn't look the type to have battled an inferno. Athletic in stature, perhaps, but he didn't exude courage, not to her anyway.

"I must have fallen," Ken all but whispered without looking up. The challenge to his weak assertion came from an unlikely source, his wife.

"Oh, Ken! When are you going to tell the truth? They aren't fools!"

Tamara was surprised. Jane, often so measured if not calculating, sounded exasperated. For his part, Janssen raised his eyebrows which was possibly the most animated she had ever seen him when speaking with a suspect or witness. Ken remained resolute in his reticence and so it fell to Jane, her frustration evident as she abandoned the coffee making, leaning against the worktop and crossing her arms in front of her.

"We came across Colin Bettany out on Holkham sands," Jane explained. "He attacked Ken."

"Why would he do that?" she asked.

"The man's deranged," Jane replied. "If I wasn't there, I reckon he would have killed him."

"That's quite an accusation," Janssen said.

"My wife is exaggerating… as usual." Finally offering some kind of reaction, Ken was dismissive, drawing a deep sigh from the other side of the kitchen. He shook his head, resigned to her ire. "The man is in pain. He's lost his daughter and is looking around for someone to blame. Somewhere for him to direct his sense of loss. He picked me. Let's not get too carried away."

Tamara glanced between the two of them. Jane was still glaring at her husband but he appeared disinterested in her theories. "In my experience, grieving parents don't generally assault members of the public for no reason."

"Victim blaming!" Jane replied. "What a surprise."

She ignored the comment, instead coming alongside Ken and sitting down. He looked across at her, quickly averting his eyes from her gaze. "Holly modelled for you. Your wife confirmed it. Is there anything else you need to tell us?" She chose her words carefully, reinforcing the point they were aware of his deceit and not mincing her words with the open question.

"Holly and I... we had a relationship," Ken said softly. "I thought I was in love with her... for a while, at least." Lifting his head, he met her gaze. His eyes glazed over, tears welling. "I miss her. *I did not kill her.*" His tone was firm, unyielding.

"What did Colin Bettany say when you allege he assaulted you?"

Ken pursed his lips momentarily before answering. "He was ranting about all sorts of bizarre things. I didn't really catch any of it. Everything happened so quickly. I stood up. We were sitting in the dunes, chatting. That's when he hit me."

"How did you respond?" she asked him.

"I didn't, not really. Jane gave him a piece of her mind."

"Was Colin aware of your relationship or his daughter's modelling for you?" Tamara flicked her eyes to Janssen, as straight-faced as ever. Ken shook his head. "How did it come about, your relationship?"

"We met through Colin and Marie. We went to theirs for dinner. Holly was animated by what I do. She spoke to me regarding my work, saying she loved it. Whether she knew about me beforehand or looked me up once her parents announced we were coming over, I don't know. She tickled my ego; I won't deny it. I was low and her attentions excited me, made me feel... alive, maybe."

Jane turned her back on them. These must be hard words for her to hear, an admission of infidelity delivered with indifference. *What reaction would such betrayal generate? How might an aggrieved partner respond?* Obviously, Jane was aware of this before today but exactly when she knew could either place her as a suspect or as an unwitting victim in the wider scheme of things.

"I know how it sounds... and how it looks for that matter," Ken continued, "which is why I didn't tell you before. I may well be a foolish, middle-aged man but I'm not a killer."

"And the baby? How did you feel about that?" She watched him intently. Ken's mouth fell open but he held her eye. If he knew, then he was quite some poker player. "Holly was pregnant. You knew that?"

"No! I... Holly was pregnant?" Ken stammered, looking to his wife.

Tamara followed his gaze. Jane was unfazed, her expression unreadable. "From what you've told us, you could well have been the father. We've also been looking into the circumstances surrounding your move away from London." Ken visibly tensed. "A number of allegations were made against you—"

"None of which led to a prosecution," Jane snapped.

"And in light of your husband's revelation along with Colin Bettany's reaction, we need to examine every potential scenario. I should caution you that you do not have to say anything—"

"I am well aware of my rights, detective," Ken stated, waving away her attempt to follow procedure. "I have nothing to hide. Ask me whatever you need to and then you can both leave!"

"Who else was aware of the nature of your relationship with Holly?"

His eyes narrowed, appearing to her as if he was genuinely thinking about the question. Whether the delay was due to his search for accuracy or a wilful attempt at misdirection was a judgement call. "No one, as far as I know. I told Jane after... Holly's passing. I haven't told anyone else. Why would I?"

She asked Jane to confirm the information.

"I knew Holly came over and that she was sitting for Ken, yes."

"And you were comfortable with him being alone with a young girl?" she asked, unable to keep the air of judgement out of her tone. Jane bristled but didn't respond. "You didn't have any doubts about what was going on, particularly after recent events in London? I find that a little hard to believe."

"Are you married, Detective Chief Inspector?" Jane asked pointedly. She was disinclined to make the conversation personal to her, merely shaking her head. "Well, when you are, you'll learn that all marriages are unique in one way or another. You start out on the same page but over time circumstances can change." She stared at Ken, he remained impassive, seemingly impervious to his wife's tangent. "Often you find out you're not married to the same person you thought you were. One, or both of you takes it a different way and you either make do and compromise or..."

"Or what?" she asked, genuinely interested from a personal perspective as well as regarding the case.

"You... accept one another for who they are and... what they need or you go your separate ways." Jane spoke the last with an air of resignation. "Perhaps, in a marriage you live with the hope that one day those paths will converge again."

"You *accept* your husband's infidelity?" The level of candour on display was such that she felt comfortable to respond in kind. Jane fixed her with a stare. They were two very different women but she had to admit, Jane held a view that many could probably relate to. Several of her mother's friends would be in wholehearted agreement. This was no framework that she could ever foresee herself agreeing to live by, though. Then again, she wasn't married yet.

"Marriages take a great deal of work," Jane said in a way that came across as condescending. Her eyes lowered to Tamara's hand, presently tapping index and forefinger on the table in front of her. "One day you might find that out." Jane must have observed the engagement ring on her finger. There was an air of superiority in the woman's manner as well as her tone. Despite what most would consider to be a humiliating conversation, what with her husband's admission, Jane Francis held herself upright, shoulders back, commanding. Defiant.

"If neither of you told anyone. How did Colin Bettany find out?" Janssen asked. It was such an obvious question, she was irritated she hadn't thought of it herself. Both Ken and Jane looked to each other but neither had an answer. "What about this fire? Presumably you had the wiring signed off?" Ken nodded. "Buildings don't tend to spontaneously combust. Old properties where the wiring is shot, perhaps, but fires like yours are rare. Any idea how it started?"

Again, neither of them offered an explanation. She indicated for Janssen to join her and they headed outside. The sense of relief at their departure was palpable within the room.

CHAPTER TWENTY-THREE

RATHER LIKE THE day following a November celebration the smell of burnt wood and smoke hung in the air. The fire was out and as they crossed the yard, the destruction within the studio became apparent. The damage was immense but largely contained to the confines of the stone structure having not spread to the attached buildings. *That will be cold comfort for Ken,* Janssen thought as he drew the attention of the station officer, notable by his white helmet. He indicated for them to wait a moment and they held their ground.

Janssen was perturbed by Ken's admission to a relationship with Holly, professing his misguided love for her and describing it as something of a mid-life crisis. That was tantamount to a dismissal of the affair as a passing moment, normalising what was a far darker reality in his opinion. Holly was seventeen and therefore a consenting adult in the eyes of the law, so Ken Francis was right not to feel shame or guilt regarding their relationship. The moral question beyond that was, however, far more nuanced. A man twice her age and married, albeit within a rather odd open marriage with some agreed sexual boundaries or lack thereof, having a physical and emotional relationship with a girl left him questioning the man's moral framework. Holly was a girl, not in the eyes of the law, but certainly in his own. Unsure of exactly when Ken would have met her, she could barely have been seventeen at the time and although in the sixth form of the school now, she was still too young. Had they become associated with one another a year before then they may well have been considering it a case of grooming and exploitation. These were how thin the margins were.

There was also the issue of consent that bothered him. Until they could find someone else to corroborate his assertion of them being in some agreed relationship, they only had Ken's word to go by. His track record of allegedly having wandering hands threw that under a different light. *Could he be trusted?* When asked the question, his response to Holly's pregnancy appeared genuine but, then again, it was also a motive for murder if Holly was ready to break cover and reveal him as the father. The motive extended to his wife as well.

The family's move to Norfolk could be viewed as a fresh start after living under the threat of prosecution or just as equally, an escape from the spectre of suspicion. He caught Tamara watching him intently. For how long she had been doing so, he didn't know.

"Penny for them," she said. He smiled.

"They are an odd couple." He looked back towards the house. Ken was standing at the window watching them or perhaps the smouldering wreck of his studio, it was unclear which. "I'm trying to make sense of them."

"You don't like them."

The statement confused him. He didn't realise he was so readable. Up until that point, he hadn't given them much thought in that sense. Personal views were best kept away from investigations as the threat of those feelings clouding judgement could be detrimental to an investigation. *Was he making that mistake here?* She was right, however. Neither of them were people he would ever choose to spend his time with, certainly not the more he got to know them. Did that make either of them a killer? No. Both were certainly capable. Ken with his controlled, secretive behaviour and his wife, angry and neurotic. People killed for lesser reasons than these two could potentially have.

The scorned wife and the younger woman. The illegitimate child threatening their status, their marriage. They were also not telling the truth. Not entirely. That thought came from instinct and he trusted it.

The station officer arrived, sparing Janssen from having to provide an answer to the question and beckoning them over to the studio.

"I figured you would want to see this." He took them to the entrance. The door was missing because they'd broken it down in order to gain access to the fire. "Mind your footing, it's a bit damp but the structure of the roof is sound. The narrow corridor led to the studio and once inside Janssen realised the fire wasn't as widespread as he first thought. The interior was heavily ingrained with smoke and the water from the brigade's hoses had increased the damage, as it commonly did, but the fabric of the building, some of the walls and the roof survived untouched by flame. His surprise must have been evident on his face. "Building regs require open timber to be treated with fire suppressing paint or coating. That gave us more time before it took hold. Another fifteen to twenty minutes and you'd find the roof would have caught and we'd have lost the structure."

"Cause?" Tamara asked, turning her collar up to the dripping water raining down on them from above.

"An accelerant of some kind, probably simple use of petrol," the officer confirmed.

Following the vandalism, arson wasn't a shock to Janssen. He half expected it. Looking around, he noted the middle of the room was darker and more heavily fire-damaged than the surrounding areas. This encompassed where the double bed was positioned. "Is this the seat of the fire?" he asked, interrupting Tamara as she was about to speak. He apologised.

"Yes, I believe so."

"Was the door forced when you arrived?" Janssen asked, scanning the windows for signs of damage. Several were indeed broken but they could easily have been destroyed by the intensity of the blaze as by a wanton arsonist.

"I'll check with the team but I believe it was locked." The station officer pointed to a narrow slot in the stonework of the wall, perhaps an outstretched handspan in width and two-foot high, common in barns of this age. Here, there were four along the southern wall, the low point being around chest height, rising to just above Janssen's head. They were infilled with glass. The one he was pointed to was broken. "That may have been a result of the fire popping the glass but, being directly positioned above the bed here, it's quite likely the petrol was poured through there. All you'd need then is a flame tossed in and you're away. The property isn't overlooked from that direction. Your would-be arsonist could sneak up unobserved."

Returning to the daylight, they left the appliance crew to their work. An investigation officer would need to examine the seat of the fire and ascertain if it was arson but it was a formality in this case. The question remained who would do it? The same person who vandalised the studio only days earlier was an enticing suspect.

"Mightily coincidental, isn't it?" Janssen said. "Holly is murdered and Ken's studio is vandalised and then set on fire. All within a few days of each other."

"Especially as he has been sleeping with her."

Any further exchange of ideas was interrupted by Ken Francis appearing at the back door. Hesitating for a moment, he hovered in the doorway before walking towards them. Each step appeared heavier than the last.

"I have something I want... I think you should see," he said calmly before turning and disappearing back inside the house. They followed and as they entered the kitchen Janssen saw a confused look on Jane's face. Seemingly, his wife didn't know what he was going to say either. Perhaps that was fear rather than confusion. Half expecting the man to confess to the parentage of Holly's unborn child, he pulled out a chair for Tamara and one for himself. He was well aware of the impact his physical presence had on people and if they were about to receive a confession, he didn't want to run the risk of intimidating the man and so took his seat quickly. Ken struck him as someone unused to sharing his intimate thoughts and feelings. "I... I haven't been entirely open with you." Ken averted his eyes from them, flicking a nervous glance at his wife. "Any of you."

"What is it you have to tell us, Mr Francis?" Tamara asked. That irritated Janssen. He would rather give the man space to talk. They could grill him later.

"I've been keeping something from my family," Ken said, "but you must understand, I did so only to spare them from worry." Janssen wasn't sure who that comment was for, them or Jane? He stepped past them into the boot room and Janssen craned his neck to see the man disappear into what looked like his study, only to reappear moments later, papers in hand. "I've been receiving these." He handed a clutch of handwritten notes to Tamara who accepted them with an incline of the head, immediately scanning the content. She passed them to Janssen, one by one. They were scrawled upon rather than neatly presented, with little care or attention to use of the printed lines. The path of the pen was erratic. Either they were written in haste or anger, it wasn't clear which. The meaning of the content, however, was dark. "Someone has it in for me… maybe us. I don't really know. They've threatened me, my work."

"How long have you been receiving these?" Janssen asked. Ken glanced at his wife again before answering.

"Several months now." He looked at Jane. Janssen followed suit and she put a hand across her mouth as if she appeared shocked by the revelation. "They started soon after we moved in. I didn't think much of it at first. Kids mucking about. A jealous local who missed out on the property. Something like that."

"This isn't mucking about," Janssen replied, holding a note in front of him and reading it aloud. *"Scum! You should burn in hell."*

"They've not all been like that… but they've been getting worse over the past couple of months."

Janssen held the note up and offered it to Jane. "Have you seen these?" She shook her head but didn't come closer to read them. He found that curious. "Do you recognise the handwriting?" Again, she shook her head. "What about you, Ken? Have you fallen out with anyone recently, other than Dr Bettany?"

"No. No, not at all. I don't really mix with people unless I have to," he replied. The last appeared most likely aimed towards his wife.

"Could it be him? Dr Bettany?" Tamara asked but Janssen

interpreted the hollow tone of her suggestion as a lack of belief in the idea.

"I don't see why he would," Ken replied. "These notes started being left at the house before I even met Holly... or any of the Bettanys for that matter." He turned to face his wife with an expression of contrition. "I'm sorry I didn't tell you, love. With everything that's been going on, I didn't want to worry you but... it looks like I got it wrong."

She crossed the distance between them and placed a reassuring hand on his shoulder, smiling weakly. "It's okay. I understand. You thought you were doing the right thing."

Ken looked back to Janssen. "Maybe this person has taken action against Holly because of my relationship with her?" Janssen saw Jane's grip tighten on his shoulder but Ken didn't seem to notice. "That would make her death somehow my fault."

"Oh, Ken. Don't be so silly." Jane dismissed the idea. Rather harshly in Janssen's view. "That's so far-fetched. I'm sure these notes have nothing to do with Holly. Wouldn't you say, Inspector?"

Janssen ensured he gave nothing away in tone or expression as he spoke. "We'll have to look into it. The fire certainly looks like it was set on purpose, so this is at the very least an arson inquiry. We'll need to take these notes with us." Ken Francis didn't object. In fact, he seemed relieved to have brought it out in the open. The idea that they could be related to Holly's murder was appealing. So far, there was no clear motive for why she was killed. It hadn't occurred to him she may not be the target and her death could have been to cause pain to others. "While we're getting things out in the open, where were you last Friday night?"

"I was here," Ken replied. "In my studio."

"Alone?"

"No. He came inside after the children went to sleep and then he was with me, watching telly," Jane said. "Would have been around nine, nine-thirty." Ken looked to his wife. *Was that relief on his face?* He didn't speak, only silently nodded to Janssen to confirm the timings.

"We'll need to make that official," he said, choosing not to press it home. It wasn't a surprise. A wife would often back her husband no matter what state their relationship was in. It was, however, a weak alibi. "When did you buy Holly a laptop?" The relief on Ken's face was short-lived. His head snapped upright at the suggestion.

"I didn't. Whatever would give you that idea?"

Janssen analysed the man's response. This was one of the few occasions where Ken willingly met his eye. "It was with some sketches she had in her possession, presumably drawn by you. They were stashed along with her own." He was stretching the truth for the artworks weren't kept with the laptop.

"Sorry. Nothing to do with me... but I did let her keep some of the sketches I drew of her."

"There was one, a charcoal picture of a girl in high heels. The sketch was monochrome with the exception of a pair of red high heels as I recall," Janssen said. "Quite... provocative."

"Stands to reason," Jane snapped. "Always dressing as if she was much older than she was." Janssen resisted the urge to make a sarcastic comment about trying to appeal to an older man. His moral judgement didn't need airing.

"The level of sexual interpretation is very much in the eye of the viewer," Ken said. Was he trying to lessen the nature of his sexual relationship or was this how artists thought? Either way, he chose not to pursue the conversation. He put the notes into an evidence bag and left the house, speaking with the brigade's station officer as they made their way to the car. The studio was taped off to await an investigator who was already on his way up from Norwich.

Janssen glanced at the house but on this occasion neither Ken nor Jane were visible. He met eyes with Tamara as they walked to the car. "Convenient. The fire and everything." He unlocked the car and they both got in. "Let's say for argument's sake that Ken is Holly's killer. She visits him on Friday night. There's an altercation or a falling out, possibly related to the pregnancy although he denies knowing about it."

"He kills her accidentally or on purpose," Tamara said, following through on the thought process.

"Ken's studio is vandalised and subsequently burned down just as details start to come out about their relationship. Both events set him up as a victim and the fire is a great way of getting rid of any trace evidence."

Tamara fell silent, thinking it through. If the theory was even close to what happened, Janssen knew they were going to struggle to prove it.

CHAPTER TWENTY-FOUR

JANE FRANCIS WATCHED the police officers talking to the fireman in the rear yard. What was he saying to them? The fire was started deliberately. They'd told them that much. A fleeting thought passed through her mind. Were the children safe? The house? The detectives appeared to be saying goodbye and she stepped away from the window so as not to be seen by them. Maintaining a calm and reserved demeanour during Ken's unfolding tale was necessary and she wondered if she carried it off. The quiet one, Tom Janssen, was focussed, clever. Whereas the other, the woman, came across as manipulative. Her ability to seize on the slightest word and interpret a narrative was clear to her. She was the one to really watch. The one to fear.

Ken appeared behind her, placing his hands on her upper arms and squeezing gently. He could be a sweet man. Undeniably intense and moody at times but with an inner kindness that he seldom showed these days. *Maybe he did to her*. Perhaps that was part of his appeal, what drew her to him. His passion for his work was obvious, he wore that outwardly. If you ever touched the part of him he kept hidden, if he let you in, then you felt an attachment to something special. A world where others couldn't go to. At least, that's how she remembered it. Ken didn't let many past the barrier. The others, the girls who came before Holly, were there for a reason. An extension of his art, he would say. Many thought they were special to him, different to other models but they didn't know Ken, didn't understand him.

Holly fitted into that category, she just failed to realise it. A baby. She hadn't seen that coming. Ken reached forward and kissed her neck. It was a light touch, one of affection rather than anything more sexual.

"I'm sorry I kept the notes secret from you." She knew she should be irritated by that but even her levels of hypocrisy wouldn't descend that deep. "I should have said." She was tense. Not directly as a result of his proximity or touch but his attempt at reassurance only seemed to heighten her angst. Forcing herself to respond, she shook her head.

"I understand," she replied. The words sounded hollow and not genuine. Ken didn't appear to notice, giving her arms a further squeeze before lessening his grip. He stepped away and she took a deep breath turning to watch his back as he walked away. "The baby... was it yours?" The words stung her as they passed her lips. How could he have been so foolish. Then it dawned on her. The obvious. This was Ken she was talking about. A man who was driven by two things, his art and his penis. Often the two crossed one another. He stopped, glancing down. *Reluctant to face me?* She heard him take a deep breath.

"I don't know. I guess it might be." The reply was unsatisfactory, bordering on pathetic. How could he not have an inclination and if he thought it possible, how could he be so naïve?

"Ken! You ought to know better." Her tone was fiery, consumed with frustration, fear and above all else, jealousy.

"Things happen, you know," he replied, turning. For a moment she thought he was going to cry again. "I didn't know she was pregnant until she showed up on Friday night. I swear."

"It would explain why Colin Bettany was so furious. How does he know if you didn't?"

Ken shook his head. "He is a doctor. Maybe he figured it out."

"And you. How did he figure out you were sleeping with his little girl?" Ken baulked at that question. Her choice of words was emotive. She knew it. She chose them on purpose. "Barely seventeen, Ken. Still a girl in my book."

"You were doing far worse by her age!" She felt a surge of anger but quelled it. Judging from his expression, he saw how that point hit home. It was true. She had. Without those experiences, there was no way she could have coped with a man as dysfunctional as her husband. "And seeing as we're not holding back, why did you lie?" She held his stare with one of her own. A show of defiance. "We didn't spend Friday night together. You didn't even see me until Saturday morning. If you doubt me so, why lie to them?"

She broke his gaze, striding into the living room. "I need a bloody drink!"

"Yeah, sure because that's going to help isn't it?" His voice was raised. He hadn't spoken to her like that in ages. "Why, Jane? Why back me up if you think I'm guilty of something?" The accusatory nature of his tone was growing stronger as he followed her. For a moment she felt something other than anger. Fear. Fear of her husband. An emotion she'd never really experienced in all their years together. Usually, she would dismiss him with a spiteful comment but something in his attitude made her think again.

Unscrewing the cap from a bottle of gin, she poured a large measure into a tumbler and added a pitiful amount of tonic water. Raising an unsteady hand, she sipped at the drink. It was far too strong and bitter but the shock steadied her. Ken cut an imposing figure, standing between her and the dining area waiting for an answer to his question. "Because you're my husband. No matter what else, we are a family and I will do *whatever* I have to do to keep us all together." His eyes narrowed. She was unsure if the reply was the one he expected or sought. Either way, he stepped aside allowing her to pass.

"You haven't asked me," he said quietly as she reached the kitchen. Turning to face him, she raised her glass again, averting her eyes from his.

"Asked you what?" She knew what he was referring to. In reality, she didn't want to know. To ask the question would be scary enough but how might she react to the truth? Her attempt at deflection failed. His frustration showed. "I'm not going to ask, Ken. I won't be put in that position."

"*Position*. What the hell do you mean by that?"

"Where I can't lie for you." She turned away, leaving him open-mouthed.

"You just did lie for me!"

"No," she said over her shoulder, correcting his assertion, "I lied for me... and the children."

Ken swore under his breath and stalked from the room, stamping his way up the stairs much like William would often do. Her head was pounding with an oncoming stress headache. Thinking on the notes, she wanted to know what was written on the others. The one Inspector Janssen held up for her was readable but the others remained on the table. She made a show of disinterest, writing them off. She had to. They must have been meant for Ken, left at the studio or on his car, different from those aimed at her. His reaction was quite telling. Had they told him what she first feared when he brought them out his response would have been very different.

She had told the truth before. Their life together was imperfect but as a whole their standard of living was better than most. Far superior to where she sprang from. There was much to be grateful for. Much to preserve. Each of them found their own ways to manage and kept the details from the other. Maintaining the family unit was important. Necessary. No matter what. The fire ensured one thing for certain. The person she kept well buried, the one she thought long gone needed to return. *Whatever you have to do,* she told herself as she finished the remainder of her drink.

CHAPTER TWENTY-FIVE

IT WAS WELL after lunchtime when Janssen returned to the station with Colin Bettany in tow. Tamara Greave was rummaging for the scraps at the bottom of a packet of crisps as he entered the ops room. They took a detour on the way back from the Francis house, stopping to buy sandwiches from a Tesco Express. The selection on offer after lunchtime was largely uninspiring but she found something. Janssen took off almost immediately upon their return, keen to bring the doctor in for a chat as soon as possible. She understood. Attacking Ken on the beach as he had done was supposedly out of character but she wasn't so sure.

Maddie alluded to the controlling nature of her parents, referencing her father in particular with his desire to know his daughters' whereabouts at all times. Arguably, that was the action of some fathers with their teenage girls. Her own, for all his views on environmental protections, liberty and humanist lifestyle, still found it hard when his daughter carved her own way in the world. A path, in his eyes, diametrically opposed to his world view. It wasn't. She just saw society in a wider context rather than the narrow perception he chose to adopt. And it was a choice. With him, everything was black and white, right or wrong. The grey areas were conversations for other people to waste their time on. In her view that was why they clashed. Her opinion differed to his and he couldn't handle it. Her mother said it was a generational thing. A catch-all description whenever family members fell out and an amicable settlement seemed far from reachable.

Thinking on what Maddie told her as well as Eric's view of the GP, she wondered how much of his behaviour was a construct of his own upbringing. A professional, educated to live a certain way of life regarding education and career, looking to ensure further continuity in the next generation. A preordained existence, structured without room to deviate. Holly struck her as someone looking for a different path, one she knew would be disapproved of by her parents. So, she kept it a secret from them, from everyone. Almost everyone. Where some teenagers came home with multiple piercings or a boyfriend wearing make-up, dressed head to toe in black, Holly chose a different path. On the surface she toed the line but once out of sight she made her own rules.

The truly sad aspect to it all were the obvious signs of her pain. The attitude at school, her estrangement from her peers and the arguments with her parents were all symptoms of a troubled mind. By all accounts the tutor was aware something was wrong as was the school. The signs were there, if only people had been willing to see. *But she hid them well, didn't she? Just like you did once.* Maybe her behaviour was judged as routine adolescent rebellion. Nothing pointed towards a reason for her to die, though. The affair with Ken and an unwanted pregnancy could lead to motive. People killed for less.

Colin's reaction towards Ken wasn't spontaneous. It couldn't be. To know where Ken would be, he would either have needed the luck of the gods to stumble across his path or he followed them to the beach. Those were the actions of a focussed mind, driven perhaps by mounting grief, anger or frustration. A need to lash out at someone. Ken would fit the criteria. They were of a similar age group, after all. She tried to imagine herself in his place. How would she react? *Badly.*

Eric snapped his lunchbox shut. The sound brought her out of her silent thought process. Looking over at him, he smiled. She indicated he had something stuck in his teeth. Whatever his mother made him that morning didn't smell great. He seemed embarrassed as he set about his teeth with the edge of a fingernail, ducking his head from view. The constable was so young, so innocent. It was hard to believe he already had the years under his belt to qualify for CID. Then again, things were changing. When she first sought to joined the criminal investigation department it was for a break to the monotony of being in uniform. An opportunity to get stuck into cases, to really make a difference in taking criminals off the streets. A good career path as well. These days, however, detectives often felt they were being stiffed by the Home Office.

Not that she would have played it any differently. Richard, on the other hand, would have her back in uniform in a heartbeat if not out of the job altogether. Her thoughts turned to her fiancé. They hadn't spoken since Sunday evening. She was avoiding the conversation if the truth were known. Richard could sulk, as well as she could, to be fair, but he would get over it and probably already had. Why he hadn't initiated a call as he usually would, was confusing.

Janssen entered. Colin Bettany was waiting for them in an interview room, a uniformed officer watching over him. She got up and the two of them went through. The interview room was windowless and warm. Uncomfortably so. The heating must still be on. Colin Bettany was turned out in his work attire. An expensive suit, cashmere and woollen blend with a shirt that easily cost upwards of a hundred pounds. She knew the difference. His cufflinks caught the light, drawing her eye to his hands and the cuts running the ridge of his knuckles. This wasn't a man used to fighting.

He was a big man, even when seated. She envisioned him playing in the rugby team at whichever private school he attended. Which he almost certainly did. The way he carried himself. The resting expression on his face, a lifetime immunity from imposter syndrome paid for by the wealth of his family. She wondered why his own children attended state school. The Bettanys appeared capable of funding a private education and chose not to. That seemed at odds with their desire for the children to attend medical school.

Colin's face was flushed. That could have been a result of sitting in the stuffy, airless room as much as from any pent-up emotion.

"Is this truly necessary? A formal interview?" He addressed Janssen. The voice was baritone, commanding.

"I'm afraid it is, Dr Bettany. Especially when you aren't where you told everyone you would be, avoiding speaking to us." She laid everything out ensuring the man opposite them was well aware who was leading this interview. It wasn't Bettany and nor was it Tom Janssen. "Then there's the assault on Ken Francis for us to discuss." Ken was adamant he wouldn't press charges, apparently well aware of how it might look to the locals and he didn't want to be the incomer adding to the grief of a grieving father. In reality, he was no doubt looking to keep his relationship with Holly out of the papers. "I understand you've waived your right to have a solicitor present."

"I have nothing to hide." Bettany remained confident, expressionless. "Madeleine informed Marie and myself of how... that... Holly used to pose at the Francis house. In my grief, I may have misconstrued the situation and lost my temper. My behaviour towards Kenneth was below the standard of conduct one might expect but... under the circumstances, I feel a magistrate would allow the matter to pass."

Moving in the circles he did, he probably knew most of the sitting magistrates in the area. "Well, Mr Francis has not made an official complaint." Bettany scoffed but said nothing further. "You should consider yourself fortunate, Dr Bettany. A dim view is taken of vigilante justice in the court system."

"*Vigilante justice.* Don't be so daft, woman." His tone was patronising. "A slap hardly qualifies."

"What about arson?" She watched as the righteous indignation dissipated before her eyes. "Ken's studio was vandalised at the weekend and subsequently set ablaze this morning. Shortly after the two of you had your... altercation. Magistrates rarely allow arson to pass, Dr Bettany. Perpetrators tend to see jail time."

"I... I... that has nothing to do with me," he stammered.

"Where did you go after you left the beach?"

"I walked for a while." All of a sudden, Bettany seemed to be far more interested in being helpful. The bluster and arrogance vanished. "Then I went home. I was there by midday. Marie will confirm it." The initial shock of the suggestion threw him but he was soon back on message. Bringing himself back upright, he locked eyes with her. "Any insinuation I had anything to do with such wanton destruction will be rebuffed with every resource at my disposal, Inspector Greave."

"Detective Chief Inspector, Greave," she corrected him, inwardly smiling at the opportunity he presented her with. The irony wasn't lost on him. "Fair enough. Now we've got that on the record, could you give me your thoughts on Holly's pregnancy." This was what she really wanted to speak to him about. The likelihood of Bettany being an arsonist was somehow unlikely in her mind. Setting a fire could be an act of revenge. However, the man before her wasn't the type. It was far too crude for a man like Colin Bettany. Upon mention of the baby, his head lowered and he closed his eyes. The first genuine expression of emotion she'd witnessed from him aside from anger obviously.

"Marie told me. I must admit, I'm finding it hard to comprehend." He raised his head, looking between the detectives, Janssen sitting bolt upright, straight-faced and silent. She was leading the interview and he appeared comfortable to take a back seat. Bettany, however, leaned towards addressing him at every opportunity. Perhaps he disliked her or struggled with female authority. It was a common enough occurrence with men of a certain type. "I didn't even know she had a boyfriend."

"What about Mark McCall?" She asked the question quickly, seeking a reaction.

"The McCall boy was a passing moment. Nothing more. I spoke with his father, told him what was what."

"And what *was* what?" Janssen broke his silence. She didn't mind, it was pertinent.

"That it wasn't on." The words tripped off his tongue as if it was obvious. "They couldn't be together. Totally unacceptable." He shook his head vigorously.

"Why not?" she asked, although, at the same time believing the answer was clear.

"Holly was going places. The whole world was in front of her. The McCall boy could well be a pleasant enough lad, after all, you don't hold the child responsible for the sins of the father... or the family, come to think of it. No, no… nice enough lad but not correct." There was so much implicit in the statement that she took a moment to let it all sink in. Every parent wants the best for their children and by all accounts the McCalls were given a wide berth by everyone but even so, for Colin, the prospect of them spending any time together was out of the question. It struck her that this man was unused to having his thoughts or actions scrutinised.

"Do you know where Holly went on the night she died?"

"Murdered, you mean." Colin Bettany fixed her with a stare. The first time he willingly met her eye. "You can say it as it is. The night someone took her from us. No. I have no idea. As far as I knew, she was in Norwich for her recital. We've told you all of this already."

"Of course. I just wanted to check you hadn't remembered anything you failed to mention before." Bettany shrugged. It was a dismissive gesture.

"Is there anything else?" He now reverted to a display of the arrogance he initially greeted them with. Taking out a folder, she opened it and withdrew some pages of paper. They were the threatening notes sent to Ken Francis. Setting several of them out alongside one another, she allowed him time to read over them. He did so casually and without any notable sign of recognition. "And these are?" He raised his gaze from the paper, sitting back in his seat and eyeing her warily.

"Is that your handwriting by any chance?" she asked.

"Certainly not!" The retort was so dismissive it was almost as if he was offended by the very idea he could be responsible. "I know doctors have a reputation for illegible script but I would be embarrassed to call myself a Wykehamist if I put my name to that. The man can't even spell. My parents would be demanding a refund." He pointed to the second sheet from the left.

She turned the paper around and saw the word he was referring to, *disgrase*, casting a sideways glance to Janssen to ensure he saw it as well. She asked him some further questions but got little useful information from him and drew the interview to a close soon after. Colin Bettany left with a firm instruction to steer clear of Ken Francis unless he wanted to see the inside of a cell for the night. He assured her there would be no repeat of his actions.

She watched as he was escorted out to the front entrance by a uniformed constable, Janssen alongside her. "What did he mean by the term *Wykehamist*?" She was unfamiliar with it but didn't want to weaken her position in front of the doctor who would no doubt have taken great pride in demeaning her any way he could.

"He went to school in Winchester." Janssen's explanation ended there but she was none the wiser. He must have realised because he carried on. "It was founded by William of Wykeham, if I remember correctly. The pupils are referred to by the founder's name. Winchester is second only to Eton as I understand."

"Oh, I see. Bristol Grammar myself."

"I won't hold it against you." Janssen smiled at her briefly. "I went to the local comprehensive. Less rugby but probably more girls." She laughed. That was the first piece of personal information he had offered since her arrival. Was he a private man who lived behind the barriers he erected or did he open up over time? She figured she would ask Eric when they were next alone.

Returning to ops, she was surprised Janssen wasn't more vocal. He seemed lost in thought and for a brief, paranoid moment, she thought his reticence might relate to her handling of the interview. She grew impatient. "What do you think?" Eric turned to look as well, keen to hear what resulted from the interview. Janssen perched on the edge of a desk, his face set in a frown. He was very circumspect.

"Honestly? I'm not sure. How much does he know about Holly and Ken? From what he offered us in there, he still seems to be in the dark." He folded his arms across his chest, thinking hard. "He offered just the right amount of anger, frustration and… contrition. Exactly what I would expect."

"Meaning?" she asked, slightly perplexed by what he was getting at.

He raised his eyebrows. "When I interview someone, I hardly ever get *exactly* what I expect."

CHAPTER TWENTY-SIX

ERIC REPLACED THE RECEIVER. Alone in ops, he cut a frustrated figure. Tracing the complainant whose allegation led to the arrest of Ken Francis was proving far harder than he ever imagined. He wasn't naïve. People dropped off the radar on a daily basis. Some because they choose to while others have little choice in the matter. Not necessarily due to anything sinister. People were transient in nature these days, particularly in a vast city such as London. The days of a job for life and living in the same house were becoming rarer in everyday life. The promise of making your fortunes in the big city were still a draw for many. The influx of people from across the country saw a constant churn. Couple that with the advance of the gig economy and sky-high rents and you had a population drifting in and out of postcodes, perhaps never appearing on electoral rolls or council tax lists.

He had three known addresses for Amanda Stott along with several telephone numbers but each lead ended with the same result. She was either no longer there, the current residents didn't know her or the phone numbers rang out. The file sent over from Canning Town had her listed as working various jobs on a part-time basis from event coordination, waitressing to bicycle courier, all allowing her the freedom to pursue what she really wanted to do which was modelling. The file listed some members of her social circle and although this bore no fruit, he was able to leave his contact details in case they came across her. Conveying at great length how Amanda was not in any way facing investigation herself, several associates sounded as if they might call if she got in touch. Amanda had dropped off the face of the earth. She could be anywhere. Sitting back in his chair, he glanced at the clock. The interview would be over soon enough and he wanted to have something useful to contribute. They weren't really looking at Colin Bettany for the murder, at least, he couldn't see it.

The interview was broadly a bush-shaking exercise from what he could gather. Casting his mind back to his study materials with precious little personal experience of a case such as this these were all he had to work with, the likelihood of Holly being murdered by a stranger was slim. Nine times out of ten it would be someone within her circle of family, friends or acquaintances who killed her. Sometimes it was the slightest snippet of information, often perceived innocuous at the time, that would lead them to the culprit.

Holly struck him as an unusual girl. There were girls like her at his school, every school probably. Popular but not overly so. There were hierarchies. The *in crowd* were the ones everyone either wanted to hang around with, be a part of or, as in his own case, be acknowledged by. Within that group there were further ranks, those everyone adored, pupils and teachers alike. Then there were the remainder who were routinely despised by the rest of the school, including Eric. They took pleasure in lording their status over everyone else, using their weight of numbers and overwhelming gravitas to inflict abuse on anyone they chose to single out. Beyond this close-knit group were disparate smaller conclaves of people who banded together in an almost tribal pact to ensure survival, perhaps six or seven strong. Safety in numbers but without sufficient strength to enable absolute security if the eyes of the pack fell on them.

Where did Holly fit into this environment? Social structures such as these weren't peculiar to his own educational experience. They were repeated throughout the country whether state or independent, in an urban or rural setting. This was how people interacted. Powerplays carried on well into adulthood, in office spaces or on factory floors. This was the nature of humanity. Sometimes where you stood in these social interactions could indicate how much of a victim you might be. Of course, this was all sociological and a construct of academia but building a profile of the victim could offer up useful insights.

Holly Bettany was popular but remained on the periphery of the central crowd. With her intelligence, personality and her looks, from the outside looking in she appeared to have it all and yet she refrained from the spotlight. Choosing to keep her distance from those around her was surprising to him. Even more so was the selection of Mark McCall as her friend and her self-imposed guardianship of his time at the school. If the support worker's views were accurate and Holly was indeed toying with Mark, what was her reasoning? To protect him from the pack of hyenas as she did only to play with his emotions herself made little sense. Unless she was driven by bouts of her own insecurity or low self-esteem which saw her punch down as many were prone to do. The further they exposed Holly's character, the greater the level of complexity was revealed.

The phone on his desk rang. It was a call from the technical support team based in Norwich. The conversation was informative as much as it was brief. The encryption on the laptop he found in Holly's bedroom was not as complex as first thought, but the data on the hard drive was far from enlightening. However, the last point raised excited him and he couldn't wait to share it with his superiors.

The two of them appeared shortly after. Tamara Greave led the way, striding purposefully as she always did. He could only hope to one day have the same confidence in his abilities as she did in hers. Tom lingered behind. There was something on his mind, Eric could tell. Janssen often fell to bouts of introspection when he was working towards something. They could last for days and it was unnerving to say the least. It was weeks before he learned not to take the silences personally for they were nothing to do with him and all about Tom and his thought process. The thought occurred how the new boss might be finding working with him. Watching the interaction between the two of them, he was intrigued. Both confident, experienced and knowledgeable but with starkly different approaches. Up until now, Tom was the benchmark, intense and focussed. Greave was different. Open, approachable and assertive but he had a sense she wouldn't suffer fools. This worried him slightly, if he was honest.

Listening to Janssen reveal his instincts about Colin Bettany was interesting. Eric found the doctor intimidating. He held a position of influence within the community, moving amongst the local politicians and land owners, living a life far above the standard he could ever hope to achieve. His mother always hammered him for his willingness to acquiesce to those of a perceived higher status. She misunderstood his attitude. He didn't see them as better than him, he knew they weren't but others didn't agree. The forelock tugging was ingrained in those around him and these people certainly had the reach to make his life difficult. Since joining the force, he found that class played a weak role in helping to differentiate between those who followed the law and those who felt it was something only for others to adhere to.

Greave didn't respond to Janssen and a short silence followed. He waited, wondering if now was a good time to speak, fearing his switch of conversation would be interpreted as a lack of understanding of the nuance to the comment. The frown left Janssen's face and he blew out his cheeks. Now was a good time. "I heard from tech regarding Holly's laptop. Good news and bad."

"Start with the bad and work up," Tamara told him, grasping a chair on castors and wheeling it closer.

"There was very little on the hard drive. No diary or email threads to read through. Offering precious little by way of insight into her life."

"That's disappointing," Tamara said, reaching for a snack pack of dried fruit on the desk behind her. She began grazing on it, looking back expectantly. Eric felt nervous at having her undivided attention, so desperate was he to make a good impression.

"However, the serial number has flagged up. It was reported stolen in a burglary a couple of months ago, in Fakenham." Both senior officers were surprised, exchanging glances. "A routine break-in. The house was turned over while the parents were on the school run. In and out in less than ten minutes. Text book."

"Any leads on who did it?" Janssen asked. The case led nowhere. In the brief time where he was waiting for them to return, all he'd managed to locate was the file attached to the crime reference number. The case was considered open but not being actively investigated.

"No. Looks cold," Eric replied. That was normal. Unless there were strong witnesses or someone being caught in the act, solving a break-in like this was unlikely. Burglars could well commit dozens, if not hundreds, of offences before being caught provided they were careful and didn't overreach. "I'll check the date with the school – see if Holly was absent – but somehow I don't see her as the type." He knew she wouldn't have carried out the break-in but it was best practice to seek clarity.

"No, you're right to check," Tamara said, narrowing her eyes. "Although, she most likely knows the person who did. Anyone we know fit the frame?"

Eric looked between them, reluctant to sound like one of the narrow-minded bigots who lived in the area but it needed saying. It was obvious. "There is one particular family who are well known for this type of thing."

"The McCalls." The response from Janssen was a statement, not a suggestion. "From what we know of Mark, he isn't the type either."

"But... he *is* a McCall," Eric replied. Janssen shot him a dark look and he realised he'd fallen into exactly the trap he sought to avoid. Seeking to reduce the damage, he thought fast. "We know Mark isn't but what of his siblings?"

Janssen slowly nodded, appearing thoughtful. "The one brother, Bradley, is inside and the other is away with the army but you're right. We can't ignore her associations. Without linking her with anyone else we should look into it. Contact the local regiment. Find out where he's stationed, if it's close by or whether a period of leave corresponds with the burglary. Likewise, check what date Bradley was put away. He could have done it pre-sentencing when out on bail."

"There's also the other one, Clinton," Eric reminded them. "He's something of a tearaway too."

"Let's not be sexist either," Tamara chipped in. "There's a daughter as well, isn't there?" She looked to Janssen and he in turn to Eric. He felt a little surge of pride.

"Sadie. She's been picked up for shoplifting previously. Quite a recreational drug user as well but burglary would be a step up for her." Tamara nodded her approval and he felt himself threatening to smile. Quelling the sense of satisfaction, he turned back to his desk.

"Any joy with tracking down the woman who made the allegations against Ken Francis?" Janssen asked.

"Not yet, no. She's vanished but I'm working on it. Damned inconvenient!"

"Not for Ken," Janssen replied, his tone belying his cynicism. "The one person who could shed some light on his character who isn't married to him... or dead, and we can't find her."

"Hey, you don't think..." Eric started but the words tailed off. He was often guilty of speaking out before forming the thought clearly in his mind. "She's not the one... come up here to ruin Ken after the collapse of the case?" It didn't sound as daft to him after he said it as it had whilst he was forming the idea. "Maybe I should check the local B&Bs and stuff, see if she's registered. She would have a motive." Both senior officers were looking at him and he suddenly felt self-conscious, as if he'd dropped a clanger. "Well, wouldn't she?"

Tamara flicked a glance at Janssen who inclined his head. "Worth a shout. Good thinking. You crack on here, Eric. I think Tom and I will revisit Callum McCall's place."

"How do you want to play it?" Janssen asked. Eric was surprised. Tom was usually so decisive, always one to lead rather than following. There was something about the dynamic between these two. It would be interesting to watch it play out in the coming days.

"I'm open to suggestions," she replied.

"I think we should execute a search warrant on their place." She seemed surprised by Janssen's idea. Eric wondered why that would be. "Callum isn't going to allow us to look around without one. If we turn up anything suspect it will give us the ammunition to put the squeeze on them. If Callum feels he has something to lose, he may well open up. The same goes for his children. It's about time someone in this case started talking."

"Agreed," she replied, smiling. Eric found himself perplexed by their exchange. There was something else beneath the surface, an unspoken communication perhaps. Watching the two of them interact was fascinating.

CHAPTER TWENTY-SEVEN

By MID-AFTERNOON the cloud had rolled back from the coast to reveal bright sunshine but hovered ominously over the North Sea, threatening to return at any moment. The wind was picking up from the south sucking warm continental air across the channel but with it came the potential approach of a storm front. Spring was tantalisingly close. The bluebells were out amongst the woods as Tom Janssen picked his way along the unmade track up to the McCall's home, a sea of fleeting colour that would be gone in a fortnight. Tamara Greave was quiet alongside him and he felt comfortable not forcing conversation.

The warrant came through around three o'clock and a short discussion ensued regarding postponing the search until the morning, giving them a full day to search and the benefits of doing so versus the risks of the delay. Eventually, they decided to act swiftly. He gathered anyone who could be spared from uniform and they set out. The revelation of Holly's computer being the product of a burglary was fascinating to him. Children of affluent parents could easily go off the rails as much as any other, so it wasn't that. Holly didn't fit the profile of a rebel, pushing back against authority. Not that she wouldn't have cause. Colin Bettany struck him as an authoritarian figure and he could see the man exerting his influence over the family. Similarly, Marie was far from the subservient wife to a dominating husband.

Loathe as he was to leap to conclusions about the McCall family, their investigation saw no other links to anyone with a criminal history. Holly's peer group was relatively small for a girl of her age. Her social media presence was small, few friends and even fewer interactions and ultimately the theory of Occam's Razor kept repeating in his mind. The simplest conclusion that relied on the fewest number of assumptions would arguably win out. They were probing and the sooner they cracked what was happening in Holly's world the sooner her killer would be revealed. So far, no one claimed to really know Holly at all.

Callum was outside as Janssen approached. If he was surprised to see him with two liveried police cars pulling up alongside, then he didn't show it. Getting out of the car, he crossed the short distance between them. Callum McCall turned his back. He stood before a small, open bonfire. A cloud of thick grey smoke was drifting into the air. The fire crackled and spat. It must have been burning damp wood and leaves to generate so much smoke. A gust of wind shifted its path in his direction and he felt the acrid taste in his mouth, blinking furiously to clear his watering eyes.

"We have a search warrant," he declared, coming alongside and offering Callum the court document. He scanned it with his eyes before thrusting his hands into his pockets. Janssen turned to Tamara who indicated for the officers to begin the search. They split up, three moving towards the residence and the remainder fanning out to search the exterior. Scattered around were various outbuildings or sheds, cobbled together from various sources, odd bits of wood, tarpaulins and throwaway materials assembled over the years.

"You'll not find it." Callum stared into the fire, sniffing hard. He seemed calm, taking their presence in his stride. After a few seconds, his demeanour shifted, glancing briefly in Janssen's direction. "Whatever it is you're looking for, Janssen. It's not here."

"What are we looking for?" In truth, he didn't expect an answer. The wind changed again, carrying the smoke away from them. Looking into the fire, he saw not only branches and leaves but also material of some description. It was dark blue, thick. "What's with the fire?"

"Having a clear out." Callum reached out, taking the search warrant from him. Another cursory examination followed before he screwed it into a ball and tossed it to the flames. Immediately the paper caught alight. "Useful for getting shot of all kinds of crap."

The creaking sound of a door opening made him turn and Mark appeared from inside. He looked rattled. The presence of the police trawling through his home probably unsettled him. Having met his eye, Mark lingered by the door before coming closer. Callum turned and acknowledged his son's approach.

"Don't bother yourself, lad. They'll be done soon enough." He put an arm around Mark's shoulder, pulling him in closer and giving him a firm shake. Mark's head rocked slightly and he offered a weak smile accompanied by a nod. "You know how it is. When the filth has nothing, they just give the McCalls a tug."

He felt his irritation rise. Not that he should expect anything different from a journeyman criminal such as Callum McCall. In and out of prison for most of his adult life, convictions for petty theft along with various other offences, he worked sporadically, labouring on farms and doing odd jobs. He wasn't a hardcore criminal merely an opportunist always looking for an angle to exploit. It was this approach to life, alcoholism and a propensity towards violence that kept him in focus not some conspiratorial police prejudice. "We're looking for stolen property, Mark." The young man glanced at him and possibly feeling the burn of his father's eyes quickly looked away. "You wouldn't know of anything, would you?" Mark shook his head.

"Wasting your time," Callum stated along with a dismissive wave of the hand. The hand was bandaged and it looked fresh, soiled slightly, no doubt from assembling the bonfire.

"That looks painful," he said, pointing it out. Callum looked at his hand, flexing the fingers and frowning before dropping it to his side. "How did you do that?"

"I don't remember. Must have sprained it or something."

The remark was throwaway. Casual. He didn't believe him for a second. Movement to his right caught his eye. Tamara was at the corner of the building beckoning him over.

"Tom. Come and have a look at this!" For the first time he saw the mask of indifference slip in Callum's expression. It lasted barely a second before the veil of defiance reappeared but Mark saw it too, his agitation apparently increasing. Crossing to where she stood, Tamara inclined her head indicating for him to follow. They went to the rear. A lean-to was constructed against the back of the property. Little more than some off-cut planks, nailed together with a grey tarpaulin thrown over the top to offer some protection from the rain. It housed split logs, presumably for a burner, a rainwater barrel, filled from the guttering edging the roof and a few wooden crates. These were a foot square and filled with odds and ends, cans of oil, some rusty tools and smaller plastic sheets folded and pressed in tight and weighted down with a rock to ensure they wouldn't blow away.

Aware of Callum McCall standing behind him, he dropped to his haunches alongside Tamara. She'd donned latex gloves for the duration of the search and now lifted one of these plastic sheets, revealing what was beneath. He couldn't help but find what he saw baffling. A pair of red high-heeled shoes were inside. The gloss applied to the finish saw them stand out, reflecting the sun overhead. They were neatly set alongside each other as if placed on a shoe rack rather than discarded alongside half empty paint tins as they were. Tamara pinched her fingers together and lifted them out, turning them over so as to inspect them thoroughly.

"The soles are worn but there are no scuffs or scrapes to the top or sides," she told him. The soles of the shoes were fairly clean although there was some dried mud on the edges of the base where they met the sides. The fading of the information imprinted on the interior showed evidence of wear but not extensively so. Whoever they belonged to they were not worn often but certainly cared for. He turned to Callum whose eyes narrowed but other than that, his expression was as unreadable as ever.

"Strange place to keep shoes, wouldn't you say?" he asked. Callum shrugged. "Why have you got these out here?"

"I've no seen them before but things get thrown everywhere. Who knows in this house and with kids like mine."

Tamara spoke up. "Not exactly your size or style, though, Mr McCall."

"You never know, lassie," Callum countered, sniffing loudly. "Anything goes these days. Besides, they're probably Sadie's. Either hiding them from me cos o' how much she paid fer them or… maybe they was her mother's. How should I know? Could be any number of reasons."

"Your Sadie, is she petite?" Tamara asked. "These would most likely fit a smaller girl." Callum shrugged once more but it was possible that he was equally thrown by the discovery, only hiding it well. It was peculiar whichever way you looked at it. A constable opened a plastic bag and she lowered the shoes inside. They were still to locate the shoes Holly was wearing on the night she died and although there was no certainty these were the missing ones they would be negligent to ignore the possibility.

Stepping back, Janssen caught sight of Mark disappearing from view. He was some distance away walking between the trees. Then he was gone. Returning to the front of the building, he was met by one of the officers searching the interior of the property. Following him inside, they crossed the living area which by anyone's standards was an absolute mess. Clothing was thrown all over the place, unclear whether it was clean or soiled. Dirty crockery was piled in the sink and every bit of workspace in the kitchen was stacked with something on top, either pans, bags or piles of junk mail. How anyone could live like this escaped him.

They entered one of the bedrooms. It was narrow with a single bed pushed up against one wall beneath the only window, itself shrouded by a net curtain. A shoulder high wardrobe was positioned in the corner, the only piece of furniture apart from the bed in the room. Clothes were stacked on top. By the look of them, the room belonged to a girl, Sadie. Next to the bed was a small bag packed with make-up, a vanity mirror on the floor alongside.

The officer knelt, picking up a shoebox that had been under the bed. Lifting off the lid revealed a small plastic bag containing cannabis.

Also within the box was a little pipe, tobacco and some rolling papers. The contents were obviously personal and far from quantities expected by a dealer. "Is this it?" The constable nodded. This was all they had to show for their efforts. Casting an eye around the room, he opened the wardrobe, scanning the clothing hanging on the rail and piled beneath. Even without meeting her, he had Sadie pegged as someone who dressed for impact, imagining heavy eye-liner and lots of monochrome. Red heels didn't strike him as her style.

Returning to the living room, he found Tamara inside talking to Callum. There was nothing here to warrant an arrest or give them cause to apply pressure to him and Callum knew it. Catching the tail end of the discussion he gathered Callum was suggesting they should leave and clearly not for the first time. There was little argument to counter his demand. The search team filtered outside, returning to their cars. Callum watched them from the doorway, arms folded and clamped against his chest.

Reaching the car, Janssen's phone rang. It was Eric. Unlocking the car, he leant on the roof with the phone against his ear watching Callum as he watched them. The man was unfazed but annoyed. That was obvious.

"I've heard back from the DS in Canning Town," Eric explained. "He's got a lead on where we might find Amanda Stott but he says he doesn't have the time to follow it up. It looks like she's been working near to where she was last known to be living."

"Well, you'll need to head down there and check it out."

"Okay, I'll go first thing. How's the search going?"

He took one more look around, doing his best to sound upbeat but, aside from the shoes, the results were disappointing. "Pretty much a bust but you never know." He hung up, climbing into the driver's seat as the other police cars drove away. Tamara enquired after the call. "Eric's off to London tomorrow in search of Amanda Stott." Starting the car, he applied full lock to the steering wheel and set off. Looking in his rear-view mirror, he saw Callum step away from the building and return to the bonfire just as he disappeared from view. Stopping the car, Tamara glanced across, surprised. "If you take the car do you think you can find your own way back to the station?"

"Yes. I expect so. Why?"

"I'm just going to follow up on something. I'll fill you in later if that's okay?"

She was curious, he could tell but she didn't press him for detail. Unhooking his seatbelt, he got out. Tamara came around to the driver's side and slipped past him into the seat. She looked up at him as he went to close the door for her.

"You're an interesting man, Tom Janssen," she said with a smile. He returned it.

"I'll catch up with you later." He watched as she pulled away. The wind was picking up and the clouds gathering above. Buttoning up his coat and putting his hands in his pockets, he stepped from the track and set off into the woods. He had a pretty good idea where Mark was heading.

CHAPTER TWENTY-EIGHT

MARK MCCALL SAT on the bank, watching the clouds rolling across the horizon. The blades of the wind turbines, far out at sea, were shrouded in a haze. Further along to his left a cargo ship was still visible as it picked its way north. He loved it here. At least, he did once. Looking over to where he used to sit, where they had on *that* night, he knew things had changed and the same thoughts and feelings would never return. The police officers at the house were frustrating. Going through his things, picking up anything they pleased without asking.

Recognising the growing anxiety within, he went to his father for safety, strange as it may seem to others. His father was a permanent presence in his life despite his obvious shortcomings. To see him so rattled by the police was odd, unsettling. Anyone who didn't know his father probably wouldn't realise. He did though. A man of few words at the best of times, for him to offer up explanations to the police was unheard of. He'd said more in those brief minutes than Mark usually heard in a day.

Then there were the shoes. Her shoes. They suited her, matched her lipstick, dress and overall style. "You used to love that colour too, didn't you?" His eyes drifted back to where he and Holly sat after leaving the beach party. Holly shivering against the cold and him draping his jacket over her shoulders. She had leaned into him and he thought about putting an arm around her but couldn't summon the courage, bottling it at the last moment. "I thought she would like it here, just as you did." He felt his eyes water and blinked back tears. Instead of picturing the vision of the two of them alone, beneath the stars, the image that came to him was of her lifeless body. Even now, the image was as clear as the morning he found her, lying in the grass, the frost covering her dress, face and her hair glistening in the sunlight. Far more serene and angelic in death than she had been in life.

Startled by the presence of another, approaching from his left, Mark made to stand. The man raised an open palm, indicating for him to stay as he was and he sat back. It was the tall detective, the one who bought him the coke and a bacon roll. Assessing the man's smile, he seemed nice enough. *You can't trust him, remember? Dad said so.* He acknowledged the policeman's greeting. He looked past Mark, over to the bank nearby.

"This is where you found Holly, isn't it, Mark?"

He turned away, as if not looking would make the image in his mind's eye disappear. It didn't. He bobbed his head. "Yeah." The policeman sat down alongside him, somewhat awkwardly he thought.

"What brings you back?"

Mark glanced at him. What was his game? Was he trying to trick him? The policeman didn't seem too bothered about being all proper and official, bringing his knees up and hooking his arms over them and turning his gaze away, looking out to sea. If he wanted to question him then it should be at a station, like on the telly. He chose his reply carefully. "I like it here."

"Nice spot. Great view, quiet."

"I come here a lot. It helps me calm down." Suddenly feeling like he was giving too much away, he inwardly chastised himself. They sat in silence for a minute. The breeze was gentle, warm.

"Who were you talking to when I arrived?" Mark felt a flash of panic. He must have been there for a while. He felt his face flush red. "You were talking to someone, weren't you?" The tone wasn't accusatory or judgemental. He felt his embarrassment subside.

"My mother used to bring me here when I was a boy. She loved the sea and it was close to home." Glancing at the policeman, he was listening not merely paying him lip service. "Sometimes, I think it was just to get away from Dad. When he was at his worst."

"You miss her?" For a moment he worried the subject had shifted to Holly. "Your mum. You must miss her." It was true, he did but what child wouldn't. "Do you ever see her?"

He was saddened to think about her leaving. In his memories there was no blame, no abandonment. They were fond recollections. "No. I've no idea where she is. I do miss her." The man was friendly, asking questions but without ulterior motive. He wasn't what his father had led him to expect. "I was talking to her. *My mum.* That probably sounds weird, right?"

"Not at all."

Is he humouring me? He didn't think so. There was something in his manner, firm and reassuring. "I tell her what's going on in my life. Whether I'm having a good day or not." Conscious of appearing mentally unstable, he sought to explain. "I know she can't hear me. I'm not mad or anything." The policeman smiled.

"I talk to myself all the time." Mark looked at him, suspicious. He seemed genuine enough. Holly said that was his biggest problem, *his big heart was too trusting.* "Sometimes it helps me to focus my mind."

"Coming here brings me close to her. Or I feel like I am anyway."

"This must be a special place to you. Did you bring Holly here?" Mark shot him a dark look.

"I didn't kill her!" Feeling threatened now, he looked around for the quickest route to run but there was nowhere. However, the thought was at the forefront of his mind now. The policeman was calm, though. His demeanour hadn't changed at all.

"I'm not suggesting you did. Only, this is a special place for you and Holly was left here. That's quite a coincidence. I'm wondering how that came to pass." He sounded sincere. "Did you ever bring her here?"

"Yes." The answer came without thinking. He shouldn't say anything. That's what his father drummed into him at every opportunity. Perhaps he was wrong about *this* one. He didn't seem out to hassle the McCalls even if the others were. "She came with me. I wanted to be here with her. Show her what she meant to me."

"Did she like it too?"

He found the question curious. After all, Holly had no connection with the place, just with him. "Nah. She wasn't interested really. Not in the place or in me either as it happens." He looked across, again wondering if he'd said too much. "That wasn't a shock. I hoped... hoped that maybe I wasn't misunderstanding our... friendship... but deep down I always knew."

"That you were only friends?"

He nodded. "Yeah. Sometimes it seemed like it was more but... I reckon Holly saw me as a kid. She didn't dress up as she did the other night for me. I don't even know why she came to the beach party. Maybe it was for me, so I could go. The others wouldn't invite me in otherwise."

"Your fellow students?" the policeman asked. He nodded again. "But she came out here with you."

"Yes, for a bit. Then she left. She said she had to be somewhere. That she had to leave."

"Did she say where?"

He couldn't say for he didn't know. Holly hadn't told him. He was so disappointed... no, angry with her for leaving that he hadn't even asked where she was going. He chose not to share those feelings. The man was nice but even so, he was still looking for a murderer. "She left me here. I stayed for a while, until I got cold and then I went home."

"Who else knew you were bringing Holly up here?"

Mark thought on that for a moment. As far as he was aware, no one could have known. They slipped away without saying anything to the others and because Holly kept them away from the fire, and therefore the group, no one else would have noticed once the beer was flowing and the party was in full swing. He shrugged. "No one." He hadn't meant for his reply to be so meek but it sounded feeble in his head.

"Was she wearing shoes, do you remember? Only she wasn't wearing any when we found her."

"Yes, of course she was. I wouldn't be able to carry her up here and it would hurt to walk without them." His mind went to the red heels found back at the house and he fell silent, trying not to look like he was hiding anything or appearing defensive.

"What did they look like?"

This time his response was immediate. "Just shoes," he shrugged, accompanying the gesture with a shake of the head to indicate he didn't know. *Was that convincing?* He wasn't sure. The policeman didn't pursue it.

"You've not been going in to the sixth form much." It was said as a statement, not a question. Now he was being nosey, interfering. His father was right after all. "The kids, are they giving you a hard time?"

"They all think I did it!" He couldn't help it, the reply tripping off his tongue before he could stop himself. They may not have spoken the words aloud or to his face but their expressions said it all, even some of the teachers. He was a McCall and a strange one at that. "They think I killed Holly." The fact that he loved her, would never intentionally harm her and would give anything to see her again didn't cut much ice with people at the school. They were looking for someone to blame and not one of them would believe him, so why would the police. "I wasn't truthful with you before." He heard his own voice, barely audible.

"About what?" The policeman was interested, his eyes brighter now. Focussed.

"About Holly... and her life. I knew she was going to see the artist."

"Ken Francis?"

"Yeah." There was no need to lie about it. If the police didn't know already then they soon would. Provided they did their jobs right, anyway, and this man looked serious, someone you would rely on if you were ever in trouble. His father told him this one was different, he would *give as good as he got*, his father had said. "Holly loved drawing, art... painting and stuff. That was what she wanted to be, an artist, but it was never going to happen around here. She thought he would help her to do it. To get away from here."

"Was she planning to leave?"

"I think so. I mean, she didn't say when but now... after what happened to her... I think she might have been saying goodbye to me that night. When she said she was leaving."

"And you reckon Holly thought Ken was going to help her?"

"She thought so... but he used her, much like everyone else."

"You say *everyone else*. What do you mean by that?"

Thinking about it, he realised he wasn't sure. "That's just what Holly used to say."

"How did you feel about her relationship with Ken? You could be forgiven for being annoyed."

He didn't want to answer that question. Nor did he wish to reveal how he would follow her sometimes when she went to see him, watching from the nearby woods. As angry as it could make him, he also found those occasions exciting. "I think she loved him."

"You know, someone's been making threats against Ken Francis. They've trashed his studio and, yesterday someone set fire to it. We're thinking it's quite likely to be the same person."

The policeman was staring at him now. He wanted to know if it was him. *Had he already made up his mind? I can't tell you what I know. I just can't.* "It wasn't me. I wouldn't do anything like that." He felt the eyes upon him, assessing him, judging. Bracing for the next question, he waited patiently, wondering what it would be but the policeman asked nothing further and slowly returned his gaze to the sea.

CHAPTER TWENTY-NINE

TOM JANSSEN'S mind was preoccupied with thoughts regarding Mark McCall as he came to the end of the path, reaching the main road. A small lorry rumbled past, the branding denoting it as one making deliveries to small food stores. Trotting across the road in between two oncoming cars he headed to his left. Tamara had offered to pick him up which he was grateful for, although the thirty-minute walk back to the station was perfectly manageable. Glancing at his watch, there was some time to kill though. The agreed meeting place was a small convenience store on the edge of the village, a landmark that she should be able to find easily enough. If not, there was always the sat nav.

He found Mark McCall a strange young man. Not a view garnered by his illness, though. It was far more than that. The family were well known amongst those who worked and lived locally. Their reputation well earned, if overstated sometimes by the locals. Stories and descriptions of events could be magnified over time making the participants appear darker, the events far more unacceptable than perhaps they were. Not that the McCalls needed much elaboration. Mark was different to his father and siblings. That was clear to him and yet Mark's distrust of those in authority was equally as strong. Thinking back to his own childhood, perhaps that wasn't so odd. As much as your thoughts and feelings towards the world could be shaped by your peers, more often than not it was your family who nurtured your world view. The arguments he used to have with his own father, infrequent though they were for they had a wonderful relationship, only came about once he reached an age to form his own opinions along with the courage and conviction to voice them. This was a rite of passage to adulthood, something everyone goes through. However, thinking on it, he still grew up to be a pretty decent carbon copy of his father with similar values and outlook.

Somehow, Mark McCall was distancing himself from how his family approached life but how far the apple truly fell from the tree, he couldn't yet determine. He was confident there was still a chance he could breach the barrier erected around the boy and get to what he really knew. Unable to force it, though, it would take time. Sadly, in a murder case, time was a luxury.

Approaching the village boundary, he came to the little shop, an old brick building converted into a store offering the basics you might need prior to making a trip to one of the larger supermarkets in town. The shop doubled up as a post office with a small counter at the far end. This was probably what made the business viable. Only two other customers were present, an elderly man was off to one side paying close attention to the magazines on display, leafing through one on fishing. Janssen passed by him and retrieved a bottle of water from the small fridge unit humming away in the corner.

The lady alongside the till was chatting to another woman leaning casually against the counter with one hand holding a crutch, keeping her upright. Not that she appeared in any discomfort as the two merrily conversed about nothing in particular. Two friends passing the time of day. The sense of intruding was strong as he approached, their conversation ceasing. It was as if they were fearful he might overhear their discussion. Placing the bottle on the counter, he smiled and the lady returned a warm greeting.

"Are you working on the murder of that poor young girl?" He was taken aback and must have looked startled judging by her reaction. "You're Tom, Annabelle's boy, aren't you?" At mention of his mother, he relaxed. "We used to work together back in the day."

"I see, yes. I'm sorry, you caught me off guard," he replied. The woman alongside chimed in as well.

"Terrible business. Are you going to find out who did it?" He was about to reply with a standard response but didn't get the chance. "I do hope it's not one of us. I doubt it is. We get all sorts passing through here at all times of the year. Getting up to no good, many of them. You'll have your work cut out if he's already moved on."

Janssen found himself smiling politely. They lived in an area with one of the lowest recorded crime rates in the country and yet fear of outsiders and crime itself was still evident. It was only a matter of scale perhaps. Certainly, if you wanted to feel depressed about the state of things all you need do was pick up a paper or put the news on the television. "The investigation is ongoing. We'll get to the bottom of it, I'm quite sure."

"I dare say you'll be speaking to that artist chap who's moved into the old Banks place." This was the elderly man talking, piping up from across the shelving behind them. He ambled around to join them. His hands were empty and Janssen figured he was killing time with the reading material while his wife talked.

"Do you mean Ken Francis?" he asked, wary of being sucked into the gossip mongering that went on in every community, particularly small isolated ones such as this one.

"That's the fella," the old man confirmed. "Up to no good out there. People coming and going at all times." Something in his manner suggested details were likely to follow. "Young girls, all dressed up."

"Sitting for his drawings as I understand it," he replied. The man scoffed, shaking his head.

"There will be more to it than that." The man's wife was speaking now and she looked set to launch into something epic. He listened politely, doing his best to appear interested but found his eyes drifting around the surrounding area, trying to occupy his thoughts with more than whatever the rumour mill threw out. His attention was drawn to the noticeboard behind the till. A cork board with business cards of local tradespeople and handwritten adverts. "Particularly with Jane coming back here." His ears pricked up at that.

"Did she leave? Jane?" The woman seemed to swell as he asked, his interest sparking her enthusiasm.

"Oh, yes. I remember Jane when she was growing up. A proper little tearaway she was too. Gave her parents all manner of trouble." This was her moment and she was revelling in it. "Went on for years until her old mum had enough."

"She made her leave?"

"Threw her out, couldn't take it anymore." The husband was nodding sagely. "She can come back here in her shiny new Range Rover sporting her fancy hairstyles and all that… what do the kids call it these days – bling, talking with all the airs and graces she likes but she's not far from the minx who left."

"How do you know? People change," he countered, curious to see what the response would be. Both of them were dismissive whereas the lady behind the counter shrugged that she didn't really know.

"She didn't look so different when I saw her a while back going at it in the car park." Defensive now, she must have thought he was challenging her view. He wasn't, merely seeking to separate fact from opinion. "There was still the anger, the aggression."

"She was arguing with someone?" he asked. She nodded furiously. Her husband picked up the narrative.

"Having a proper slanging match with that odd fellow. The Highland gypsy fellow from the woods."

"Do you mean Callum McCall?" He must have failed to keep the surprise from his tone.

"Yep, that's the one and it wasn't pleasant either, the way it was shaping up." The man's brow furrowed as he clearly tried to revisit the memory. "I thought someone was going to get hurt."

"McCall threatened her?"

"No! Quite the opposite." The man's eyes lit up. "I thought she was going to do *him* some damage. The poor man was on the back foot. I felt for him. Well, for a moment."

"Until you remembered who he was," his wife added.

Janssen was intrigued that none of this had come up in the many conversations with the respective parties. "Any idea what it was about?" They both shook their heads. That was the end of the anecdote and he figured he'd got as much from it as he would. His eyes moved to his bottle of water, prompting the till to be rung up. Handing over a note, looking at the noticeboard again. The handwritten notices describing items for sale, exchange or offered free were all on the same lined cards, the ones commonly found in an indexing box. There was one in the bottom corner that stood out. He indicated to it, asking for a closer look. The lady gave him his change and reached behind her for the card, passing it on to him.

The advert was an offer of availability for general handyman services, gardening, odd jobs, labouring, that type of thing. The handwriting was poor as was the punctuation. However, it was a close approximation to that found on the threatening letters left at the Francis place. The card had a mobile number but no name. "Who put this up?"

"I'm sorry, I don't know. Martin, the owner, takes care of those. Often he puts the name on the back so he can keep track." Janssen flipped the card over but it was blank.

"May I keep hold of this?" She could easily have said no and he would have taken a photo with his phone but she didn't seem bothered.

"Having some work done?"

He nodded, not wanting to add fuel to the gossiping that would no doubt continue once he left. Stepping out of the shop, he saw his car rounding the bend and he waved her down. Tamara stopped and got out as he unscrewed the cap on his water and drank from the bottle.

"I presume you want to drive?" she said, coming around and opening the passenger door. "The restaurant will be opening soon and you can fill me in on what you've been up to all afternoon."

He agreed, getting into the car. Alice was busy tonight anyway, Saffy having swimming lessons and by the time that was done and the bedtime routine completed she'd be too tired to see him. Not cooking for himself seemed like a bonus.

THE RESTAURANT WAS HALF empty that evening. The guest rooms of the hotel weren't full to capacity and walk in trade was light. Janssen figured that wouldn't be the case for long. The evening was warm enough for them to sit on the terrace overlooking the marshlands and the approach to the harbour at Brancaster Staithe. Small fishing vessels and pleasure boats were at anchor. Those out working on the water would return during the evening. Looking over at Tamara's seafood salad, he felt greedy tucking into his steak. No wonder she managed to stay so slim, she never appeared to eat a great deal. Where she found her energy reserves he couldn't figure.

Tamara sipped at the glass of wine accompanying her meal. Declining an alcoholic drink himself, because he was driving, Janssen added to his own glass from a bottle of mineral water. A waiter passed by checking their meal was to their satisfaction and continued on circulating the room.

"What did you make of Mark McCall then? Funny lad," she said, placing her glass back on the table.

"He's a complicated character." Sitting upright in his seat, he rolled his shoulders momentarily and frowned. "Not quite as overawed by Holly as many seem to think." Putting the boy's motivations in an order where they could anticipate his actions, or past actions, was tricky. "Don't get me wrong, I think he loved her. Even if it's only the adoration that comes from a teenage boy having a girl take an interest in him. And I think they had a relationship of sorts."

"Do you think he is capable of killing her?" Tamara's gaze was upon him, her eyes narrowing. The question came across as something of a test, assessing his ability to interpret a suspect's intent.

"Quite capable, yes." The reply was firm, confident. "That's not to say I think he did it, though. I don't see the child as being his. The reaction has been all wrong from the point of view of how I'd expect."

"And what would you expect?"

"A greater attempt at avoidance, more misdirection... anger maybe." His mouth was dry and he raised his glass, sipping at the water. "Crimes of passion take a toll both mentally and physically.

Arguably, he could still be guilty but I don't see it." He reached into his jacket pocket, hanging on the back of his chair. Placing the card he took from the shop on the table, he slid it across towards her. "I found this in the local shop."

"Similar writing. Whose is it?" He shook his head. "We can have a comparison done. In the meantime, look up the number. We might get lucky and find it's on a registered contract." She sounded optimistic.

"It'll come back to Callum McCall." Now he had her attention. She was both curious and impressed. He could tell from the slight smile creeping up at the corners of her mouth. "He was seen arguing in public with Jane Francis recently. How that came to pass I don't know. Possibly Callum was looking out for his son, knowing he was seeing Holly. If, and it's a big *if*, Callum knew Holly was knocking about with Ken Francis, he may have told Jane in order to put a stop to it. By all accounts she was pretty upset."

"Would also go some way to explaining the threatening letters, too, if it was him... Callum," Tamara said, glancing at a passing boat, "but why not mention his accusation, if that's what it was? I understand why she wouldn't initially – not wanting to cause ructions at home, but not now everything is out in the open."

"Unless... not everything is out in the open," he countered. She inclined her head, seeking elaboration. He was wasn't sure he'd ironed out a theory yet. Not one that would hold up under scrutiny at any rate. "We know Jane has accepted Ken's... dalliances, should we say and to that end, Callum revealing her husband's affair wouldn't be news to her, so why would she be so upset? It doesn't make sense."

"It makes sense if he was threatening to reveal it or blackmailing them. From the general consensus of opinion everyone has regarding Callum McCall that isn't beyond the realms of possibility."

He sat back in his chair, thinking it over. He had to concede her point. "And how would he know about what Ken was up to?" Thinking aloud now, picking his way through their established facts. "Mark admitted to me he knew about it, so *may* have told his father. Did you see how Mark reacted to your finding the shoes? Took off shortly after."

"You think they're Holly's don't you?" she asked him. Clearly, she thought so. "I've sent them off to the lab this afternoon. They'll test for DNA, fingerprints, anything on the sole or heels that could indicate which area they were walking in recently. I checked with the pathologist and they would fit Holly. If they do turn out to be hers that brings both Mark and his father front and centre."

"Would either of them be stupid enough to keep them around stashed some place where they will easily be found?" It was too much of a gift to them and that niggled him. "Plus, Callum's not the sharpest but he has enough experience to ensure he doesn't make a mistake like that."

"Petty crime, though," Tamara said. "Nothing on this scale."

"Motive?" As far as he could see, Callum McCall had no reason to kill Holly and if he had done so, the likelihood of his placing her in the location where his own son spent a great deal of time was possible but far from plausible. Unless he would rather see Mark sent down than return to prison himself. Tamara hadn't responded to his question suggesting she had no answer. "Jane is local, too, which I wasn't aware of. Eric didn't mention it. His local knowledge isn't an inexhaustible resource but she would have left when he was barely a teenager, so he probably didn't know her. Maybe we're missing something. A connection with Callum McCall from elsewhere in her past." He knew he was thinking aloud, trying to understand the link between them better.

"Seeing as we're speculating," Greave began, nursing her glass of wine. "If they are Holly's shoes and neither of the McCalls are involved... how did they wind up where I found them?"

"The killer is trying to direct our attention towards one of the McCalls, either Callum or Mark, deflecting our focus away from them."

"Possibly." From the tone of her response she was unconvinced leading to him doubting the idea. It was obvious. Maybe that was the problem. "I'm looking forward to seeing what Eric turns up in London tomorrow." He turned his thoughts to unravelling Ken's recent past. The man was running from his choices but the consequences appeared to be following him. It struck him that the man was prone to acts of self-destruction brought on by personal moral failings. But was he a killer, an arsonist, or merely an unfortunate man of dubious character? Maybe Eric could find something not in the files that might steer them either way.

CHAPTER THIRTY

ERIC WAS at the station in Norwich far earlier than he needed to be. Waking with a growing anxiety about not being able to find suitable parking and subsequently missing his train to London saw him out of bed before sunrise. He showered as quietly as he could, doing his level best to avoid waking his mother. Unsure if he was successful in the attempt, he didn't know, but he heard no signs of movement once he was dressed and crept downstairs. A bowl of cereal and he was out of the door.

The 8 A.M. train from Norwich was bound to be busy. Although the majority of those commuting to the capital would have caught earlier connections, the station car park would be full by the time he arrived. Norwich was an infernally awkward place to navigate at the best of times with the thriving modernity of the present juxtaposed on the layout of centuries past. Once England's second city, with its wealthy agricultural heritage, the ravages of the Industrial Revolution were bypassed leaving the area untouched by the mass influx of labour and enterprise. Eric liked that history. Although he knew for a time the area suffered as a result of clinging to the past it was now very much forward-looking with a creative industry to celebrate. He just hated travelling on a deadline.

On the train, he found himself sitting next to a curious man. At first wary of him, heavily tattooed with the sides of his head shaved and oiled hair swept back in a quiff that would make *TinTin* jealous, Eric figured they would have little in common and didn't seek to make conversation. As it transpired, the man felt the opposite. He was an engineering contractor, working on construction projects around the world. He was travelling to London to catch a flight to Schipol, in The Netherlands, before continuing on to Angola.

"It's pretty hectic, what with all the travel and pressure to meet timescales but I love it when I'm back here. Every time I tell myself it'll be the last trip but..."

"But?" Eric asked, interested. The man smiled.

"The pay cheques are good and I think my wife would go mad with me under her feet. What about you?"

Eric briefly explained his role as a junior accountant. The last time the question was asked he stated he worked for the forestry commission. If at all possible, he avoided telling strangers how he made a living. Not that he wasn't proud of it, he was, but many people reacted strangely to him when he said so. There were those who mistrusted the police, possibly resulting from a guilty conscience but in most parts just interpreting officers as always looking to make an arrest. Probably they'd been spoken to during their life coarsely in a routine traffic stop or for some minor misdemeanour. That was a failure of understanding. Police officers were trained to be polite and cordial but at the same time authoritative. It went with the warrant card. It still made decent people wary.

The man next to him listened politely but Eric sensed he was either disinterested or unconvinced by his story. The conversation lapsed, eventually ceasing altogether as headphones appeared from the man's travel bag and soon after his eyes closed as he dropped into his own musical world. What it was, Eric couldn't tell but it was loud. Far removed from his own softer tastes. Arriving at the recently refurbished Stratford Station shortly before ten, Eric shuffled off the carriage between those remaining on the train and the line of people queueing to board, all jostling for position amongst each other with backpacks and suitcases. This was why he hated large cities. Everyone was always in such a rush.

His mobile vibrated in his pocket and he stepped out of the flow of people on the platform, finding a safe space against one of the supports. It was a text from his contact in Canning Town advising him to take the DLR for the six-minute journey on from Stratford rather than the Jubilee Line. Looking up at the overhead signage, he saw it was a short walk across the concourse. The throng dissipated and the train he arrived on pulled out of the station continuing on to Liverpool Street. Crossing the concourse an announcement was made regarding a delay on underground services bringing a smile to his face.

The knock-on effect was an increase in those using the DLR and Eric was grateful to reach Canning Town station and get off. The iconic skyline of Canary Wharf lay off to his right. Monuments of sparkling glass towering over London's east end. The text advised they meet at the coffee shack but looking around, he couldn't see one by that name. There were several concessions, each doing a roaring trade with people milling about. Ringing the number back, it was answered immediately and he located the detective nearby.

Not sure what to expect from DC Frank Chambers, he found the man from Canning Town station to be somewhat curious. Estimating him to be fifteen to twenty years his senior, he was a round man, in both face and frame. His cheeks were cherry red and his skin bore a sheen of sweat as one might develop on a summer's day. However, it was early spring and not particularly warm today despite the sunshine. They were unable to shake hands for both his were occupied by a cup of coffee in one and a steaming pastry of some description in the other. Catching a whiff of the smell drifting from the nearby stall, Eric's mouth watered. His cereal seemed a long time ago. Not that he often ate such foods, preferring the healthier options but even so, every now and again the appeal of convenience was there. A keen runner, he was well aware of the effect diet had on him. The man standing before him was a poster boy for moderation.

"My tip has Amanda working out of a hair and beauty salon just down the road in Plaistow," Chambers advised him as he led them towards the exit. "It's not far." They left the station and slipped between oncoming buses, crossing the main road to where the car was parked on double yellow lines outside a recently constructed hotel. Chambers wiped grease from his fingers with a paper napkin, chewing the last mouthful of his pastry as they approached the car. Picking up a half-full bottle of coke and an empty packet of crisps from the passenger seat, brushing crumbs into the footwell, he offered the seat to Eric. He got in, noting a strange smell that he put down to general untidiness rather than a lack of hygiene. At least, he hoped so.

Chambers started the car and pulled away from the kerb into traffic. The docklands were behind them and he saw signs for the Olympic Park. He had seen it on television many times since the construction and thought he might like to visit one day. Having been a teenager with a great deal on his plate at the time when London hosted the games, he didn't think to apply for tickets. Now he realised how close it was, he felt a tinge of regret at not bothering.

The small run of shops was alongside the main road, nestling in between a terrace of brick residential houses and opposite a modern block of flats. The salon was located between a florist and a greengrocer. Eric found it extraordinary how the latter could survive in London with the competition from big business. Farm shops were plentiful in Norfolk and did a roaring trade with access to local produce but here, he was unconvinced by the viability. Again, Chambers parked illegally. This time pulling the car half onto the pavement directly outside the salon. A passer-by shot them a dark look as they got out of the car and Eric was embarrassed, but the local detective didn't appear to notice either the disdain or his discomfort.

The woman on reception smiled as they entered. It was obvious neither were there for treatments. Three beauticians were busy with clients. Two were undergoing manicures and the third Eric could only guess at. Something to do with eyelashes or brows, he didn't know. Everyone present was heavily made up and he found it off-putting. Evidently, this was the style these days. For some.

"We're looking for Amanda," Chambers said, offering up his warrant card.

"Sorry, she's not in today," the woman replied. Eric didn't pick up any negative vibes from her as some were prone to when the police came calling. "Amanda only works a couple of days a week."

"Yeah, we know she has a few jobs," Chambers said, looking around. "Any idea where we can find her?"

They left moments later with an address. It meant nothing to Eric. He was yet to find his bearings. His knowledge of London was scarce, little better than the tourist highlights of landmarks, monuments and attractions. Back in the car, they were passing through built up areas. Everywhere he looked appeared built up. There was a lot going on for him to take in. Cranes towered over vast construction sites set alongside rundown streets and what looked like newly opened cafés and boutique shops were competing for frontage with independent shops whose signs were weathered and appeared decidedly outdated.

"Gentrification." Chambers answered an unasked question as if reading his mind. "You'll not recognise this place in a few years." He sounded regretful. His area was changing around him and the future looked very different. Eric thought the uplift might be a good thing but having never been here before, he didn't feel entitled to hold an opinion, let alone voice it. He sat in silence, eyeing the surroundings as they passed them. Even the largest hotels on the coast were dwarfed by many of the buildings around him now. He was glad of that, feeling grateful to hear the daily sound of gulls and the crash of waves rather than the rumble of traffic and the smell of diesel.

Arriving outside a block of flats, four-storeys high, Chambers found a parking bay on this occasion. Eric noted it was restricted for resident permit holders but his concerns were dismissed. The flat was on the third floor and without lifts, Chambers was breathing hard having climbed the concrete stairs as they made their way along the open walkway overlooking the car park. "These used to be council." Chambers bemoaned in halting speech. Eric glanced over his shoulder, slowing the pace and thinking it would be better for the man if he refrained from talking but he didn't. "Now it's mostly private residential and a bit of housing association. Sky-high rents and long waiting lists. No place for the locals now."

Eric looked around. Just as many were moving to the city others were leaving it, thinking about the influx of Londoners relocating to parts of Norfolk over the recent years. Always assuming they were fleeing the city life, he hadn't considered it might not be a relocation through choice but of necessity. "You live locally?" He stopped, turning to place his hands on the brick wall and looking at the view across the neighbouring buildings towards the Thames. It was a good opportunity to give Chambers a chance to get his breath back.

"Yeah. Fourth generation," Chambers replied, his chest inflating with pride. "My grandfather and his father worked the docks whereas my old man the warehouses. Changed a lot I can tell you, even from when I grew up."

"How come you never thought about leaving?" Eric realised his tone must have struck the wrong chord because he read the look of irritation at the question. "Not that you should move. I just meant—"

"Yeah, son. I know what you meant." Eric felt a little aggrieved. There was no intent in the comment but his disdain for city living may have accidentally shown through. "If she isn't here, you're on your own. I've got a full caseload I'm working on and this is as much time as I can spare."

"Fair enough," Eric replied, smiling, trying hard to convey gratitude in the face of the perceived slight. They resumed course to the flat, two doors and barely four metres away. There was a window to the front shrouded in a net curtain and a half-glazed front door. Eric rang the doorbell, hearing it sound inside. They waited but there was no movement. He pressed it again, holding it down for altogether longer than was polite. Leaning forward, he tried to see through the obscured glass.

"I guess that's that." Chambers thrust his hands into his pockets. "You're more than welcome to hang around here but I've got things to —" A shadow appeared on the other side of the glass and the door was unlocked. A bleary-eyed woman cracked the door open, peering at them warily. Her general appearance was dishevelled and it was clear they'd woken her up.

"Police," Eric explained, opening his wallet to reveal his identification. "Amanda Stott?" She nodded, glancing between the two of them before unlocking the chain and pulling the door open. They followed her inside. The flat was in a bit of a state, bearing the remnants of a heavy party the previous night. There was one living room, the kitchen and then another door presumably leading to the bedrooms. The air stank of stale cigarettes. Several ashtrays were dotted around, each full to overflowing. There were empty beer and wine bottles, takeaway cartons and associated crockery with dried on remnants of food.

Amanda offered them a seat. Eric wasn't keen, worried he might sit in spilt alcohol, food or worse but didn't want to appear impolite. Not twice in as many minutes. He cut to the chase. "I'm here to ask you questions about Ken Francis." At mention of the name her eyes widened, if only slightly, and she took a deep breath.

"That's all done. I've said everything I have to say on it. I made a mistake." As she said the words, she averted her eyes from his and Eric knew he'd caught her off guard but she was more awake now, alert.

"We're not here to reopen the case, if that's what you're thinking," he explained. "I'm down from Norfolk. We're investigating another matter and Ken has surfaced in the inquiry. I'm trying to get some background, that's all."

"What do you want from me?"

"I'm not looking to apportion blame nor make trouble for you but I need to know about the nature of your relationship with him. With Ken."

"*Relationship*. That's an interesting description for the pervy old sod."

"Then why did you back out of the prosecution?" Eric asked. She didn't strike him as one to be cowed. Ken Francis was an athletic man but hardly intimidating. Not to him at least. She met his eye before casting a nervous look towards Chambers. He was leaning on the doorframe, looking disinterested. Eric followed her gaze. Chambers took the hint.

"All right. I'll wait outside," Chambers said, sighing. Moments later they heard the door click and the two of them were alone. Eric was pleased. They could have an off the record conversation. He didn't mind. Anything she said that could be used in a case would be useless anyway. Her prior withdrawal and change of statement would render her credibility highly suspect.

"You got a smoke?" she asked. Eric shook his head. He'd never smoked. Amanda looked disappointed. "It's like this... I needed the money. I don't like Ken and I know his type, acting all new-age and presenting as some kind of guru. He's nothing but an egotist with a streak of misogyny running through him." She started rummaging around the detritus on the table and opening cigarette boxes. The third proved a positive result and she found a couple of cigarettes inside. Offering one to Eric, he declined. She sparked one up, taking a stiff draw. "I'll admit, I found him interesting. I thought he was into me, too, until I realised he would quite happily go at it with anyone who came into his studio. Randy old sod!"

"You wanted to get even?" There was no suggestion of judgement in his tone. It was clear she was hurt by his actions and people dealt with that in different ways.

"At first I was just angry. I had a go at him. He couldn't care less but then..." She sat back, blowing smoke from her nose and shaking her head slightly. "I was so angry with him. I went back with the intention of hurting him the only way I could think of."

"Which was?" Eric sensed reticence but anything she told him would be inadmissible for he was alone with her and she hadn't been read her rights.

"I was going to trash his stuff. The pictures he did of me, at least." She sneered and Eric thought she was reacting to the art.

"You didn't like it?"

"Looking back, he had such a fetish for red, always wanting me to wear it. Red lipstick, dress, skirt... whatever. He said it was his *signature statement* or some other crap like that."

"Takes all sorts," Eric said with a smile. "Did you? Trash his pieces?" She shook her head. Maybe filing a claim of assault looked far more damaging and offered less personal risk.

"I went back but when I got there this girl came out." Amanda's knee was vibrating as she shook her leg. It looked involuntary to him. "This girl, that's what she was, a girl... can't have been older than sixteen, maybe even younger. It's hard to tell sometimes, isn't it? Anyway, she was crying. I looked after her. Took her away."

"He assaulted her?" Eric asked, immediately regretting putting words in her mouth. She shrugged. "Is that what she said?"

"He tried it on, yeah. I don't know how far it went."

"Did she report it?"

"No. Way too frightened. Wouldn't let me take her to the police or anything, not even tell her family. So, I thought I would."

Looking her in the eye, he knew he was getting to the truth. She made a false allegation. What he couldn't tell was if it was driven by revenge or, in part at least, a misguided attempt at seeking justice for the girl. "But you dropped it."

"I did, yeah." Amanda looked down at the floor. "Probably shouldn't have done what I did anyway. Don't get me wrong, he deserved it. I'm not proud of it... making it up like, but why I backed out is worse than that... I needed the money. Five grand is a lot to someone like me."

"Ken paid you off?"

"Not him." She shook her head. "The woman. His wife."

CHAPTER THIRTY-ONE

TAMARA LISTENED PATIENTLY to Eric's description of his trip to London, tuning out the young constable's embarrassed recanting of offending the locals. She was certain it wasn't as bad as he feared. If the detective was as sensitive and easily hurt as Eric thought then he was certainly in the wrong profession. Few people joined the police to be popular. The wider society may well respect the police but on a day to day basis, the people they moved amongst were quite the opposite. Her thoughts about Ken Francis were merely confirmed by what Amanda confessed to Eric. What she hadn't seen, and was surprised about, was Jane's reaction. Although, she shouldn't have been. The evidence was there to see. *What else was she capable of?* Apparently, others were thinking similarly.

"If Jane Francis is prepared to pay someone off to keep her husband out of court, particularly in light of knowing what he's up to, what else might she do?" Tom Janssen asked. Eric's brow furrowed. She couldn't tell if he was in agreement with Tom or not.

"I'm intrigued to know more about this falling out she had with Callum McCall," she said. There was more to Jane than she let them see, dropping a cloak of ambiguity on every meeting they'd had so far. She had the sense that she was quite capable of using her femininity when required. A skill wasted on herself, forcing her to fall back on restrained silence. Next time she would have to allow Tom to take the lead with her. She may unwittingly open up to him and he might get a better result.

"Should we go for the direct approach?" Janssen asked. She shook her head. A woman like that wouldn't respond well to being forced. She would be more inclined to retreat further. After all, it was only hearsay. There was something else behind his question. A sense of frustration. She shared it. They had been investigating Holly's murder for nearly a week now and although they all felt the killer was known to them, putting a face and a name let alone a motive to them, seemed tantalisingly just out of reach. They could make a circumstantial case against several people but that was it.

"I think we should be as prepared as we can be before we take it to her," she said, scanning the information board on the wall. This community was so entwined within itself. The charade of privacy, of keeping to your own affairs seemed practically impossible. Someone knew something that would break this case, she was certain. An elderly couple were as familiar with Jane's personal affairs now as much as they were a decade ago. Any gaps in the actual detail could be filled in with exploratory gossip. How anyone could keep a secret here was beyond her and yet, here they were, grasping. "Let's try to find out who's been sending these notes to Ken. I can't help but think it's all tied in somehow."

"Any ideas on how we do that?" Janssen asked. "The phone number on the card in the newsagent is attached to a prepaid burner. All I've got is the serial number of the handset and that it was purchased here in Norfolk. Credit top ups are done in cash and not online nor with a credit card." He sounded despondent. It was the first time she'd heard him so. "The company said they'll provide a list of locations where the top ups were purchased. If it's local then we may get lucky with a member of staff remembering the buyer, if it's frequent enough."

"Any chance of CCTV?" Janssen's response was irritating. He laughed.

"This is still Norfolk." He must have seen her reaction. His expression changed slightly. "If he went through one of the bigger supermarkets then it's possible but we'll have to wait and see. Similarly, the handwriting analysis came back as inconclusive."

"In which case, we have to consider that all options are still open." A pause. All eyes were on her. "We'll have to chalk them off the old-fashioned way. Tom, you and me will go to the school and see if we can see a sample of Mark's handwriting. Then, we can go to his father and have him write it out if needs be. These two are the most likely even though I accept we don't fully understand Callum's role in all this."

"What do you want me to do?" Eric asked expectantly.

"Head over to the surgery. We told Colin Bettany we wanted a sample of his handwriting. You can pick up an example of Marie's while you're there as well, if only to rule them both out."

TAMARA DID up her coat almost to the top, wishing she'd brought something thicker with her forgetting she hadn't been home in ten days. The heaters in the car were set to cool and she reached over shutting the vents facing her. Janssen didn't appear bothered, concentrating on the road ahead. Didn't he feel the cold? The head of a storm front rolled in overnight on a strong easterly carrying cold air across the North Sea from Scandinavia. The marshlands were shrouded in thick fog and the sky overcast when she got up this morning and even now, as both slowly burned away, the surrounding area took on an entirely different persona to the one she'd experienced thus far. The vitality of early spring was muted by an overbearing greyness, a brooding presence dominating the landscape.

Her thoughts drifted to Richard. Finally, they'd managed to speak the night before but it was a stilted conversation, one where he failed to ask her when she'd be coming home. He was still upset. Arguably more so than she initially realised. He seemed cold towards her on the phone. It would pass.

Pulling into the school grounds, they passed a number of pupils lining the approach road. There must be a break in classes. Janssen found one of the few remaining spaces and parked the car. The sun was threatening to break the canopy overhead now, the warmth on her skin was pleasant as she got out. Mounting the steps to the reception, she caught a glimpse of a familiar face. It was Maddie, Holly's sister. She was standing off to their left with a couple of friends. She thought to acknowledge the girl, maybe enquire as to her wellbeing, but she appeared in conversation and possibly wouldn't want to draw attention to herself with the police in front of her peers, so she decided to leave it.

Tamara found Mark McCall's tutor to be an interesting man. Somewhat easily distracted and fidgety, he appeared relieved once they were satisfied the handwriting couldn't be Mark's. Even to the untrained eye it was clear whoever had penned the threats was someone other than him. His letters were far too neat and ordered. She wasn't perturbed by the knowledge. It had been expected. "How is Mark? What's he been like since he found Holly?" The tutor appeared as if he was looking directly through her. For a moment she wondered if he'd heard the question.

"We've hardly seen him. I think he attended for the first time yesterday. Very quiet, preoccupied. Unsurprising, seeing as he was so sweet on the girl."

"You could see that?"

"You'd have to be blind not to."

"And today?" Janssen asked.

"He turned up for morning registration but never made it to his first class. I've no idea where he is."

They signed out in the visitors' book located in reception. The scene outside was in stark contrast to when they arrived only a short time ago. The fog had dissipated, possibly receding back towards the coast with them being further inland. The sky was brightening but the air still felt damp as they crossed to the car. Janssen stopped to answer his ringing phone, mouthing to her that it was Eric, probably calling from his visit to the surgery. In the corner of her eye, she caught sight of a figure peering around the corner of the admin block they'd just left. It was Maddie Bettany. The playground and surrounding paths were deserted. Classes must have restarted.

Leaving Janssen behind, she casually strode over towards the girl who was nervously glancing at the main entrance. "Skipping class?" Speaking barely above a whisper, keeping her tone non-judgemental. The last thing she wanted was to scare the girl away with the threat of discovery. Maddie retreated around the corner into a group of mature trees, shielding them from any of the windows of the nearby classrooms.

"I know I shouldn't but..."

"What is it, Maddie?" She felt the need to reach out and place a reassuring hand on the girl's arm. The girl seemed rattled, on edge. Hardly a shock under the circumstances. To find her in school so soon was surprising. "I'm sure no one will give you a hard time if you felt you needed a break from class—"

"No! You don't understand, it's not like that. I insisted on coming back to school. Anything to get away from the house."

"It must be difficult for all of you." The urge to give the schoolgirl a tight hug was fought back by the need for professional distance. There was a bench nearby, set beneath a willow tree and she led them there encouraging Maddie to sit down. The girl looked lost, sitting with her legs crossed at the ankles and her hands cupped in one another across her lap.

"It's been totally mental since... well, since Holly..." The words tailed off. She couldn't bear to utter them. "Mum and Dad argue all the time. I think they blame each other... or me."

"How can they blame you?" The thought was preposterous.

"Maybe not *blame* exactly... but Dad would rather it was me than her." The words were bitter, tears welled in her eyes as she spoke. Tamara ignored her training as instinct took over. She put an arm around Maddie and the girl sank into her.

"Don't ever think that, Maddie. Whatever your parents say, they are hurting too and... will lash out. It's irrational but very human." Warm tears fell onto the back of her free hand as she stroked the child's cheek.

"Dad's lost it now," Maddie continued, sitting up and wiping her eyes, sniffing loudly through a weak smile. Taking out a tissue, Tamara passed it to her. Maddie took it gratefully. "He always used to be bad, what with wanting to know where we were, who we were seeing and stuff but now... he's on a whole new level of OCD."

"He's lost a daughter," Tamara said. It was obvious but maybe it was difficult to see the effect grief was having on her father. "Who knows how that can make a parent feel?"

"Do you have kids?" She shook her head. How would she feel if and when she did have a family? How much effort would she put into protecting them from the horrors she came across on a daily basis? These were scenarios playing over in her mind every time Richard, or his family, started going on about it. As a child she was granted almost unrestricted freedom to venture wherever she chose, disappearing for the entire day with her siblings and her parents barely noticed. They certainly didn't come looking. If they were late home it would be another story, albeit one where they were in trouble rather than the consideration of something bad having happened. Were times different then? *No, that was nonsense.* Statistically, children were in no greater danger now than they were in her own youth. Attitudes had changed, that was all. Perceptions maybe. How *should* a parent behave these days? "I wanted to come back to school to have a break. Like, at least here I can talk to my friends and stuff."

"How are you finding it... them?"

Maddie shrugged. "It's okay. Everyone's being weird... exceptionally nice, especially the teachers but my friends are normal. Well... almost." The schoolgirl fell silent, her expression looked pained as if she was dwelling on something. She waited for her to speak, giving her all the time she needed. "I can't help but think if I had been with her... then none of this would have happened."

"You can't think that way, Maddie. Holly was supposed to be in Norwich seeing her tutor and preparing for a recital the following day. There was no way you could have been with her." Maddie looked at her, straight into her eye and there was something there, a revelation she wanted to speak of. "What is it, Maddie?"

"I knew... I knew she wasn't going to Norwich on the Friday night. I got her in trouble." Tears fell. "It's my fault."

"I don't understand."

"I was supposed to be at a friend's house. We... we went to the beach party. All the fifth and sixth form were talking about it and we wanted to go, so we told our parents we would be at the other's house and went along."

"Ahh… I see." They wouldn't be the first teenagers to play that trick. She'd done similar. "How does any of this come back to you?"

"Dad found us there," she said, looking at her feet. "He dragged me away… in front of everyone. It was so embarrassing."

"What about Holly?" It was odd that the Bettanys failed to mention this. They were supposed to be attending social functions that night, not dragging a wayward daughter away from a beach party. Colin was all about image and status, though. Perhaps he didn't want it becoming common knowledge.

"I don't know. I didn't really see much of her. She was off with Mark. I argued with Dad."

"What about?"

"He was ranting about me being there. It wasn't fitting… stuff like that. He's old-school, my dad. I didn't think it fair I should be pulled away when Holly got to stay out."

"Did she? Get to stay, I mean?"

"Dad put me in the car and then called her on the phone. She didn't answer. Probably saw him kicking off and did a runner. Usually she would stand up for me. I don't blame her this time. He was really angry. He wanted to go and find her. We sat there in the car for at least twenty minutes while he stared at his phone before we went home."

"Maddie, how did he know where to find you?" she asked, puzzled. And why would he lie… not lie, that was too suggestive. He certainly wasn't open and truthful about his movements.

"I don't know. We didn't tell anyone where we were going." Maddie sounded unsure. "Maybe he called Abbie's mum or the other way around."

"Have you got your phone on you?" Maddie nodded, reaching into the pocket of her blazer. "May I?" she asked, holding out her hand. Maddie unlocked the handset with her fingerprint and passed it over. It was a smartphone, fairly new judging by the slim design. Flipping through the screens at the standard icons one would expect alongside a collection of social media apps, she recognised most but there were some unfamiliar to her, probably popular with teenagers alone. There was nothing unusual. Ideally, she wanted to have a more tech-savvy person take a look. Maybe Janssen would know, more likely Eric. However, it would likely be noticed by Colin and judging by his recent reactions he would probably kick up a fuss. Handing the mobile back, she smiled. "Thanks. I don't suppose Holly's phone turned up at home, has it? We still haven't located it."

"No, sorry. Not that I know of. She would have had it with her. She never went anywhere without it." A bell sounded inside the school buildings and Maddie looked over her shoulder. "I should get back. I have maths next and Mr Fothergill is less forgiving than most."

"I'm sure you'll be just fine." She wanted to reassure the girl, tell her that everything would be okay. "I could come with you if you like?" Maddie shook her head, although with an appreciative smile at the gesture. "Call me if you want to speak again." The girl turned and headed up the path and through the nearest door, disappearing from view as the voices of children freshly released from class, carried to her.

CHAPTER THIRTY-TWO

MARK WAS UP WELL AHEAD of usual. His father stirred on the sofa as he ransacked the kitchen looking for a clean bowl in which to make breakfast. Giving up, he found one from the previous day and gave it a cursory rinse under the tap. There was no hot water again, the third time this week. The baffles on the wood burner had gone, only this time his faith in his father's ability to fix them was waning. A man quite adept at repairing almost anything, even his skills would be far stretched on this occasion. Wiping the inside of the bowl with the sleeve of his shirt, he filled it with cereal and milk. Picking up a spoon, he crossed to where his father lay and put the bowl on the occasional table next to the sofa.

Placing a hand on his shoulder, he gently rocked his father awake. "Dad. There's some breakfast for you." Bleary-eyed and with a deep frown, his father sat up. He'd secured some work on a neighbouring farm, just manual labouring. Old man Carlisle needed a barn cleared to make way for some new machinery he had arriving and couldn't spare anyone else to do it. It was menial but it paid cash and they needed the money. There was only so long they could go on boxes of cereal and cold showers. The least he could do was to help his father keep the little work he managed to secure. Callum McCall coughed, then stretched his arms in the air and yawned. The man's pores oozed the distinct aroma of alcohol. An empty bottle of cheap scotch or vodka lay on the floor alongside the sofa. He wondered how his father would get by without him. Maybe Sadie would step up. She hadn't come home again last night and he couldn't blame her. Dad may well have to get by on his own soon.

Skipping his own breakfast, he made a show of picking up his schoolbag and setting off. Having been up for most of the night, his appetite had deserted him. Agonising for several days over what he should do, he'd finally reached a decision the previous night. It was the right thing to do. Making the phone call, however, was hard. Not slipping out in the dead of night so as not to wake his father, that was easy. The man was hammered as usual. No, it was the uncertainty. He knew what he was looking to achieve but there was a lot at stake and if he'd pitched it wrong then he was in trouble. His father didn't speak as he left the home.

At this rate, he would be early for school and not wanting to draw attention to himself, he slowed his pace. Upon reaching the gates he slipped into the throng of arrivals. The sixth-formers entered through a different door to the uniformed kids and he kept his distance from the others. Not that many of them spoke to him much of the time anyway, now they positively avoided him. He knew what they were thinking and undoubtedly saying, and it was never going to stop. Even if an arrest was made and successfully prosecuted there would be those who still didn't believe. They never would. Unless it was him, a *McCall*. Well, if they wanted a genuine reason to fear him, then they would get one soon enough.

Morning registration passed without incident. Not a word was said regarding his lack of attendance the previous day when he came in, the first since Holly's murder. A couple of the teachers even asked how he was. Today was normal. Much like any other. The notices were read out, something about grief counselling aimed in his general direction, or at least he thought so, but he wasn't really listening. The clock was ticking by slowly. When the bell went to indicate morning classes, the scrape of chair legs across the floor and instant break-out of multiple conversations masked evidence of his growing anticipation and anxiety. He felt himself flush, sweating profusely. No one seemed to notice.

Joining the massed ranks queueing to get out of the classroom, he lingered at the rear. Once out into the corridor he ambled to the stairwell, the last person to enter. As students peeled away towards their various classes, he continued on to the ground floor, passing out of the fire exit into the overcast morning. It was still cold as it had been on the walk in, but the sun was threatening to break through. Glancing around, no one was in sight. He'd left via the eastern exit, the one unfavoured by anyone because there was no route out of the school without walking around the building. Unless you were going over the fence as he was. Confident he was unseen, he tossed his bag over and then followed. It wasn't particularly challenging, being barely above waist height and he made it with ease.

The walk home usually took half an hour but he could cut that by a third if he upped his pace. His father should be away to work by now and Sadie would reappear when she ran out of money or her latest turfed her out, whichever came first. His route took him along one of the main roads and a few cars passed by him but no one paid him any attention. Once back home, he approached with caution just on the off chance his father decided to go back to sleep rather than put in a shift. Everything was quiet when he opened the door, peering in and listening for signs of movement. There were none.

The door swung closed behind him, banging against the jamb. The latch didn't take as the frame was warped and ill fitting. They never locked it anyway. What was the point? They had nothing worth stealing. Heading straight to his father's bedroom, not that he slept there much preferring the sofa or bunking in with Sadie, he crossed over to the wardrobe. Moving aside a stack of magazines and an old carrier bag containing some random cables, he reached to the rear and found what he was looking for, an old canvas duffle bag. The dust disturbed by him taking it down brought tears to his eyes. From the weight of the bag, he knew what he was looking for was still there.

The bag was two-foot-long, with a double handle and a shoulder strap. Placing it down at the foot of the bed and unzipping it, he eyed the contents. Looking over his shoulder, he feared discovery as if everyone knew what he was planning. Taking a deep breath, he steadied himself. Returning to the wardrobe, he rooted around towards the back and found a small cardboard box. It rattled as he pulled it to the front. Opening it, he tipped the contents into the canvas bag and fastened the zip once more, slipping the strap over his shoulder.

Stepping out of his father's room, he went through to his own. Dropping on to all fours, he extended his arm under the bed and blindly rummaged around for a few moments until he felt his fingers brush against the cold glass of the screen. Teasing it into reach, he pulled the mobile phone out, holding it in his palm. Pressing the power button, he waited for it to power up which took a matter of seconds. A musical tune sounded as the company logo flashed up soon to be replaced by the lock screen and he typed in the four-digit pin. There was no going back. Not now.

Leaving the house as quickly as he could, a strange sensation passed over him. It wasn't nerves. He didn't suffer from that type of thing. Exam stress, peer pressure... people talked about that stuff all the time but it never bothered him. This was an alien feeling though, one he couldn't interpret. Maybe this was what other people felt, his brothers. One going into battle, the other heading to prison. Was it anticipation, excitement... fear? Whatever it was, he didn't like it and tried to push the feeling aside. However, the intensity of the sensation only grew with each step he took through the woods.

CHAPTER THIRTY-THREE

RETURNING TO THE STATION, Tom Janssen found an excited detective constable waiting for them in ops. The handwriting examples collected for comparison would be sent away for confirmation but even a cursory inspection proved conclusive. Neither of the samples collected from the Bettanys came close and Mark McCall's were a definite bust. Despite this, Eric was bouncing as he entered with Tamara only a step behind.

"You must have had a positive experience at the surgery for you to be so enthusiastic," he said as Eric bounded over. Knowing how Colin Bettany intimidated the young man, he seemed remarkably upbeat. Eric tried to hide his insecurity around dealing with professionals, doing well in the most part. However, to someone proficient in reading people the effect it had on him was fairly obvious. Eric would get better with experience. "How did you find Colin and Marie?" The question wasn't a test, he found the Bettanys a curious family.

"Didn't see them to be fair. I called ahead and they had samples ready for me at reception. Odd though. I figured they would take every opportunity to speak to us about the case, find out what's going on but they were both in surgery."

"I thought they were getting locums in," Tamara said, leaning against a desk and folding her arms in front of her.

"Alice said they've struggled to get locums to cover the entire surgery so both are seeing patients as and when required," he replied. Thinking of Alice, he hadn't seen her in days such were his preoccupations with the case. She seemed to understand, though, and it's not like he had a murder inquiry every week. "What's got you so excited then?" Eric was shifting the weight between his feet, clearly frustrated at the deviation in the conversation.

"I got a voicemail on my way back from the surgery from the mobile network. The one Holly's phone was registered to. It's active. For the second time today."

He exchanged a quick glance with Tamara and she recognised the significance as much as he did. Slapping Eric on the upper arm, he inclined his head. "Well, why didn't you say so?" The tone playful as much as it was sarcastic. "When?"

"Last night, around 2 A.M., it popped up on the network connecting to a local cell tower. That lasted for only four minutes before it dropped off again. The provider said the handset made a call lasting less than two minutes."

"Switched on to make the call and then off again, I should imagine. Do we know who the call was to?" Janssen cast a sideways glance to Tamara, seeing the hope and expectation in her. Eric shook his head.

"Not yet. The call was made to someone registered with a different provider. I've put in a request off the back of our previous court order. Still waiting to hear back."

"You said it was recorded twice." Eric nodded. "When was the second?"

"Just before half past nine this morning," Eric replied, turning to his computer and bringing up a map on the screen. There were two circles, shaded in burgundy, and they partially overlapped at the limits of each tower's cover. "This is where the signal connects to these towers, alternating between the two, hence the crossover. The key thing is, it's active now."

Pulling out a chair, Tom sat down weighing the rationale behind the information. "Why now, after a week? And why make a call in the middle of the night, to whom?" It was an odd turn of events, completely unexpected.

"Do you think someone found the phone?" Eric suggested. By the look on Tamara's face, she was unconvinced. So was he. The detailed search of the area turned up nothing. If the phone was mislaid or discarded, then it wouldn't lend itself to someone stumbling across it. Eric broadened the idea. "Or maybe someone stole it and thinks they're safe to turn it on." The second idea was far less probable than the first.

"Unlikely," Tamara replied, her brow furrowed in concentration. To Janssen it looked as if she was piecing something together. "I was with Maddie earlier. Her phone was passcode protected. She said before that her and Holly were given new phones recently. Most people are security conscious regarding their mobiles these days. It's probable that Holly was equally so."

"Whoever has the phone knows her pin," he said in response. Tamara nodded. "Or she passed it on before her death." The likelihood of that struck him as a slim possibility. The motive for Holly's murder wasn't robbery as far as they could tell. Turning his attention to the map, it covered quite an area. One advantage Norfolk had with regard to network coverage was the landscape. There were few hills to block signal, so as long as the transmitter on the tower was powerful enough the reach was decent. This left them quite a large area to cover. "The question is, who was close enough to Holly to have her pin… and lives in this zone? Let's face it, if you are making a call in the middle of the night then you're unlikely to have ventured far from home."

The three of them huddled together but it was apparent only one name fitted the criteria. Mark McCall. That realisation was painful. Trained to maintain a level of detachment from people within an inquiry, it remained a large part of being human to empathise and he was perhaps guilty of wanting Mark to be free of suspicion. Every reading of the boy's body language when they'd been together suggested he was a troubled soul but not a murderer. Was he mistaken? Even now, to give credence to it was tough to accept. "He cut class again today. We need to speak to him, find out what he's up to."

"Agreed," Tamara replied. "The McCall's place is slap in the middle between those two towers. That's where we'll go. I know it's tough for him but the boy is going to have to open up to us otherwise he'll wind up our chief suspect."

THEY MADE the drive out to the McCall place in relative silence. Janssen found he was still mulling over Mark's role in this whole affair. What Tamara was contemplating he couldn't tell. He found himself wondering whether she harboured the same doubts about the lad's involvement and if she was also considering whether they took the investigation in the wrong direction. Turning off the main road, a figure appeared from the shadows of the trees ambling along the unmade track towards the house. It was Callum. Upon hearing them approach, he glanced over his shoulder, stopping as soon as he recognised them. His jacket was slung over one shoulder and a sheen of sweat covered his face. Both it and his clothes were grimy. He must have been working.

Bringing the car to a stop, Tamara lowered her window. Callum eyed her with a cold stare, his usual. "We're looking for Mark," she said.

"He'll be at college." The reply was curt, rough. She shook her head.

"We were there earlier. Mark skipped class straight after registration this morning." Janssen saw Callum's eyes narrow, if only slightly, the closest the man would ever get to revealing a tell. He was surprised. "You seen him?"

"No. Maybe he's back at the house." Callum looked up the track. "What do you want with him anyway?" There was an edge to the question. He was concerned. That registered on Janssen's radar. Callum wasn't easily bothered by the police. He was hardened but something was troubling him.

"Probably best for us to speak to him directly," Tamara replied. "Get in, we'll take you the rest of the way."

"Nah. You're alright. I'll see you there," Callum replied under his breath, stepping back and resuming the remainder of his walk home. Janssen moved the car off. Looking in the rear-view mirror, he got the impression Callum was walking with more purpose now.

Pulling up in front of the property everything looked quiet. He half expected Mark to be sitting outside, idling the day away. Or was that what he hoped? Getting out of the car, they looked for any sign of movement from inside. Tamara indicated towards the outbuildings and he went to check the interior. Net curtains on every window obscured the view of the interior and so he tried the door. It was unlocked and he gently opened it. Peering inside, he looked around. No one appeared to be home. Stepping up, he entered.

"Oi! You've got nae right!" The shout came from distance, beyond the parked car. He knew it was Callum. Ignoring the protestation, he went further, allowing the door to swing to behind him. There was a strange smell inside, part damp, part decomposing food and lingering body odour. They didn't open windows often nor clean up by the look of it. The door flew open and a red-faced, out of breath Callum McCall charged in. "You've got nae business searching ma home, not without a warrant," he said in halting speech, waving a finger at him pointedly whilst trying to catch his breath.

"We're not carrying out a search, Callum. We're looking for a suspect in a murder investigation and when we find Mark, we intend to arrest him." Callum was dumbstruck, standing open-mouthed with fists clenched defiantly at his sides.

"My boy's a good lad. He's nothing like the rest of us and he ain't no murderer, Janssen, you hear? And you bloody ken it too."

"Where is he, Callum?"

"How should I know?"

"Here's me thinking you're his father." Callum made to reply but dropped it. His nose twitched and his top lip curled into something of a snarl as he advanced towards him. For a brief moment, Tom thought there was about to be an altercation and he braced himself. In no doubt he could handle a partial drunk such as Callum McCall, for his peak days were well past him, he still knew better than to take the prospect lightly. Instead, Callum brushed past him and disappeared into one of the rooms beyond.

Watching the man for a moment longer before resuming his search for Mark, he didn't expect to find him. Were he to be there he would either have revealed himself already or made a break for it if he felt the need to flee. Moments later, Callum reappeared at the threshold to the living area. His expression seemed conciliatory which was intriguing so soon after his outburst.

"Why are you on Mark's case all of a sudden? You've already searched here. If you were going to arrest him, why wait until now?"

"There's been a new development."

"Ahh… cut the crap, Janssen. Spill it."

They needed to find Mark and unless he was hiding nearby, they were unlikely to do so without help. Callum might be a lousy role model but he did seem to care for his son. At least, when he wasn't searching for the bottom of a bottle. "Someone activated Holly Bettany's mobile phone last night and again this morning." Callum took it in the stoic way he processed everything, running his tongue across the inside of his cheek. He appeared thoughtful.

"And you reckon this was Mark?"

"Someone did it from this location." That wasn't strictly true but he figured Callum's knowledge of cell towers would be limited. "Unless it was you, that leaves Mark. Why would he do that do you think, keep her mobile from us and then make a call with it last night?" Callum looked over his shoulder into the room he had just come out of and when he turned back lowered his gaze to the floor. He was nervous. "What is it?" Lifting his head, Callum indicated for him to come and see for himself.

Janssen approached, Callum stepping aside when he reached him allowing access to the room. There was a double bed pushed up against one wall but even so, floor space was limited. The bed was unmade, a duvet piled on top of the mattress. A wardrobe was in one corner. There was a small cardboard box on the floor. It was empty. Not knowing what he was expected to see, he looked back at Callum. The man wouldn't meet his eye, standing there biting his lower lip and shaking his head. "What's going on, Callum?"

"This is my fault," he muttered under his breath. "I shoulda seen it coming."

"Callum, spit it out man!" He was losing patience. "If there's something I need to know, then now is a good time."

"Ma boy... he takes things too literally. I should have kept my mouth shut." Callum continued to berate himself. "Look... I ken how things work. Your lot... you look for the easy solution. People like us are easy targets. You ken it as do I."

"Also, you keep breaking the law. Makes it easier for sure."

"The laws ain't the same for everyone, that's all I'm saying." Callum went on. He decided to give the man space to speak. It wasn't often he had anything to say, not without a solicitor present at any rate. "If you went to the right school, ken the right people... then the courtroom looks a little different when yer in the dock, yeah?" Janssen had to concede the point. It shouldn't matter but it was true. If you could muster some positive character witnesses with a high social status for the defence then it could cut some ice with the judge at sentencing. "I may have given Mark the idea that... Holly's killer might not get what they deserve."

"You're not usually this forthcoming. What else?" Despite the new found openness, there was still reticence. "Callum, if you know something that will help Mark then you need to tell me."

"Ma shotgun is missing... along with the shells."

Suddenly incensed, Janssen couldn't believe what he was hearing. "How the hell have you got a shotgun?"

"I use it for rabbiting."

"Poaching more like," Janssen bit back. Callum glared at him but didn't dare issue a rebuttal. "Well, he won't get far with that." Again, Callum looked away.

"I adapted it," he said barely above a whisper.

"You mean you've sawn off the barrels?" Callum nodded, grimacing as he rubbed absently at his jaw. "So, he can easily conceal it. Where's he going? Tell me now before it's too late!"

"He's a good boy, Janssen. He wouldn't do any harm—"

"Except he's wandering around Norfolk with a loaded shotgun. How many shells does he have?"

"Half a dozen. Maybe more. I don't really keep count."

"Where's he going?" They locked eyes and for a second he thought Callum was going to clam up but after a brief pause, he relented.

"To see that ponce Ken Francis, I expect. Mark thinks he killed Holly... and so do I."

CHAPTER THIRTY-FOUR

TAKING a firm hold of Callum's upper arm, Tom Janssen practically dragged the man across the living room before bundling him out through the door and outside. He didn't voice an objection. Tamara Greave came across to them and seeing his face, realised the situation must have escalated.

"What's going on?" she asked as Tom released his grip on his charge.

"Callum here, has an illegal firearm and it looks like Mark's taken it and is set on getting justice for Holly." Her inquiring expression was mixed with concern. "A shotgun with who knows how many shells. Callum thinks he has Ken Francis in his sights."

"He believes Ken killed Holly?"

"Too right he does!" Callum stated aggressively. "And he'd have it coming too."

"How the hell did we miss that on the search?" Tamara asked, furious. Callum chuckled.

"I stashed it once I ken you lot were snooping around after Holly died. It was only a matter o' time until you rocked up at ours. I'm nae as daft as you lot think. Once you'd been, I figured I could bring it back."

"In the car, now," Tom commanded and Callum begrudgingly got into the rear. He opened the driver's door, catching Tamara glaring at him across the roof. "What is it?"

"Do you think it's wise taking him into a volatile situation?"

"Normally, I would agree it's a risk but not this time," he explained. "Mark believes what he's told by those he respects or trusts. He wouldn't open up and talk to me. If I have to talk him down I will do my best. Perhaps his trust in his old man will be needed to stop him doing something catastrophic."

"We should call in an armed response unit as well as a trained negotiator."

"Make the call on the way but we'll get there before them." Anxious to get moving, he got into the car and started the engine before Tamara even opened her door. Accelerating away, he knew time was pressing. Mark must have planned what he was going to do, going into registration until his father would have cleared out of the house to work, allowing him to slip back unnoticed and retrieve the shotgun. "Call the Francis house. Let them know we're on our way." Tamara nodded and once through requesting the nearest ARV, she redialled the Francis house. After a few moments and no apparent answer, she retried. There was still no answer and she looked across. He read her look as one of consternation. They could already be too late.

Speeding up, Tom glanced in the rear-view mirror at Callum sitting behind Tamara. He was staring out of the window, his expression unreadable. "Why don't you tell us about it." Callum knew the question was directed at him for he glanced forward, locking eyes with him in the mirror for a brief second before he returned his gaze to the road. "You know what I mean. What's the story between you, Ken and Jane? We know there is one." Callum stared straight ahead, as if he was looking through Tamara in front of him and eyeing the road ahead. His gaze drifted back to the landscape passing alongside them.

"Aye and what would you know?"

So far, he wouldn't take the bait but Tom was certain that he had captured Callum's attention. "We know about you and Jane." Tamara cast him a sly sideways glance, circumspect but clearly willing to let him run with it. "How long has that been going on?" Choosing his words carefully, not wanting to overplay his hand.

"You should nae be listening to gossip, Janssen," Callum replied, looking forward once again. His tone dismissive. "That was all a long time ago."

"A few weeks back wasn't so long ago, was it?" There was a softening of Callum's expression rather than the hardening of it that he'd anticipated once scratching the surface. "Jane's not one to hold back." Still no response was forthcoming. "I guess she took offence at the letters you've been leaving?" The suggestion was something of a gamble but delivered with confidence, masking his fishing expedition.

"She told you about that, huh?" Callum sniffed loudly, drawing the back of his hand across his nose. "Sometimes it's the only way to get tae people, make 'em see what they're doing wrong. Jane and that daft husband of hers."

"Sending them threats is a bit... childish for you, isn't it?" Janssen eyed the mirror. The accusation hit home. He could tell by the sideways half-smile crossing Callum's face.

"Is that what she said?" Janssen glanced over his shoulder at him. "I'll bet there's a lot about the lass you din nae ken." Callum shook his head, glancing out of the window. "I never threatened her and that's the truth. Her husband... now that's a different matter but he deserves it."

There was a steadfastness to the response that set him thinking. All the letters they'd seen were threatening in both words and tone. However, all were aimed squarely at Ken with no mention of his wife. From what they understood Jane learned of the letters from Ken at the same time as he told the police. Callum's reaction was indicative of an altogether different turn of events. The short drive to the Francis house took less than five minutes with Janssen pushing hard. Approaching, he pulled the car to a stop on the grass verge fifty yards short of the property. Jane's Range Rover could be seen parked to the rear with the charred remains of Ken's studio taped off beyond it.

"Wait here," Janssen said to Callum who was preparing to get out. He began to protest but it tailed off as Janssen glared at him. Tamara got out and came around to his side of the car.

"The ARV is ten minutes away," she advised. "We could wait or..."

"A full tactical unit could spur him into doing something rash. Let's remember he's still a kid. This isn't his type of thing. We stand a better chance of talking him down with a softer approach."

"What if he's already been?" He could sense stress in her voice and she was right. If they were too late, Mark could have been and gone leaving a trail of devastation behind. Alternatively, he may not have arrived yet and could be in the surrounding trees keeping watch for a moment of opportunity.

Taking out his mobile, Janssen called the house one more time. The call was picked up by the answerphone. He looked to Tamara and shook his head. "To stay or to go?"

"We go," Tamara replied. He was pleased. Looking back at Callum, he pointed at him making it clear he was to stay in the car. "Let's head to the rear. We'll get a far better view of the interior from there."

Aware that under a watchful eye their approach would be easily seen, they walked briskly through the gate and into the rear yard, hugging the wall of the main house just in case. Thankfully, the children would be at school. That gave them some measure of comfort. The first window they came to was positioned in the hallway leading to Ken's home office. That door was closed and they could see into the boot room, the main access point into the property from the rear. The angle of view gave them only a slither of sight into it and the kitchen beyond. A shadow moved in the interior but who cast it was unknown.

Moving further along, they reached the entrance door. Janssen slipped past it and sidled up to the windows lining the kitchen overlooking the yard. Casting a last glance at Tamara for approval, she nodded and he chanced a peek into the house. Jane was in the kitchen, preparing some food on a chopping block, knife in hand. He let out a sigh of relief. Ken Francis was at the dining table, poring over a newspaper. Smiling at Tamara, he stepped away from the wall giving her a silent thumbs up. In doing so, he became visible to Jane and she was startled by his presence. Her reaction alerted the dog which hitherto now was asleep on the sofa. It rose and ran into the kitchen barking. The surprise on Jane's face turned to a frown as she crossed the kitchen to the rear door.

They met her as she drew it open. "You've got a nerve skulking around our property!"

"Mrs Francis," Tamara said, "may we have a word?"

Jane took a step away and turned, passing back into the kitchen. Ken raised himself and came over to see what was unsettling his wife. "What is it? Do you have some news about the fire?"

"No. Sadly not," Tamara explained. Janssen came alongside, scanning the interior before training his eyes on the surrounding outbuildings, watchful for Mark's approach. "It's come to our attention that Mark McCall could be set on causing you harm, Mr Francis." The man baulked at the suggestion, seemingly a genuine response.

"Why on earth would the boy wish me harm?"

Janssen picked up the narrative. "Mark had something of a relationship with Holly Bettany. It seems he has it in his head that you're responsible for killing her. Why would that be, do you think?" Ken shook his head, open-mouthed. Janssen glanced at Jane but she averted her gaze, looking at the floor. It was telling. "Apparently, he's not the only McCall to have something of a grudge with you two, is he, Jane?" Ken recognised he was in the dark with something passing between his wife and the policeman.

"Jane. What the hell is going on?" Ken asked, his brow furrowing. There was a disturbance behind them and they turned to see Callum McCall standing at the threshold to the kitchen. "What are you doing here?" Ken asked.

"Me?" Callum replied with something of a smug expression. "I've been doing yer wife, that's what. Just like old times." He seemed emboldened by the fact his son wasn't here and also somewhat relieved.

"I thought I told you to wait in the car," Janssen stated, annoyed by Callum's wilful antagonism. The man shrugged, apparently revelling in causing discomfort. Jane looked crestfallen. To Janssen, it was as if her world was about to fall apart. Ken stared at Callum before his eyes drifted across to his wife.

"Aye, that's right, Ken. You've been knocking off my son's girl and I've been revisiting yer missus. We go back a long way, me and Janey. Isn't that right?"

"Shut up, Callum, for Pete's sake!" Jane broke her silence, glaring at her lover and avoiding Ken's stare. His reaction struck Janssen as unusual, not visibly angry or upset but neither uncaring or apathetic. The man looked lost, confused. "I should *never* have allowed it to happen—"

"Probably right... but you did though, frequently!" Callum was enjoying this moment. An opportunity to reveal their affair, have it out in the open and also to rub his rival's face in it. This triangle of affections crystallised in Janssen's mind what was really happening here. Suddenly, the random events took shape and made perfect sense.

"Threatening letters to Ken whilst sending what... love letters... obsessive demands to Jane, is that it?" Janssen theorised. Tamara met his eye and he could sense she was thinking along similar lines. "So, what was the setting fire to the studio about, Callum? Evening the score on behalf of your son or just more childish jealousy? You don't torch a building to win over a lover."

Callum bristled. "Aye, and what would you ken anyway? I've seen him at night in his studio, touching up young girls. He's a bloody nonce and if you were any kind of policeman worth anything at all, you'd have nicked him by now. But *you have nae*, have you Janssen. Why? Because he's a rich man, arty type, eh? Mates with all the right people and yet you've come here not for him but for ma boy! You'll happily bang him up."

"If he's planning on carrying out an act of premeditated murder, too right I will." At the mention of that, Ken's confusion lifted and he appeared overcome. Jane crossed to him and pulled out a chair. Placing a hand on his arm to help him sit down, he forcibly shrugged it off and took the seat by himself. Jane remained where she stood, her expression showed she was hurt. Janssen thought she might cry. "The two of you," he indicated Jane and Callum, "picked up where you left off before Jane moved to London but let's face it, Callum, you don't have much to offer."

"You can come back here in your flash car and make-up, Janey but you're still you," Callum argued, largely ignoring Janssen at this point. "You haven't changed and I know who you are and what you want. Your husband might be able to give you a better reputation than you left with, a nice house and money to spend but he din nae ken yer like I do, lass. *Never will."*

"You don't! We're finished, Callum. *I told you that!"* Jane hissed.

"And yet you keep coming back for more!" Callum replied with a smug grin. Janssen couldn't see the appeal but he'd given up deciphering the wants, needs and attractions of other people years previously. Decisions made by many bore no relation to logic or reason in his mind.

"This is fascinating but none of it is helping us find Mark," Tamara said, establishing an authoritarian position and quietening the group. "Has he been here today, or have you seen him nearby?" Both Ken and Jane shook their heads. "Why didn't either of you answer the phone? We've been calling you non-stop."

Ken answered. "Some journalists in London have got wind of the fire and are sniffing around, calling and asking questions. It won't be too long before they put it together with Holly's death and make some nonsense story about it. We've been ignoring the phone. I dare say someone in your station is probably making a profit from leaking information." The last was said accusingly, daggers aimed at both of them.

"Well, if you have any evidence of that, Mr Francis, please do make a complaint and it will be objectively assessed," Tamara replied evenly. Ken scoffed at the suggestion. "No doubt we'll be reopening another case related to the investigation of sexual assault back in London as well."

"That case was over. I had nothing to answer for," Ken protested.

"Not you, Mr Francis but your wife." Ken looked at Jane, his eyes narrowing. Tamara continued. "Witness tampering is a very serious offence. Even if the witness turns out to have been lying after all, bribing them to withdraw testimony is still an offence."

"You didn't!" Ken barked at his wife who couldn't help but retaliate.

"If I left it to you then we'd have been ruined. You are bloody useless at times, Ken!"

Callum laughed. Janssen wondered whether it was genuine humour or pantomime in nature. So often considered to be the community pariah by many people, Callum was undoubtedly pleased to see those considered better than him falling from grace in front of his eyes. How his reaction would have differed if he wasn't publicly rejected by what Janssen figured was the love of his life, he didn't know. Jane either had leftover feelings from her youth for Callum or seeing him again rekindled those emotions at a time of great stress in her life, what with her marriage being somewhat unorthodox in nature. Maybe she was in denial about her feelings or it was a badly misjudged fling. Either way, what was once in the shadows was now visible for everyone to see. Janssen turned to Callum whose face dropped as he read his expression.

"Courts don't look kindly on arsonists either, Callum."

"Prove it!" Callum replied, crossing his arms in front of him. He knew how things worked. Without a confession or a witness, he would be in the clear.

"You must have spent so much time spying on Ken from the woods, how else would you know what he was up to?" Janssen said, changing tack.

"Public land. I can be where I like. Not my fault if he's putting it about in clear view with the young lassie." Jane bit her lower lip at the description. She must have been living in her own world of ignorance or denial, possibly for years.

"Tell us what you saw the night she died then," Janssen asked. "You saw something otherwise you wouldn't be so adamant he's a killer."

"I'm not a murderer!" Ken protested, suddenly animated. "I didn't kill Holly."

"Aye, right!" Callum said, dismissively. "She was here, in your bed that Friday night. Din nae lie, man. I bloody saw her with ma own eyes. I saw her here, with you."

"I didn't kill her! She was here but she left. Perhaps if you'd stayed perving on us for a bit longer you would have seen that just as clearly!" Ken's demeanour shifted from fearful victim to accuser in his own right. "Maybe you did see her leave and saw a chance to get even, a chance to get a clear shot at my wife." He looked at Jane who stood passively at his side. "Not that she puts up much opposition by all accounts. That's how my friends described her when we first met, after all." His tone was callous, cutting. She swiped a hand across his face. He didn't flinch, fixing his eyes on her.

"And you told this to Mark?" Janssen asked. Callum nodded. "And yet he isn't here."

"Maybe he changed his mind or bottled out?" Tamara suggested. Janssen thought about it. That was too simple. Mark struck him as a focussed young man, not merely as a result of his Asperger's Syndrome. He was driven but what that meant in this scenario he didn't know.

"Callum, you said in the car how you told Mark that Holly's killer wouldn't see justice." Callum nodded. "Largely because you figured Ken, being who he is, would escape our attentions. Who he is, his name would shield him from us?"

"Aye. That's about the size of it."

Janssen indicated for Tamara to join him and he led the way from the kitchen, Callum turning sideways and making room for them to pass. Almost as an afterthought, he turned back to address the three of them. "You lot behave until we come back inside. There are enough charges to go around without adding any more to them." Callum grinned, evidently still enjoying his moment. No one spoke as he and Tamara stepped outside. The storm front was moving back in, the wind picking up and rolling the fog in off the sea. The earlier brightness was rapidly being replaced by an all-encompassing darkness as if by an onset of a solar eclipse.

"What are you thinking?" Tamara asked him.

"That we're in the wrong place. It's not Ken. I don't believe he killed Holly."

"He's just admitted she was here on the night she died and Callum as good as stated he saw them having sex but..." She held her breath for a moment, her eyes drifting across the surrounding woodland. "I think you're on to something. As neat as it is, this doesn't sit right with me either."

"What Callum said to Mark may well have influenced his actions but I reckon Mark hasn't told us everything he knows, nor did he tell his father."

"So, who's the target?"

"I'm not sure but I think I know where we'll find Mark," Janssen said with confidence. The sound of a siren carried to them from distance. Assistance was approaching. "The question is, will we find him alone?"

CHAPTER THIRTY-FIVE

TAMARA SHIVERED, the drop in temperature accompanying the shift in the weather felt dramatic. Her phone rang and she answered it. It was Eric. She noticed Janssen's interest as she listened intently. Her expression must have conveyed surprise. Still processing the recent revelations in the case, she mentally beat herself up for not having seen the interactions sooner. There were few suspects within Holly's circle and all of them had secrets to keep regarding their relationships with the teenager as well as each other. Janssen was growing increasingly frustrated. He wanted to be off in the search for Mark McCall. For all the good of his restrained, methodical approach, once he'd come to a decision, he seemed to be driven to the point of ignoring risk. They still didn't know what they were walking into. She hung up.

"That was Eric. He's on his way out here but wanted to let us know Holly's phone is active again. Connected to the same two towers as last time, has been for the last thirty minutes." Janssen's brow furrowed. He was thinking the same as her. This was Mark's endgame. At least he hadn't already played it out. "We still have time."

"What makes you so sure?"

"If it was done, I think he would have turned the mobile off, or chucked it." Janssen appeared to agree with her. Looking over her shoulder at the police car approaching them up the access track, a jumble of possibilities bounced through her mind. "You said you know where he will be?"

"I think so. Mark always goes to one place in particular if he's stressed or looking to get away. It's where his mother used to take him," Janssen said, gesturing to the uniformed officers, clambering out of their car, to stand down. They acknowledged him and waited for further instruction. "It'll be faster to walk it from here, across the fields. There's a bridleway."

"In this?" she asked, referencing the fog closing in around them. Getting lost or surprised by a potential killer wasn't appealing.

"It's a more direct route. We can send the uniform along the road but they should hang back at the entrance to the path until we know what we're dealing with. Similarly, we don't want to spook the boy into doing anything rash." It was a sensible suggestion although the counter argument that he'd already passed that point could easily be made. Nothing about Mark struck her as indicative of a killer but there were many people she'd come across in her career who made one lapse in judgement and spent years suffering the consequences. "I know the way. It's not far." His confidence swayed her and she agreed. "What should we do about them?" Janssen indicated back towards the house.

"I reckon they have enough to talk about until we're done." The love triangle between Ken, Jane and Callum was worthy of the best gossip the village could produce. Throwing in the extra dimension of Ken's sexual involvement with Holly, Callum's son's girlfriend, added an even greater twist that would no doubt be the talking point to entertain for years to come, provided that is that Mark wasn't about to outdo everything that went before. The more she learned about these people, the more she felt they deserved each other. "Mind you, it's probably a good thing Eric's on his way here to supervise. Callum has admitted to arson, Jane to tampering with a witness and who knows what will go off if Callum works out she tried to fit him up."

"The red heels?" Janssen asked. She nodded. Jane must have known her husband was with Holly on the night she died. Even if she thought he was innocent, although possibly even if she thought not, her desire to cover up for Ken in the past pointed to the stark reality she put her needs and those of her children ahead of the truth. Jane wouldn't think twice about planting Holly's shoes at the McCall house. Whether to frame Mark or Callum, she wasn't sure. Callum was stirring things up and posing something of a threat to her marriage, the family security. Seeing him sent down at the same time as clearing her husband removed two problems with one simple action. "I doubt her prints will be on the shoes. She's too calculating for that."

"You're right. We might not be able to prove it." Even when they knew what was going on, with everything slotting into place, the frustration would be ensuring admissions were on the record. The evidence was circumstantial and that irritated her. Janssen instructed the armed officers in where they should place themselves and firmly ordered them to hold back unless they judged them to be in imminent danger.

Janssen indicated the way they should go and they circumvented the house, leaving through the rear gate to the yard. At the front of the house, he led them to a stile and they climbed over and set off along the path. Janssen's rolling gait and large strides set quite a pace and soon Tamara was struggling to keep up. Her calves burned as the path inclined steeply uphill towards the coast. She didn't ask him to slow down, for one she didn't want to lose face and at the same time figured he probably wouldn't listen such was his desire to get there. Their route appeared to bear to the left but it was hard to tell as the further they went the thicker the fog became, decreasing their visibility to barely a few yards. The sun was obscured now, a blurred smudge in a dense bank of grey.

"I'm cutting across here," Janssen said, abruptly coming to a halt. She looked around, there was no fork in the path and he made to climb over a stone wall that looked likely to collapse under his weight. "If I go this way, I'll come in above him. Stay on the path and you'll come in from his right." Testing the steadiness of a particular stone, he hoisted himself up not waiting for a reply.

"We should stay together, Tom! We don't even know if Mark's there." Dropping to the other side of the wall, he looked back with a stern expression on his face.

"He'll be there and I don't want to give him two targets." With that, he disappeared into the gloom. The density of the moisture in the air muted sounds and soon any sign of his presence had vanished, eaten up by the fog. She swore under her breath. All her career she'd needed to manage men like Tom Janssen. Somehow they felt protective over her, as if she needed to be kept out of harm's way. In one sense it was touching, ingrained in every generation by society but not a virtue she enjoyed considering herself equally as capable as any of her male counterparts.

Resuming her course, the sound of her breathing hung in the air around her with every footstep, every broken twig, magnified by the oppressive surroundings. The path cut sharply to her left as Janssen said it would and she found herself slowing. Telling herself she was merely being cautious the truth was she was frightened. Her heart rate was increasing as she approached an unknown threat. The sound of the nearby sea crashing against the base of the cliff face could be heard even if the edge was invisible through the fog. She was near. The path wound along the cliff top, sixty feet above the churning sea below thundering against the rocks. Not far now. If Janssen was right, she was within shouting distance.

Stopping to listen, she focussed on a point somewhere in the gloom ahead. There was nothing beyond the sound of the waves along with that of her heart hammering inside her chest. Edging forward, she maintained her vigilance straining to hear any telltale noises in front of her. Voices carried, muffled and inconsistent. How many she couldn't tell but thought it likely to be no more than two. For a second she thought Janssen may well have come across Mark and they were talking but as she approached, two figures grew out of the darkness. Neither of them was Tom Janssen.

As she inched closer, stooping low and careful to avoid stepping on anything to give away her presence, she saw details emerge as the shapes took form. One figure stood upright, straight backed extending an arm towards the second figure who was cowering nearby. Only it wasn't an extended arm, it was a double-barrelled shotgun pointed directly at the second person who was shuffling backwards precariously towards the cliff edge. Whether he was aware of that was unclear. He had both hands held out before him in supplication, turning his face away from the weapon aimed at him.

She looked for Janssen. Where could he be? Would he risk making a move on the gunman or would he double back and bring in the armed unit? She was in no position to do so. The two men locked in their deadly stand-off were between her and the armed unit. If she made a phone call it would give her presence away. Stepping away and making the call from a position of safety would no doubt be too late. This was going to play out in the coming seconds. She cursed her indecision. The figure holding the gun stepped forward encouraging the other to back further away. The ground beneath his feet shifted as part of it gave way under his weight toppling to the sea below. Suddenly realising his position, he yelped and begged. "Please... don't..." Tamara was thrown. She knew that voice. It was Mark's.

Another figure loomed out of the darkness, tall and imposing. "Don't worry, Mark. It'll all be over soon enough." The gunman turned on the newcomer. It was Janssen striding forward. "You'll not be needing the gun anymore." His voice was calm, authoritarian. Tamara realised then that Mark must have lured his intended victim to this place and either failed to go through with his plan or was overpowered and disarmed. That made sense. The weapon was now trained on Janssen who halted his approach. The gun was not lowered. Perhaps Tom had miscalculated, assuming the intended victim was keeping the gun raised in self-defence but now, now he was pointing it at him. Unless that was the intention all along, to protect Mark. *Damn him for putting himself in danger!*

Mark rose tentatively, taking a step away from the edge. The gunman turned his head in his direction. The gun moved slightly towards Mark. Was he considering which target was the greatest threat, Mark McCall or Tom Janssen? The gunman's moment of hesitation must have been what Janssen was looking for as he surged forward. The man brought the shotgun to bear just as Janssen engaged him, thrusting the barrels up and away from him as the weapon discharged. The flash lit the pair up momentarily and the thundering boom drowned out the crash of the water below. Instinctively through fear, Mark stepped back, losing his footing and teetered on the edge of the cliff. Throwing himself forward as the soft earth of the cliff edge fell away beneath his feet, a primeval scream followed as he reached out, clutching at anything that might prevent him from falling.

Tamara ran forward, hurling herself at Mark and grasping for his flailing arms, the material of his coat, anything that would stop him slipping over the edge. He looked into her eyes and she saw abject terror in his, a fleeting glimpse into the mind of a young man who believed he was about to die. She lurched forwards towards the edge as his momentum pulled her off balance. She lay flat on her front, both hands clamped firmly on Mark's. The sound of the sea crashing against the cliff face was ever present as her hold on him grew ever more precarious as they slipped further towards the drop. She redoubled her efforts, managing to take a better hold and arrest his descent. He was panicking and scrabbling around in desperation. "I've got you, Mark, and I won't let go." She tried to sound confident, as authoritarian as Janssen had been but she could see in his eyes a lack of belief.

Glancing to her left she saw the two figures grappling a short distance away. Janssen was a big man, strong and powerful but so was the other combatant. It was impossible to tell who had the upper hand, one endeavouring to detain and the other focussed only on victory at any cost. They stumbled away into the gloom and within seconds they were lost to the fog. Mark yelped as the earth displaced around his elbows dug into the ground around him and he slid further from safety, his face a picture of fear. Tamara felt the muscles in her upper body tense under the strain. Her arms burned and for the first time she feared this was beyond her, picturing in her mind's eye the image of the teenager plummeting to his death on the rocks far below. For a passing second she saw herself falling with him.

Another boom carried to her as the shotgun discharged for a second time only now, powerless to move and unable to see, all she could do was listen. Her concern for Janssen grew. The armed response officers would be on their way. Her mind churned over the possibilities. Were they where Janssen had agreed and if so, how long would it take for them to approach? If Janssen was overpowered by his assailant, would the support arrive before Mark and herself became his next victims? Thoughts of self-preservation flashed through her mind. She was defenceless at the mercy of a killer. Mark was right. Whoever he lured here killed Holly and was more than willing to silence Mark along with anyone else who stood in his path. Releasing her grip and allowing the boy to fall to his death was the only way she stood a chance. Retreating into the relative safety of the fog the only advantage she had.

Mark must sense it. He must know. The expression on his face told her that. Clenching her teeth, she mustered every ounce of energy she could and channelled her efforts into pulling him back up and to safety. The exertion brought sharp pain to her arms and quickly she realised it was futile. If ever she had the required strength, now it escaped her. All she could do was hold on. The two of them locked in situ, her grip being the difference between life and death. *Where were the uniforms? They should be here by now. Where was Tom?*

CHAPTER THIRTY-SIX

MOMENTS PASSED that felt like minutes but could only have been a matter of seconds. Her grip was loosening, Mark slipping further away from her. In her mind she tightened her grip but, in reality, she had nothing further to give and an involuntary thought to let go came to her, the physical relief that action would bring was inviting. Digging in, she focussed on Mark… on keeping him alive. Then a shape formed in the gloom, morphing into a figure that came towards her at speed. One arm pointed down, appearing out of proportion to the other. Realising it was the shotgun, Tamara's heart thundered inside her chest both through fear and anticipation. Tom Janssen materialised out of the fog casting the weapon to the side of her and, dropping to his knees and reaching past her with his massive hands took a hold of the stricken youth. Together, and with a monumental effort on her part, they hauled him up and back over the edge to safety. The three of them collapsed to the ground.

Tamara's arms felt light. The release of the muscles was a relief but the strain on her body left her breathless. Mark lay beside her, curled up into the foetal position. She realised he was crying. Placing a comforting hand on his upper arm she rubbed it gently, looking to Janssen who was up on his haunches, hands resting flat on his thighs and breathing hard. He was sweating, looking pained and relieved in equal measure.

"We've got him," Janssen declared, running a hand through his hair and answering the question before she managed to ask. "Colin Bettany is in custody."

In her mind the pieces came together all at once. She wasn't surprised. Everything made sense. Two constables in high-visibility jackets came into view and she encouraged Mark to sit up. He was in a state of shock and they needed to get him checked out. Whatever his plans were for this encounter it was fair to say they probably didn't work out as he intended. Janssen stood and helped both her and Mark to their feet. The teenager wiped his eyes with the back of his sleeve, his gaze settling on Tamara as he cleared them.

"Can I have Holly's mobile now, please? You took it from her when you found her body, didn't you?" She took great care to ensure no hostility carried in her tone. The boy had been through quite an ordeal, facing death on two occasions at the hands of Colin Bettany and Mother Nature. He reached into the pocket of his hoodie and brought out a mobile phone, passing it to her. His eyes lingered on the handset. It was a symbolic moment, almost like he was giving away the last piece of Holly he'd clung to since her death. "You found the tracking software Colin put on her phone, didn't you?" Mark nodded.

"At school, Maddie told me how her dad turned up at the beach party, dragging her home. He always seemed to know where they were, Holly and her sister. I figured he came home that night and looked up where they were, realising they were up to something and came out looking."

"But you didn't see him that night." Mark shook his head. "You and Holly had already left."

"You lot never mentioned him turning up at the beach party. I knew either he must have kept it secret or... or there was something else going on. After what my dad said..."

"You were worried we were covering up for Colin and looking to pin it on you or your father?" she asked, feeling for the boy. He must have been in a terrible state of confusion tying himself in knots this past week.

"Especially when you found Holly's shoes at our place," Mark said, his eyes flitting between the two detectives. "After Holly left me, I went home. Dad was there when I got in. There's no way he could have killed her. When you found the shoes I thought everything he told me about the police must be true."

Placing a comforting hand on his, Tamara smiled. "There's much more to the story than just what you know, Mark. Your father is connected to events that have been going on around here but you're right, he didn't kill Holly. Come on, we'll get you somewhere safe." She passed him over to the waiting constables who led him away. Janssen knelt and retrieved the sawn-off shotgun from where he'd tossed it in his rush to their aid. "Are you okay?"

"A little bruised," Janssen replied with a shrug.

"Your body or your ego?" she asked playfully. His face split into a broad grin. "I dare say I'm annoyed with myself for not putting it together sooner. What's the betting that we will be able to match the DNA from Holly's baby to her father." Janssen appeared shocked. It was the first time he'd given such an emotional reaction since they'd met.

"I hadn't thought of that," he admitted. "I gathered he was controlling but..."

"Stands to reason, though." Glancing along the path she could make out flashing lights through the fog. It was beginning to clear as the breeze coming off the sea picked up. "She was popular but reclusive, dreaming of running away from her life to start over. She dressed herself as a much older woman which, to be fair, many teenagers do but she also sought out the company of older men, such as Ken Francis. Was she used to older men, feeling strangely comfortable around them because she'd been so well groomed by Colin? Let's face it, her interest in boys her own age, like Mark, was passing at best."

"That's tragic, don't you think?" Janssen replied with a shake of the head. "From the outside looking in, she had everything going for her."

"Maddie spoke of how Holly looked out for her, protected her... I didn't realise how significant that was. I wonder if she was planning a way she could get her out as well at some point in the future. I wouldn't be surprised. Colin probably felt threatened as Holly was growing up and moving away from him, particularly after he searched for her that night. Maybe he didn't find her with Mark but more likely at Ken's house. If Callum McCall could see what they were up to then it is just as likely Colin would have too."

"Then he confronted her after she left," Janssen suggested.

"Whether the thought of losing her or, more likely, losing his power and control over her saw him intentionally kill her or he went too far in a fit of pique… who knows… but the upshot of it was she was dead and he had to think of something, fast. He may have seen that Holly was with Mark along that path or it's a coincidence, I don't know, but placing her there put Mark in the frame."

Janssen's brow furrowed. He was walking it through in his mind, she could tell. "There must have been something of an altercation with Ken. When she left him, Holly was barefoot and the soles of her feet were still clean when we found her body. She can't have walked far. I imagine she met her father near to the house and he killed her shortly thereafter. A man of his size could easily carry her out here. Holly was such a slight girl it wouldn't have been difficult for him and at that time of night he was unlikely to be discovered doing so."

"Do you think Ken will give up exactly what went on that night for her to leave without her shoes? I mean, now their secrets are laid bare." Janssen shrugged. No one in this case appeared able to tell the truth. The paternity of the child would remain a theory until it could be proven either way for it could just as easily be Ken's child. "Needless to say, without Mark's rather clumsy attempt at justice we may never have figured it out."

Janssen nudged her in the side with his elbow as they set off along the path. "We'd have got there eventually, I'm sure. It's going to be interesting to know what Mark said in the late-night call to get Colin out here."

"Maybe he didn't have to say anything much at all. Colin couldn't know for certain what evidence was stacked against him and a man with such a desperate need to dominate needed to be sure. Finding Mark alone… he probably couldn't resist the opportunity of tying off the loose end, even taking the chance of putting you down as well.

Had he dropped the gun and pleaded a case of self-defence we would have been hard-pressed to make any kind of a case. As it is, he was far too impulsive for his own good."

Janssen stopped walking. "Men like him always are." It sounded like the words were spoken from experience, the tone was harsh and edged with bitterness. She chose not to press him on it. "I wonder how much his wife, Marie, knew? Maddie was afraid of revealing what she knew to you but she confided in Mark."

"Yes. She trusted Mark. You were right about him all along. As for Marie, she'll have questions to answer but abusers like Colin don't just groom their victims, they groom everyone around them. At what point does Marie cease to be a victim and become an enabler?"

"I know what you mean," Janssen replied, meeting her eye, "and maybe I'm being far too simplistic but… for me, that moment is when he enters your child's bedroom." He turned away and resumed his course up the path. Tamara quickened her pace to keep up with his stride.

CHAPTER THIRTY-SEVEN

TAMARA GREAVE STOOD at the entrance to her hotel, handing her case to the taxi driver when she caught sight of Tom Janssen's car pulling off the highway. He brought the car to a stop and climbed out. Before acknowledging her, he showed the driver his warrant card and took the case from him offering the man a five-pound note in exchange whilst telling him he was no longer required. The driver glanced at her and she smiled, indicating it was okay by her. Janssen gave the man a soft clap on the shoulder and came to stand before her, still clutching the handle of the suitcase. The driver seemed unhappy at losing the fare but didn't protest.

"You didn't think I was going to make you get a cab to the station, did you?" Janssen said with a smile.

"I don't see why not." She returned the smile, appreciating the gesture. After a pretty intense week, she still found Janssen to be something of a closed book. Just when she thought she had him figured out he would throw her off again. During their time working together Janssen appeared to approach cases differently to her but at no point did he ever imply his was a superior route nor did he undermine hers. Aware of her own inability to work closely with others, their time together had proved something of a success. "I've stretched out the overnight bag as far as I could." He laughed then. "Don't worry, I'm not leaving you with all the paperwork. I'll be back in a couple of days."

"Oh, in that case, I needn't have bothered coming," Janssen said, taking the suitcase and putting it in the boot of the car. "Eric and I played rock, paper, scissors for the trip."

"Who won?"

"Now, that'd be telling," Janssen replied, getting in his side as she opened her door.

The child's seat was back in the rear and she broke her own rule about intruding on her colleague's private life. "Tom, do you have a child or do you slip that in occasionally just to confuse people?" He laughed again. It was as if the successful conclusion of the case had eliminated the stress of the previous seven days. Janssen came across as a different man to the somewhat broody, reticent one she first met at Downham Market the week before.

"Alice, my partner does."

"Ah... they live with you?"

"No and I don't see that happening any time soon either."

"Sorry, I didn't mean to pry." Looking out of the window across the estuary as Janssen started the car, she realised she would miss the place, although she'd return soon enough. Janssen glanced across at her as he pulled away.

"A boat isn't an ideal place for children to spend their time," he said quietly, pulling out into traffic.

"You never said you lived on a boat." That was novel, quirky. Somehow, he didn't seem the type. There was so much to him that she was unaware of that could easily have come up in conversation. Although, she was often accused of being someone who was unwilling to listen. Tom also struck her as one who was reluctant to share personal information. They held that in common. Her thoughts drifted to Richard and how he would respond to her popping home for a day or two before leaving once more. She wasn't sure, doubting it would be news warmly received. The anticipation of an argument threatened to dampen her mood and pushing the thought from her mind, she turned her attention to Maddie Bettany. "How did it go with Marie?" Janssen sucked air through his teeth.

"What we were expecting. She's closed ranks with her husband and is flatly refusing to cooperate."

"Even now… having established beyond reasonable doubt that he killed their daughter?" Janssen confirmed the assertion. A flash of anger passed through her before she set it aside, her heart reaching out to Holly's sister. A troubling period lay ahead whatever the outcome of her father's prosecution. People talking, always pointing the finger. Maddie and her mother, if she proved not to be complicit, would always carry that burden unless they decamped to pastures new. Even then, the ways of the modern world and its tabloid nature would make this part of their lives very difficult to leave behind. "The poor girl." She almost whispered the words.

"What's that?"

"Nothing… I was just thinking about the innocents affected by all of this." She stared out of the window at the passing landscape. "And Callum. Is he still not talking?"

"Not a word. Nor are Ken and Jane Francis. We've rumbled a dysfunctional group that's for certain. I dare say Callum will keep it zipped but the other two may well turn on each other at any moment."

She laughed at that. Janssen was underestimating their attachment to the status quo. The lengths Jane went to in order to preserve a marriage that was little more than a mutually beneficial arrangement were incredible but then again, weren't all marriages similar in one way or another? Once the initial passion of a relationship subsided, what remained were two people keeping each other company as they passed through life. *Is that where they were, her and Richard?* Shuddering at the thought, the journey home suddenly made her feel anxious. Janssen must have noticed a subtle shift in her demeanour because he took on a concerned expression.

"Are you okay?"

She smiled weakly. "I'm fine." He didn't seem convinced but didn't offer further comment. After the events of the week, the last thing she wanted was more drama and that was her expectation. Richard was a man used to getting his own way. Not so much with her despite his best efforts. Perhaps they were too different or maybe in some ways too similar.

Janssen took the turning into the train station. Pulling up in the drop-off zone, he got out. There was a train already at the platform. They were cutting it fine. She was pleased to have already arranged her ticket. By the time she got out, Janssen was already alongside the car having retrieved her case from the boot. Taking the offered handle, she thanked him. They exchanged pleasantries and she set off towards the station entrance as he returned to the driver's side. She called after him just as he opened the door. "I never thanked you for being there the other day, when I was holding on to Mark. For a moment... I wasn't sure it was you coming at us through the fog."

Janssen inclined his head. "You can hold your own, I'm sure. We make quite a team, you and me." He smiled warmly. "Maybe you should put your hand up a little more often."

"I might just do that, Inspector." Her face split a grin. "Besides, I'm dying to see that canal boat of yours." She turned and walked through the double doors and onto the concourse without looking back. If she had, she would have seen Janssen watching her go until she disappeared from sight, absently drumming his fingertips on the roof of the car. He lingered there for a few moments until a taxi driver conveyed his irritation at Janssen's blocking of the zone by sounding his horn.

"I'll be seeing you DCI Greave," he said under his breath. Glancing at the taxi, he got into the car, restarted the engine and set off back to the station.

FREE BOOK GIVEAWAY

Visit the author's website at **www.jmdalgliesh.com** and sign up to the Reader Club and be first to receive news and previews of forthcoming works.

Here you can download a FREE eBook novella exclusive to club members;

Life & Death - A Hidden Norfolk novella

Never miss a new release.

No spam, ever, guaranteed. You can unsubscribe at any time.

Enjoy this book? You could make a real difference.

Because reviews are critical to the success of an author's career, if you have enjoyed this novel, please do me a massive favour by entering one onto Amazon.

Type the following link into your internet search bar to go to the Amazon page and leave a review;

http://mybook.to/One_Lost_Soul

If you prefer not to follow the link please visit the Amazon sales page where you purchased the title in order to leave a review.

Reviews increase visibility. Your help in leaving one would make a massive difference to this author.
Thank you for taking the time to read my work.

BURY YOUR PAST - PREVIEW
HIDDEN NORFOLK BOOK 2

THE EASTERLY WIND whipped sand into his face. The clouds parted momentarily revealing the new moon and a brief glance to the horizon saw the shifting light of the coming dawn. Time was limited. The fallen trees, a result of the violence of the previous night, left many local roads impassable with residents hunkering down in their homes to wait out the storm. Many heeded the warnings and travelled inland away from the coast, thereby avoiding the worst of the damage and disruption. Others, however, didn't fare as well. Coastal flooding struck several communities overnight according to the news report he heard on the radio. The power was out across much of the region with no indication of when things would return to normal, Norfolk's eastern coast battered back to the stone age in the space of a few hours.

Now amongst the dunes, he caught sight of another soul braving the lull that followed the previous night's events, walking their dog along the deserted beach. Dropping down he found some shelter from the elements with the dunes acting as a natural wind break and the relative calm allowed him to hear the sounds of the nearby breakers crashing onto the beach. Reaching into his knapsack, he took out his small bundle tightly wrapped in linen. Laying it on the ground, he carefully unfurled the material to reveal the contents. A small circular mirror, slightly smaller than the palm of an adult hand, was put to one side. Alongside this he placed a black candle, a length of string and a piece of cinnamon bark. Lastly, he set down a smooth oval rock the size of a closed fist that he'd collected from the shoreline.

Taking a marker pen from his jacket, he picked up the mirror and scribbled a word upon it. Laying it in the centre of the linen he retrieved a cigarette lighter from his pocket and, protecting the wick from the breeze with his body, lit the candle. Once the wax began to melt, he angled the candle in order to allow three drops of wax to splash down onto the surface of the mirror. Then he allowed the breeze to extinguish the flame. Nervously casting his eyes to the east, the sun threatened to breach the horizon at any moment. The reddish backdrop to the tumbling angry clouds promised yet another day of turbulence. Putting the candle aside he reached for the cinnamon. Snapping the bark into smaller pieces in the palm of his hand, he closed his eyes and sprinkled it over the mirror whilst softly mouthing an incantation long committed to memory. Taking each corner of the linen in turn, he folded them into the centre creating a pouch of sorts and tied the corners together with the string. Working with more haste now, he used both hands to dig in and push the sand aside in order to fashion a hole roughly six inches deep at its centre. Then, he lifted the pouch and laid it carefully inside.

Picking up the rock, he hefted it above his head and looked out to sea once more. As the first glimpse of the sun crested the horizon, he brought his arm down as fast as he could, hurling the rock into the hole. The muted sound of the mirror smashing under the impact carried and without a moment to lose he refilled the hole as fast he could, smoothing over the topmost layer of sand with the palms of both hands. He left them flat against the ground, stretching out his fingers into the sand and feeling the slight warmth of the rising sun on his skin. Closing his eyes, in that very moment, he was certain the elemental power of the earth coursed through him.

The sound of a dog barking came to him on the wind, erratic and shrill. Something about the animal's intensity piqued his interest and he stood, slowly clambering up to the crest of the dune and looking down along the beach. Barely forty yards away, the dog, a black

Labrador, was standing as if on point barking to alert its owner, occasionally stopping and leaning into the ground, pawing at the sand and tugging on something at the base of the dunes. Curious, he moved closer, watching as the dog's owner, an elderly man, drew near, pulling the animal away by its collar. For its part, the dog continued to bark excitedly.

Making his way toward them, he watched as the man knelt and appeared to be trying to retrieve something from the ground. Approaching, he saw whatever it was, it was wrapped in a piece of material and apparently well buried in the sand. The receding water lapped at their feet leaving a frothy residue as it dragged sand away from their discovery with each tidal sway. The dog came over to inspect the newcomer and he held out the back of his hand to allow the animal to smell him. The creature became rapidly disinterested and returned to its owner. Coming to stand alongside, he watched him recoil from the discovery before rising and backing away. They hadn't met before. The old man's face was ashen and pale, his eyes haunted. Looking past him, he wondered what he'd found.

"I… I better call the police," the man said, fumbling for his mobile phone. Intrigued, he stepped past and dropped to his haunches to inspect the find. Once white, the material was now heavily stained and discoloured by exposure to the elements. "Damn it. I haven't got a signal." That wasn't a surprise. The storm had brought down both trees as well as power lines and there was no reason the cell towers wouldn't also have been disrupted. Meeting the old man's eye, he recognised the expression. Not merely apprehension but true fear invoked by the discovery. *People are so scared of what they don't understand.*

Returning his gaze to ground, he lifted the material to reveal what lay beneath. Folding it back he drew a hand across his mouth. The skull and a portion of the neck were given up from its sandy grave. The eye sockets stared up at him, empty and lifeless and the dawn sunlight glinted from a silver necklace hanging between the vertebrae. He leaned closer, lifting the pendant for a better look. "Do you think you should be doing that?" A nervous voice said from behind. He ignored him, inclining his head sideways and trying to imagine the face of the person buried in the sand, he pursed his lips. "I'm going back to my house. Maybe the landline will work from there. I really don't think you should be touching that." Summoning his dog, the man set off without another word.

Looking over his shoulder, he watched the retreating figure as he walked away. Once he was out of earshot, he returned his focus to the human remains once more and smiled, releasing his hold on the chain and allowing the necklace to drop. "I always knew one day you would be returned to us."

Bury Your Past
Hidden Norfolk – Book 2

ISBN - 978-1-80080-994-9

ALSO BY J M DALGLIESH

The Hidden Norfolk Series

One Lost Soul

Bury Your Past

Kill Our Sins

Tell No Tales

Hear No Evil

The Dark Yorkshire Series

Divided House

Blacklight

The Dogs in the Street

Blood Money

Fear the Past

The Sixth Precept

Audiobooks

Read by the award-winning Greg Patmore.

Divided House

Blacklight

The Dogs in the street

Blood Money

Fear the Past

The Sixth Precept

Audiobook Collections

Dark Yorkshire Books 1-3

Dark Yorkshire Books 4-6

CPSIA information can be obtained
at www.ICGtesting.com
Printed in the USA
BVHW030048170421
605144BV00014B/722/J